THE FEI

A DCI JACOB MYSTERY

ROB JONES

Copyright © 2025 by Rob Jones

All rights reserved. No part of this publication may be used, reproduced, distributed or transmitted in any form or by any means, electronic, mechanical, photocopying, recording or otherwise, without the prior written permission of the author or publisher, except in the case of brief quotations embodied in critical reviews and certain other non-commercial uses permitted by copyright law.

THE FERRYMAN is a work of fiction. All names, characters, places and occurrences are entirely fictional products of the author's imagination or are used fictitiously. Any resemblance to current events or locales, or to persons living or dead, is entirely coincidental.

This book is sold subject to the condition that it shall not, by way of trade or otherwise, be lent, re-sold, hired out or otherwise circulated in any form of binding or cover other than that in which it is published and without a similar condition including this condition being imposed on the subsequent purchaser.

ISBN: 9798316454457

For my family

"The croaking raven doth bellow for revenge."

— **Shakespeare**, *Hamlet*

PROLOGUE

The weak autumn sun painted the sky and lit the cloud deck a coral pink, lighting up the ancient fallow fields until they glowed amber. In the summer, the surrounding fields, gold with wheat, would ripple as the evening breeze brushed over the crop waiting for harvest, but today the land was stripped bare and dormant, waiting for winter. As the sun dipped below the farmhouse, Lucy Ricks walked over to the man standing out in the open, watching the landscape change colour in the sunset.

"You're late," he said.

"Sorry, got caught up in some traffic," she said, looking around the fields beyond the old house. "Are you sure we're supposed to be here at this time of night?"

"I bought it. It's mine now."

"So, it's okay for us to be here?"

"I just said so, didn't I? You worry too much."

There was no defence against this. She knew he was right – she always worried too much and had done her entire life. It was just who she was. She would always find something to concern her or cause her anxiety, no matter how small or tenuous. It was her nature and she hated it, but she didn't appreciate the tone he had used when telling her.

"Well, I'm here now," she said, smiling.

He warmed up. "C'mon, let's go down to the pond."

She took his hand and followed him down a slope and past a barn half-filled with this year's hay and then a smaller outbuilding on their left. They crossed a gravelled footpath and then made their way down a steeper grass slope until they reached the edge of a large lily pond. She stood and took in the view of the smooth water, shimmering in the low sun, and the darkness of a small copse running around its west bank. Startled by some birds, she turned and tracked them as they crested the slope leading up to the farmhouse behind them, then they dipped across the pond and flashed out of sight behind the trees.

"What were they?" she asked.

"Swifts."

"In that case that was an awful lot of swifts!"

He turned and met her eyes. "Scream."

She returned his dreamy gaze. "I'm sorry?"

"It's a scream of swifts," he said. "The collective noun for swifts is a scream."

She looked back to the woods, but the birds were gone. "Why do they call them that?"

"Because of the noise they make."

"File that under *Things I Never Knew*."

He made to walk around the pond, heading for the trees. "Walk with me."

Lucy saw something in his eyes. Her heart told her he knew, but her head said this was impossible, that there was no way he could have any idea of what she had done. With some reluctance now, she took a step closer and walked around the pond beside him. When they entered the small woodland that traced around the western edge of the pond, she felt the temperature drop enough to take the jumper she had tied around her waist and put it on. She reached behind her head and pulled her long hair through the collar, shaking it free.

"Let's go back to the house," she said at last. "It's getting cold."

"I thought we could go all the way around the pond. It's so beautiful, after all."

Far away, the hoarse, high-pitched bark of a fox cut the twilight like a scalpel, making her jump. "I hate it when they do that."

"It's signalling danger," he said, pulling up and facing her in the gloom. "Alerting other foxes in the vicinity to a potential threat. Maybe it's warning me about you."

She looked up. He was towering over her, his face dark in the woodland shadows. "What does that mean?"

But she knew what it meant. It meant her heart had been right after all.

He knew.

"I could forgive a lot of things, Lucy, but not this."

Looking into his eyes, she was reminded not only of what she had done, but also how cold he could be, and what a distant, difficult man she had realised he truly was, despite only knowing him for a few months. She took a step back but felt her back brush up against a tree trunk. He drew closer and put his hand on her chest, pinning her against the tree.

"Not a nice thing to do, all told," he whispered. "Was it?"

The man reached into a pocket in his blue sports coat and pulled out a silk scarf.

"What's that?" she asked.

He said nothing but began wrapping each end around his hands.

"You're frightening me, Den."

The man said nothing and moved fast, wrapping the scarf around her neck and pulling tight on it, squeezing her throat until she felt like her eyes were going to burst. She reached up, desperately clawing at the scarf with her fingernails, cutting into her flesh to save her life. It was no use. The man was too strong. He stared at her with soft, dreamy eyes as he slowly choked her to death. She felt her windpipe collapsing as the force of the tightening scarf crushed down on it. She saw stars swimming around her in the twilight woods. Her vision narrowed, and the sounds of the birds receded into nothing. The world grew dark and then, taking one last glimpse at her killer's eyes, she felt everything slip away from her.

CHAPTER 1

Mist hung in a flat sheet across the graveyard at Malmesbury Abbey. The sun was low and watery and it would take another hour or so before the air cleared. The man inside the filthy white Ford Transit van wished he could stay inside it with the heater on all day, or better still get back home and switch on the electric fire. As it was, he had a job to do, so he turned off the ignition and climbed out of the van, clicking the door shut behind him. Then he climbed inside the platform of the trailer-mounted cherry picker he was towing and used the controls to raise the platform until it was level with the top of the trees on the graveyard's perimeter.

The abbey was beautiful and though he had driven past it thousands of times, local arborist Dave Butcher had never seen it from so high before. He was even able to see some of the lower, sloping roofs on the abbey's south side, an angle only the birds could enjoy. He adjusted the platform with his controls, raising it a little higher and then moving it across to the left by a few inches until he judged it was in the correct position to start work. The contract with the abbey was to inspect the trees for signs of damage after a recent storm and high winds, but also while he was up here to look for any signs of disease and generally clean the trees up, removing limbs that crossed one another. He also planned on doing some trimming to tidy them up, particularly this one which was getting too close to some power lines.

He saw at once what the groundskeeper at the abbey had told him about – a heavy branch had broken off and was hanging precariously in the middle of the tree. The abbey authorities were concerned that it would eventually fall to the ground, possibly striking someone and harming them. Dave manoeuvred the platform a little higher and closer to the broken branch and with some effort was finally able to pull it free. It crashed to the ground with a heavy thud and Dave was free to begin working on the main job of the morning – crown reduction. This involved trimming the tree to stop it from getting too close to the overhead powerline. Dave was considering the best way to tackle the job when he caught sight of something out of place on the far side of the graveyard, near part of the abbey that was in ruins.

It looked to Dave like a rolled-up, white dustsheet, which wasn't right. The rest of the abbey's grounds were immaculate, as always. Someone dumping litter in a place like this made Dave's blood boil with anger but when he looked closer, he reconsidered and decided that it wasn't litter at all. It looked like some kind of sleeping bag, and there was someone asleep inside it. Dave had never seen a white sleeping bag before, but he guessed such things must exist. His mind leapt to the possibility of a homeless person who had taken shelter overnight in the graveyard inside the abbey's ruins to stay out of the high winds. But that didn't seem right either.

He decided to take a look a closer look and lowered the platform back down until it connected with the trailer hitched to the back of his van. He climbed out of the platform, closed the cage back up and powered everything down. Then he made his way round to the main entrance of the abbey grounds in the west, opening the gate and stepping inside. He then walked gingerly through the misty graveyard around the abbey's south side, pausing to look up at the great old building. Dave Butcher was not one of the world's greatest readers, and he hadn't learnt anything about history since he left school at sixteen, but being a local man, he knew a little about the famous abbey.

He knew that as a religious house, it was one of England's oldest, going right the way back to the 7th Century when King Henry VIII ordered the dissolution of English monasteries. It was originally a Benedictine Monastery founded in 676 AD by King Ine of Wessex's nephew, a religious scholar and bard called Aldhelm, but it was most famous in Dave's mind for something his father told him when he was a boy. Around a thousand years ago, a monk named Eilmer built himself a set of wings and leapt from the tower, sailing through the air for over two hundred yards before crashing into the grounds and breaking both his legs. He asked his father so many technical questions about the wings that his mother had to warn him not to try anything similar.

Dave smiled at the memory, but it soon faded into the mist as he walked past the old stone lichen-covered sarcophagi dotted here and there in the graveyard. He felt a shiver go up his spine and began to wonder if he should have just called Hendricks, the groundskeeper instead. He looked at the graves and heard his late grandfather telling him some of his favourites. *It's later than you think*, was one. *You're a long time dead*, was another. Dave didn't like to dwell on such thoughts while walking past so many graves. He continued skirting around the south side of the abbey until reaching the section of ruins at the eastern part of the building and here he stopped for a moment, almost too nervous to peer around the side of the wall, so uncertain was he about what he might find on the other side. Deciding it must have been an old dustsheet after all, he stepped around the corner and walked over to the white shape, knowing in his heart more clearly with every inch he drew closer to it, that something was very seriously wrong.

The grass, heavy with dew, squelched under his work boots as he moved slowly through the mist, nearer to the strange wraith-like object languishing on the damp ground. His heart began to thump in his chest, banging like a funeral drum as he went forward, realising suddenly what it was he had really seen from back up on the platform at the top of the tree. He edged nearer again, the sound of the blood rushing in his ears and making him feel almost dizzy as he looked down and saw what was unmistakably a human body wrapped inside some kind of shroud. He almost forgot to breathe, but then fumbled for his phone and called the emergency number for the police.

*

Twenty miles south, just outside the pretty Wiltshire town of Bradford-on-Avon, Detective Chief Inspector Thomas Jacob was in the midst of domestic chaos. The kitchen was the epicentre, with the large oak table now being used as a staging area for Dr Sophie Anderson's short trip abroad to attend an international psychology conference.

"Do you really need all this stuff?" Jacob asked, slowly lifting a spare pair of folded jeans and finding beneath them a portable travel pillow, a rain poncho and a dog-eared copy of *Crime and Punishment*. "You're only going for five days!"

"You never know," Sophie said with a serious face. "You have to pack for all eventualities."

"Like the one where you're caught out in a flash flood with an irresistible urge to read nineteenth-century Russian literature?"

Sophie flipped the suitcase lid over and tried to zip it up. "Stupid thing won't do up."

"Maybe lose the art supplies."

"I am not packing art supplies. That's a notebook for the conference."

"Old school. I like it."

"It's in case my tablet runs out of battery."

Jacob bowed over and peered through the side of the bulging case. "Maybe you could pack a couple of spare tablet batteries instead?"

Sophie finally zipped it up. "There! All done. You were saying?"

Jacob sustained her notoriously effective 'ignore him' gambit with admirable cool, showing not a flicker of emotion. "I was saying I hope the weather is nice while you're there."

"Rome in November is always lovely," she said with a glint in her eye. "It's just a shame you're not coming. We could talk about the wedding when I'm not attending the conference."

"That really *would* be wonderful, but sadly I have to work."

"Sarcastic bugger," she said. "We have to talk about it sometime, Tom. May is only eight months away."

"Only eight months left, eh?"

She gave him a play-slap and slid the case off the table. "I'll pretend you never said that."

Jacob checked his watch. "You should get going soon or you'll miss your flight. What time have you got to be at the airport? I can't remember what you said."

"The flight leaves Bristol at twenty-past one," Sophie said, also checking her watch. "I think they want me to be there two hours earlier than usual. How long does it take to get to Bristol from here on a Thursday morning, do you think?"

"Not long, I shouldn't think. It's been so long since I've made that trip, I'm not entirely sure but I think it's less than an hour for sure. If you leave now you'll be there in plenty of time."

"You're not trying to get rid of me are you?" Sophie asked with a smile.

Jacob was about to reply when his phone rang. He looked at the screen and saw it was work. "What the hell? I'm supposed to be on holiday this week. I have to take it."

"Go ahead," Sophie said, checking her bag one more time and making sure her wallet and passport were packed and ready for the trip.

Jacob took the call. "Jacob, go ahead."

"This is Chief Superintendent Kent, Jacob. I need you back at work."

Jacob felt a surge of disappointment. "Sir, I booked this leave months ago! I'm meeting Sophie in Italy at the weekend."

Kent sighed painfully. "Not anymore, you're not. We've got a suspicious death on our hands out at Malmesbury Abbey and I want you on it straight away. Your leave is cancelled."

Jacob knew Kent well enough to know there was no point arguing with him. "Any details?"

"All I know is a body was found in the abbey grounds this morning, wrapped in a sheet and dumped there."

It was Jacob's turn to sigh. "I'll be there in half an hour."

"Good job, Chief Inspector. Keep me informed."

After the call, Jacob and Sophie's eyes met; each knew what the other was thinking without any words being spoken. Eventually, Sophie told him to forget about meeting her in Rome on the last day of the conference. "There'll be other chances."

"I guess so," Jacob said. "But this week of all weeks!"

As if on cue, their black Labrador bounded into the room, all smiles.

"What about Drifter?" Sophie asked, looking down at the happy dog as he padded around the kitchen. Her job as a university lecturer at Bath allowed her to spend a good deal of the week at home and she normally walked him, but this time Jacob was on walkies duty. "Maybe we could ask Vincent?"

Jacob thought for a second. "I'll call him."

Vincent Miles was a handyman who lived down the road. He was a bit of a dropout who had turned to being the local DIY guy after a failed attempt at day trading left him bankrupt. He was in his thirties but looked ten years older.

"Gotta go!" Sophie said, extending the handle on her case and kissing Jacob on the cheek. "I'll phone you when I get to the hotel. You two men stay out of trouble," she added, stroking Drifter on the head.

Jacob watched Sophie drive her Audi across the gravel drive and past the brick gateposts out into the lane. When she was out of sight, he picked up his phone and called his neighbour down the road.

"Vincent – you all right to come and walk Drifter? I've been called away for the day."

"Sure."

"Just take him down to the river at the end of the garden and back as usual," Jacob said. "You can use the side gate. Maybe take him over the bridge into the field and make sure he gets a good run. You know how lazy he can be."

"No problem," Vincent said. "I'll leave him in the boot room like normal?"

Jacob nodded. "There's food and water for him there."

Jacob thanked Vincent, then went upstairs and changed into a suit and tie and slipped on his watch. Then he went downstairs, stepped outside and locked the door behind him before walking over to the garage. He braced himself for the day ahead. *Anything but a murder investigation*, he muttered as he opened up the garage's old wooden double doors. *Anything but that.*

CHAPTER 2

Jacob climbed into his car, a vintage powder-blue 1962 Alvis TD21 drophead coupé and reversed it onto the gravel drive. The car technically belonged to his father but was on a kind of long-term loan on the condition Jacob restored it to its former glory. It was a labour of love but Jacob had found sanding rusty metal and searching online for rare parts an excellent distraction from his police work. It had gradually come together over the years until now it looked like a brand-new car, freshly rolled off the production line back in '62. He never really spoke about it to anyone because it wasn't his style, but he was proud of his work and quietly enjoyed the look on people's faces as he cruised past in a classic car.

He pulled through the gates Sophie had used just moments ago and as soon as the lane outside was straight enough for some speed, he pressed the throttle and opened up the powerful three-litre Straight-6 engine, producing a satisfyingly throaty, vintage growl beneath the polished bonnet. As he pushed the old car through the light mist still lingering in the country lanes, his mind turned to what Kent had told him on the phone. Someone had called in a body wrapped in a sheet and dumped on the grounds of the abbey up in Malmesbury. Something didn't sound right about that. Wiltshire was a low crime area with only eight counties in England and Wales recording lower violent crimes. Only two or three people were murdered per year, or less, so he considered other possibilities. Accidental death of a homeless person was a possibility, except homeless rates in the area were very low, and sleeping out in the streets in a town like Malmesbury would be extremely rare.

He hit the main road at Melksham and turned north, cruising past Lacock Abbey and then skirting around the west side of Chippenham before driving over the M4 and slowing for the honey-coloured buildings of Corston. He arrived in Malmesbury in good time, leaving the A-Road at the Burton Hill roundabout and then slowly rumbling the vintage motorcar down the town's busy High Street. All look normal, with smiling pedestrians, dog walkers, and people carrying shopping bags. Red and ochre leaves blew down the street, but the trees still had plenty of foliage in their canopies. It was a pleasant scene, but he knew all that was about to change.

He pulled to a stop at Market Cross and waited for some people to use the zebra crossing before turning left and immediately seeing the bell tower of St. Paul's Church, its beautiful spire stretching up out of the mist and showing everyone below the way to God. Jacob drove past it and the famous abbey grounds opened out to his right behind a black-painted wrought iron fence. He pulled up in between a marked police car and a white Ford Transit van with a trailer-mounted cherry picker hitched to its tow hook. He switched off the engine and climbed out of the car, walking through the gates and heading over to the action, which in this case was a police CSI forensics tent newly erected at the far eastern grounds of the abbey. That meant Mia Francis, the senior SCI officer was probably already at work inside. A good start.

As Jacob approached the tent, Detective Constable Laura Innes appeared at its entrance and stepped over to him.

"Good morning, Constable," Jacob said.

"Morning, sir."

"What have we got?"

"Victim's name is Tansy Babbington, sir. Forty-one years old."

"How do you know?"

"She's famous, or sort of famous, sir."

"Sort of famous? What does that mean?"

"She's an author. I've read all her stuff. I recognised her as soon as I saw her. Very distinctive face, curly blonde hair, bright blue eyes."

"Local woman?"

Innes nodded. "She lived locally but was originally from Cornwall. I've followed her on social media for years."

Jacob raised an eyebrow. "Did your cyber-stalking allow you to glean her address?"

"Yes, but only because I know the local area. She often posted pictures of her home on her socials, especially Instagram. While she never came out and said where she lived, I could tell right away as soon as I saw the pictures. It's a very large house with a lake on the grounds, in between Brokenborough and Tetbury. Just a couple of miles from the King's Highgrove Estate."

"An impressive neighbour to have. I'm guessing that doesn't come cheap."

"She bought the place for four million a couple of years ago. More stalking, sorry."

"I can see you're a fan who really cares, but that is a lot of money for a house, even for one with its own lake."

"And a maze and formal gardens, too. The whole package comes in at around fifteen acres."

"What did she write?"

"She specialised in 18th Century bodice-rippers."

"I didn't know you read that sort of thing."

She shrugged. "A bit of a guilty pleasure, if I'm being honest. Her publisher describes them as a cross between Poldark and Sherlock Holmes."

"Jesus."

"They're great, actually."

Jacob wondered about that. "Thanks to the house, I'm guessing she was successful."

"Very, but not everyone was a fan."

"How so?"

"She was always very busy on social media and had one of the country's biggest Instagram accounts. She had an opinion on everything and wasn't shy about letting the world know what it was, no matter the subject."

Jacob watched one of the CSI officers walk out of the tent and go back to the van. "She liked ruffling feathers, then?"

"It seems so. One of her favourite gripes was that no one in the industry took her books seriously and I know from her socials that she complained about it a lot. Everyone was to blame but her, she thought, and she crossed swords with a lot of other writers as well."

"Any stand out as potential killers?"

"Only one – Meredith Ash. A has-been contemporary romance writer who was last famous back in the nineties. He also spends a lot of time on social media and they often had words on there. Recently, he replied to one of her posts on Instagram calling her – and I quote – 'a sad, narcissistic windsock who never knows when to shut her mouth."

"It's shut now," Jacob said. "What caused Mr Ash to write that?"

"Ms Babbington had gone on a rant about how everyone was stealing her work, then Mr Ash replied to her, pointing out how a scene from one of her early books was what he called a 'carbon copy' of a scene in a 1970s American detective show. He illustrated this point-by-point with a certain amount of relish. After that, it went ballistic between the two of them and turned into an online brawl. It ended with the windsock comment."

"Which was posted when?"

"Two days ago."

"Where does Meredith Ash live?"

"That's the thing, he's local too. He lives in Cirencester, just up the road."

"Twenty minutes away," Jacob said.

Innes shook her head. "If it was him, then he's one weird bastard."

Jacob pulled up and looked at him. "Why do you say that?"

"Take a look for yourself, sir," Innes said, lifting the flap of the tent.

Jacob stepped inside and felt his skin prickle. He was looking down at a corpse wrapped in a white shroud from head to toe. His mind was instantly filled with visions of a killer from a long time ago, someone whose ghost he thought he had buried forever.

Mia Francis, the senior CSI officer was on her knees beside the body. She had already unwrapped the head and part of the upper body allowing him to see that whoever had wrapped her in the shroud had crossed her hands over her chest and put a dark, black feather in her right hand. Jacob's ghost came at him stronger now, flooding his mind with the horrific memory of Professor Alastair Keeley, the notorious murderer dubbed the *Ferryman* by the press. Keeley slowly choked his drugged victims to death before wrapping them in a shroud and placing a coin in their mouths. The ritual was about paying the Ferryman Charon, a figure from Ancient Greece, a coin to take the dead women across the River Styx and into the Underworld. After a lengthy killing spree that terrorised women in London and triggered the largest manhunt in British criminal history, he was eventually caught by the Metropolitan Police and given a life sentence without parole at his trial. The thought of this woman being another victim of the Ferryman lingered on his mind, but he knew that was absolutely impossible.

"Morning Jacob," Mia said. "What did you opt for this morning, toast or cereal?"

"Just a coffee this morning, Mia. Sorry to disappoint you."

"You should make sure you eat a hearty breakfast, especially if you're going to spend the day working. It's the most important meal of the day."

"So they say," Jacob said, walking around the corpse until he was looking at it from another angle. "Found anything to help us out?"

"Nothing so far," Mia said. "I can tell you that the body was dumped here late last night before dew formed on the grass."

"Any clue as to whom dumped it?"

"There is no forensic evidence that we've managed to track down yet, and I wouldn't get your hopes up on that score either. Someone walked across here in the night and dumped this body here, that much I can tell you. I've already searched thoroughly for footprints and found absolutely nothing, and no security footage covers this part of the abbey grounds. The only things that might be of interest to you immediately right now, are two objects that I found on the body."

"I can see the feather, what's the other one?" Jacob said, almost not wanting to ask. When Mia answered, he wished he hadn't.

"I found a coin in her mouth."

Jacob's stomach turned over.

"What kind of coin?"

"I'm no expert, but it's clearly an ancient coin. I will however take it back to the lab for forensic testing."

Mia now pulled the coin out of the dead woman's mouth and held it up in her nitrile-gloved hand for Jacob to see.

He stared at the small bronze coin, seeing the profile of some kind of ancient ruler on it. "Turn it around please."

Mia turned the coin so he could see the other side. Jacob saw the figure of a man standing holding something in his hand.

"That's not a honeybee," he said. "This just doesn't make sense. The shroud is right, but the feather and the coin are wrong. The whole thing is impossible anyway. None of this is right."

She got up to her feet. "What are you talking about?"

"It should be a silver coin and there should be an image of a honeybee on it."

"You've lost me, Jacob. Are you thinking about Keeley?"

"I don't know what I'm thinking about," Jacob said. I don't know *what* to think."

He then heard the booming voice of Dr Richard Lyon outside the tent talking to Innes. The jovial Home Office pathologist now poked his head inside the tent.

"Morning chaps!" Richard said, entering the tent with his small, black medical bag. "What's the skinny?"

"The *skinny*," Jacob replied, "is a dead writer in her forties, wrapped in a shroud with two calling cards left on the body – a black feather and a coin."

"Poor woman." Dr Richard Lyon sighed as he looked down at the body. "Another day another dollar, I suppose."

"I need an approximate time of death, Richard," Jacob said.

"All in good time. Hello, Mia."

Mia went back down to the body. "Richard."

Innes joined then and pulled her notebook out from her pocket again, ready to capture anything of interest from the doctor. "If it helps, she was found this morning by a dog walker, very early, so we think she was killed last night."

"Hazardous business," Richard said.

"Being out on your own at night or being a dog walker?" Jacob said.

Innes clicked her pen open. "Dog walkers certainly seem to find a lot of bodies these days."

Richard crouched down beside Mia and began examining the body. "Neither. I meant doing my job for me and diagnosing the time of death."

Jacob cocked his head. "Are we wrong?"

Richard paused and leaned in closer to the dead woman's head and neck for a more detailed visual inspection. "Very wrong, presuming we all understand 'last night' as being around twelve hours ago. I'd say she's been much dead longer than that. Perhaps twenty-four hours or more. She also has substantial bruising on her head that would have hurt a great deal. That's just instinct following a cursory visual examination. I'll know more after we've processed everything through the lab. Wait for the report, is the best advice."

Jacob felt even more confused. "Thanks, Richard."

"As I say, after I get it back to the lab and do the full monty on it, I should be able to tell you more. Whatever I find will be expedited to you the moment the report is finished."

Jacob nodded his understanding and stepped out of the tent with Innes following a step behind him.

"I don't like what I've seen this morning," he said. "I don't like it at all."

Innes peered back inside the tent as the two professionals tinkered away around the body. "What do you want to do next, sir?"

"I want to talk to the man who discovered the body and then to whoever is in charge around here. After that, we're going to take a drive over to the dead woman's home and see what we can find there. We have to work fast. Instinct tells me we could be in real trouble here."

CHAPTER 3

Jacob found Dave Butcher standing inside the entrance to the abbey, talking quietly to another man with a thick silver moustache, who was wearing a wax jacket and a flat cap. There was a uniformed police constable there Jacob recognised as James Tanner. Butcher seemed calm and composed, if perhaps a little surprised by the events of that morning.

"Mr Butcher?" Jacob asked.

"That's me."

"My name is Detective Chief Inspector Jacob. I'm from Wiltshire CID and this is my colleague Detective Constable Innes. If you feel up to it, we'd like to have a few words about what happened here this morning."

"Yes, of course. That's fine."

Innes stepped forward and wheeled the man out of the abbey's west entrance and back onto the path outside so they could get some fresh air and talk in private.

"Is this the first time you've done groundwork for the abbey?" Jacob asked.

Butcher nodded. "As a matter of fact, it is. I've been an arborist for thirty years but this is the first time I've ever worked here on the abbey grounds. The groundskeeper told me their usual man has got too expensive so they thought they'd try someone else."

"Is that the man you were talking with at the abbey entrance?"

He nodded. "Hendricks is his name."

"At what time did you arrive here this morning?"

"Nice and early," Butcher said. "I always like to get to my jobs nice and early because you never know what's going to unfold. Things can get out of hand maybe or one thing leads to another and the next thing you know you've run out of daylight. I suppose I was here about eight this morning."

"And everything seemed to be in order?" Jacob asked.

"Of course," Butcher said, a little surprised by the question. "Malmesbury is a quiet place. Not much usually goes on around here. I pulled up in the van just as I had arranged with Mr Hendricks and then I set up my little cherry picker – it's a little trailer-mounted unit you can see out the front. I elevated it up so I could get to work on the pruning and trimming and that's when I saw it. It was a dreadful shock, I can tell you."

"So, you saw absolutely nothing else anywhere around the grounds that was unusual?" Jacob asked. "No other sign of movement of other people anything like that?"

Butcher's face scrunched up for a moment and lifted to the sky as if he were seeking an answer from God. "No, I don't think so. After I saw the white sheet, I went straight back down to the ground and walked around to get a closer look. I saw no one else on the grounds or even in the street."

Jacob was making notes. "No unusual vehicles anywhere?"

"Cars and vans park all over the place up and down here, so I didn't pay any attention to that."

Jacob nodded, thinking it was barely worth putting down in his notepad, but he made a note all the same. *Butcher did not take note of vehicles in street.*

"And you say that's the groundskeeper back in the abbey entrance, with the flat cap?"

"That's right yeah. Mr Hendricks. Nice chap. He cut the grass here late yesterday, that's why it all looks nice."

Jacob nodded, certain that Butcher was telling the truth and had nothing further to add. Deciding not to waste any further precious time on the interview, he took full note of Butcher's details, including date of birth, telephone number and address and told him to make sure he was available for the next few days in case the investigation returned to him.

"Returns to me?" Butcher looked shocked. "I don't know what you're talking about! All I did was turn up to work and see that body over there. I had nothing to do with it."

"Nonetheless, Mr Butcher," Jacob said, "you never know what you might think of over the next few days that could be of essential help to the investigation. I would appreciate it if you could make sure that you're available."

Butcher nodded reluctantly and walked back over to his van. Jacob watched him switch the ignition on, signal and pull away, towing the cherry picker behind him until they vanished out of sight into Malmesbury's honey-coloured streets.

"Not much to be had there, sir?" Innes said.

"No indeed. Maybe we might get some more information out of Hendricks. And after that, I want to talk to the gaffer. What's his name?"

Innes now referred to her notebook, flicking through some pages for a few seconds before finding what she needed. "The Right Reverend Julian Squires. He's the vicar."

"Where is he now?"

"He's waiting inside the abbey, I think."

"All right, well let's do Hendricks first, then Squires. Work our way up the food chain, as it were."

They walked back up the path towards the abbey and saw Mr Hendricks give them a reluctant nod and wave before stepping over to them.

"Nasty business," Hendrick said.

"Indeed it is, sir," Jacob said. "I take it you're Mr Hendricks, the groundskeeper?"

"That's right. I'm Peter Hendricks."

"What time did you get here this morning?" Jacob asked.

"I'm normally here at nine, but I got in a bit early today after all of this kerfuffle."

"I understand you mowed the grounds yesterday, late in the afternoon. Is that correct?"

Hendricks nodded. "Yes, that's correct. I did it not too far off of sunset. I went around because the grass was quite dry and the weather report was saying there was going to be a lot of mist and dampness today."

"And there was definitely nobody or anything else unusual on the grounds when you did that?"

"Not at all, Chief Inspector. Everything was just as usual. I went around and mowed in exactly the same way I always do and nothing was out of place."

"And can you be a little more precise with what time you did that?"

He considered. "I suppose it was around five in the evening or thereabouts. It was my last job of the day before going home."

"And you're certain you saw nothing unusual?"

Now it was Hendricks's term to look confused, but Jacob felt it was natural confusion and not being put on for the cameras. "Now you come to mention it, there was a woman who walked up the path and went into the abbey as I was packing up my equipment into the van. But people do come and go."

Jacob looked up from his notes. "So why did you mention it when I asked if you saw anything unusual?"

"I suppose just because I didn't recognise her and she looked a bit furtive like, you know – looking over her shoulder before she went inside and closed the door behind her."

Jacob and Innes exchanged glances then Jacob dismissed Mr Hendricks with the same caveat he had given Dave Butcher a few moments ago. When Hendricks disappeared down the path and walked away to his car Innes spoke first.

"Our first break, sir?"

Jacob was reticent to comment too deeply on the matter. "Could mean anything."

"Still, it might be interesting to find out what the Right Reverend has to say about it. After all, it is a little suspicious, isn't it? The groundsman saying he saw a woman behaving suspiciously on abbey grounds at last light yesterday and then this morning, a body is found here?"

"Let's just go and talk to the man."

Jacob and Innes stepped inside the western end of the abbey's impressive nave. Much of the building was destroyed during the dissolution five centuries ago, but the western part is still used as a church today. As such, it was well maintained, clean, tidy and warm with pews and Bibles and other books positioned neatly for worshippers. Jacob looked up, mesmerised by the beautiful stone vaulted ceiling high above him and followed it the full length of this part of the building until he saw a seventy-foot high brick wall blocking the used part of the building from the ruins beyond. Here his eyes made their way down the wall to the altar and kneeling before the altar was a man dressed in the black garb of a vicar.

As they walked towards him, the vicar heard their footsteps on the smooth flagstones and finished his prayer, bowed his head, turned and walked towards them. His face was sullen and stern and coloured with a mixture of bewilderment and dismay as he extended his hand to shake. He was tall and thin with a thick mop of silver hair and penetrating grey eyes, partly hidden by bushy eyebrows the colour of wire wool.

"Thank you so much for coming," he said softly.

"You're the Right Reverend Julian Squires?" Jacob asked.

"Indeed I am, and you must be Detective Chief Inspector Jacob."

"That's correct and this is Detective Constable Innes, my colleague in Wiltshire CID."

Jacob was amused by the vicar's gratitude that they had turned out as if it was an optional extra and they were doing him a favour rather than attending the scene of a suspicious death and establishing the beginnings of a murder investigation. Nonetheless, it had already given him a small understanding of the man's personality.

"Reverend Squires, do you live very close to the abbey?"

"Nothing like this has ever happened before, Chief Inspector," Squires said. It's simply dreadful, isn't it? Do you know who the poor woman was? Do you know why she was left here?"

Three questions in one sentence, Jacob considered; these things never passed him by without his making a mental note of them. Often, compulsive or obsessive questioning was a delay tactic designed to give the questioner more time to prepare themselves and think of a manufactured response to what they were being asked. Not only that, Squires had dodged Jacob's original question.

"We'll come to all that later, Reverend," Jacob said. "Do you live very close to the abbey?"

"I suppose you could say so. The rectory is not far from here, perhaps five minutes' walk. Why do you ask?"

"I ask questions, Reverend Squires," Jacob said with a smile. "I suppose you spend most of your life talking to God, but I spend most of my life talking to suspects."

"Am I a suspect, then?"

"Everyone is a suspect at this stage." Jacob decided to ask three questions. "Were you working here at the abbey yesterday evening? If so, what time did you go home last night? Did you hear or see anything suspicious last night or this morning?"

Squires immediately became flustered and then started fiddling with his cassock. "Well, I was here yesterday of course and I went home, I suppose at six o'clock or thereabouts. I did hang around a bit later than usual because Hendricks was mowing the grounds and I wanted to ensure that it was all done properly before going home. So, let's say about six. I got in this morning early because I received a telephone call from Mr Hendricks. Mr Butcher phoned the police about what he had seen, and then he phoned Mr Hendricks and Mr Hendricks phoned me. So I suppose I was in here before eight-thirty, but that's not unusual. We normally open at nine-thirty – as a historical abbey for the tourists, you understand. The church is open more often for worshippers."

"And you were here on your own after Mr Hendricks left last night?" Innes asked.

"Well, of course," Squires said to Jacob.

Jacob noticed Innes glance at him but did not look at her or pay her any attention. He kept his eyes fixed on Squires.

"One has to make sure everything is locked up properly, Chief Inspector. Takes me time to finish my business here, both liturgical and administrative. You do realise we were robbed not so long ago? Thieves broke in and stole a lot of silver that we use during communion. I remember telephoning the police at the time and speaking to them and they didn't seem particularly bothered about it. Now it looks like you want my help instead."

"All right, that'll be all for now, Reverend Squires. I take it you have no plans to leave the area in the foreseeable future?"

"Of course not! I must tend to my flock, Chief Inspector. My superior is not the sort of man one wants to disappoint," he said glancing up at the vaulted ceiling. "But all in all, I would say he is a real joy to work for."

*

"That Bloke gave me the creeps," Innes said to Jacob when they were standing outside.

"I think he was just a bit nervous, that's all. The problem is, maybe he's got a good reason to be. If Hendricks was telling the truth about him seeing a suspicious-looking woman walking up the path and going inside the abbey at around five, and Squires was telling the truth about staying till six, then he was lying about being alone for that hour."

"Why didn't you press him on it, sir?"

"I'd rather get an advantage first and I don't feel I have enough information. For a start, Hendricks could be lying. Maybe he's a nasty piece of work with a grievance against Squires and realised he had an opportunity to drop him in it so thought he'd do some stirring. Maybe not. I want a full check done on all of the town CCTV. Whoever dumped that body in the abbey grounds must have been caught on camera somewhere, especially if they brought the body into the town in a vehicle of any kind."

"There's not that many CCTV cameras around in Malmesbury, sir."

"I realise that, Innes. They plan on increasing the number of cameras here substantially following an increase in vandalism and anti-social behaviour – if you can believe it in a place like this."

"It's everywhere now, sir."

Jacob wondered about that. "However, there are some cameras dotted around here and there. I want you to do a door-to-door around the abbey, say a two or three-hundred-metre radius. While you're doing it, make a note of all the CCTV cameras that have any kind of access to any of the roads leading to the abbey. I don't believe whoever dumped that body carried it in over their shoulder from out of town. There's going to be a vehicle and we're going to find it.

"Yes, sir."

"And try and find out who the mystery woman is who paid Mr Squires a visit last night."

"Shall I do that now, sir?"

Jacob shook his head. "No. We're visiting Tansy Babbington's house now. I want answers and there aren't too many around here."

CHAPTER 4

The drive northwest out of Malmesbury up towards Tetbury was through pleasant and beautiful countryside. This was Cotswolds country and everything was starting to look very chocolate box. Jacob barely noticed, because his hometown of Bradford-on-Avon was also one of the most beautiful towns in the country. On the road today, there was little traffic and Jacob cruised the vintage car through the thin mist until Innes pointed up the road towards the next turn.

Jacob turned left and drove his old car down a narrow winding country lane wide enough only for one vehicle. This was always a bit of a nightmare because there was always the risk of meeting another car and then having to reverse back to a passing place. As it happened, there were no other vehicles and they were soon at Tansy Babbington's country pile and pulling up to a closed five-bar gate.

"Do the honours please, constable," Jacob said.

Innes hopped out of the Alvis and tottered through the thinning mist. Jacob watched her open the five-bar gate and swing it open then he gently pressed the throttle and nosed the car through the gate. After Innes had shut it behind her again, she climbed into the car and they continued down a sweeping gravel driveway lined on both sides by horse chestnut trees until finally reaching the sumptuous house.

They exited the car and Jacob took a moment to survey the property. Judging from the fairly short drive from the gate to the house, he deduced most of the fifteen acres lay behind the property, which was a beautiful Edwardian manor house built of honey-coloured stone with beautiful bay sash windows. The entire front façade of the house was covered in wisteria, which in the springtime he imagined would be something to behold.

They walked to the front door. Tansy Babbington's body had been found naked apart from the feather and the coin. There had been no wallet or purse or car keys, so Jacob now picked up a terracotta pot with an extravagant fern beside the front door and walked around to a sash window in one of the bays. He smashed the bottom pane out with the terracotta pot, then after removing dangerous shards by pulling them out of the putty and knocking more obstinate ones out with the pot still in his hand, he climbed inside through the window.

Innes climbed in behind him and the two of them found themselves in a beautifully appointed study, presumably where Tansy did most of her work. Although the room contained many beautiful period features, such as the fireplace, mantelpiece, and ceiling rose, Jacob saw an enormous amount of new money had been spent restoring and modernising the space. He guessed the rest of the house would present him with a similar display of the wealth and taste he saw here in this room. There was a large polished mahogany writing desk set one-third into the room, with the sash windows behind it, so the writer sitting at her desk would be looking into the room towards the door leading out into a hallway. The walls were painted in a beautiful soft green colour, and there were tasteful black and white photographs of the Wiltshire countryside, three in a row on the far wall. On the left-hand wall was a long three-seater studded leather sofa, with beautiful silk scatter cushions on it. Jacob wandered closer to the desk and saw a laptop computer, shut down and closed.

"Pick that up. We'll take it back to forensics. They can go through it later."

"Yes, sir," Innes said, picking up the laptop.

Jacob scanned the luxurious space. "You see a mobile phone anywhere around here?"

"Not in this room, now. But the damned things are so small, they could be anywhere."

Jacob shook his head. "Not in my experience. They're always left somewhere handy. The most obvious deduction is that our killer took it, but we might get lucky. Search the rest of the house."

They stepped out of the study into the corridor, and Jacob ordered Innes to go upstairs and search the top floor while he made his way around the ground floor. His self-guided tour included a drawing room, some kind of salon, a ludicrously appointed dining room with a table for twelve people, a large sitting room with two three-piece suites arranged in it, one around an enormous fireplace, the other in a sort of reading nook by some French windows. On a marble mantlepiece, he saw more photographs of the county and one of Tansy standing in front of the Eiffel Tower. He wondered who had taken the picture, but then realised due to the proximity of Tansy to the lens that it was almost certainly a selfie.

There was a shelf beside the mantelpiece, with precisely nineteen books on it, held in place by bronze elephant bookends. When he tipped his head and looked along the spines, he saw these were Tansy Babbington's chef-d'oeuvre. The magnum opus that had built the empire whose heart he was now standing in. He pulled the first one from the row, opened it and saw it had been signed by the author. He read the blurb: *Tristan Abercromby-Fairfax, the tenth earl of Northshire, retreats to his English castle after being savagely wounded far away across the sea during the American War of Independence. He is only partly healed when a murder on the sprawling estate drags him back into a world of secrets and betrayal from which only true love from a woman with a pure heart can save him.*

Jacob frowned, put it back and then picked the second one out which had also been signed. They had all been signed by her but were sitting on the shelf above the mantelpiece, where no one could see them but her. They were all brand-new, and barely handled, with not a single crease in any of the spines and perfectly flat pages, as smooth and unused as a fresh blanket of snow.

Innes stepped into the room. "Did you find anything, sir?"

"Only the home of a very lonely woman. There are no photographs here of anyone but herself. No sign of anyone else at all. I wouldn't be surprised if no one ever visited this place. What about you?"

"Yes, or at least I think so. Upstairs, there's a second study that looks out over the maze. There were no computers in there and I think it was supposed to be a sort of an internet-free space. I found a kind of journal and in it is the personal address and phone number of her agent."

She had handed it to Jacob.

Jacob looked at the details and almost smiled. "This is good work, Innes."

He looked at the details and saw the agent's name was Delia Wagner.

"Think she's related to the composer?" he asked

Innes looked confused, her brow furrowing. "Sorry, sir – what do you mean?"

"Never mind." Jacob pulled his phone from his pocket and made a call to the agent.

"Good morning, this is Delia Wagner."

"Good morning Mrs Wagner," Jacob said.

"It's 'Ms' actually. I find 'Mrs' rather oppressive."

"My apologies," Jacob said, always noting everything that was said, no matter how small or seemingly irrelevant. "My name is Detective Chief Inspector Tom Jacob and I'm calling from Wiltshire CID."

"My goodness! What's happened?"

"Are you the literary agent of the author Tansy Babbington?"

"Yes, I am. Is everything all right with Tansy?"

"I'm sorry, but I have to tell you Tansy Babbington was found dead earlier today by a member of the public."

Silence.

"Ms Wagner? Are you still there?"

"Yes, of course, I'm still here Chief Inspector. I'm sorry, it was just such a shock. Are you sure?"

"Sadly, yes."

"But how did this happen?"

Jacob noted Innes was now going through the neat row of books on the shelf.

"That is what we're trying to establish. We're treating her death as suspicious."

"That means murder doesn't it?"

"Yes. I wonder if you wouldn't mind answering a couple of questions this morning. We can do it over the telephone."

"Yes, of course, Chief Inspector. Anything that will help, but this is all simply appalling."

"When was the last time you saw Tansy?"

"Weeks ago, no one ever sees her."

Jacob took note. "What do you mean by that?"

"She was the archetypal reclusive writer, Chief Inspector. She never saw anyone, she never went anywhere. She did travel a little once, a few years ago, but always on her own. I'm afraid to say that for the past few years, she rarely left the house. We do most of our meetings over Zoom and most of our discussions on email. She even signs her contracts, scans them and emails them to me. It's just the way she is."

"I see, and did this reluctance to speak to other people extend beyond her professional life into her social life?"

As he spoke Innes was now examining the elephant bookends.

"I don't believe she had much of a love life if that's what you're asking."

"Not specifically, Ms Wagner. I'm just interested in if she had any kind of family or social life."

"Neither," Wagner said flatly. "I'm afraid poor Tansy was an orphan and she had no knowledge of who her parents were. She had no family at all. She had no friends, except those she made at university many years ago but she never saw them. As far as I'm aware she'd never really had any significant other until…"

"Yes, Ms Wagner?"

"She had talked a little bit on email lately about a local man named Den, but she never went into any detail. I knew better than to ask her."

"Did she say if this was a friend or something more?"

"I can't tell you, although I suppose the way she was talking about him one might deduce more than a friend. But we're talking very recent."

"When exactly did she start talking about this Den?"

"Only the past few months. I wouldn't get excited, she barely mentioned him."

Jacob paused, realising Wagner was trying to be helpful but had little more to offer.

"Thank you, Ms Wagner. You've been very helpful. If I need you again, I'll call you on this number."

"Of course. Anytime."

Jacob thanked her, hung up and then turned to Innes.

"Did you get anything from her, sir?"

"Tansy Babbington may have recently met a man named Den. Other than that, nothing. Just a line of dead ends. She didn't have any family, she grew up in an orphanage, with no friends, and no real significant other over the years. She was in the words of her agent, the 'archetypal reclusive writer'. Now she's dead and we've got nothing but dead ends everywhere we look."

"Apart from the M.O., sir?"

Jacob said nothing. He knew that Alistair Keeley couldn't have killed Tansy Babbington and whoever had done so was trying to make it look like the Ferryman. But something about that didn't sit right with him. They were only hours into the case and already things were becoming tangled and opaque.

"C'mon. Let's get back to HQ," Jacob said. "I need to speak to the Chief Super before all of this gets totally out of control."

CHAPTER 5

"Keeley is dead. He was killed in a car accident in the Austrian Alps a year after he escaped from Wakefield Prison. He is a dead man so don't even *think* about going there, Chief Inspector. I want none of your crackpot theories clouding up this case."

Jacob had run through the conversation with Kent in his mind on the drive back down to Devizes. So far, it was going pretty much the way he had imagined, except for the temperature in Kent's office, which was even hotter and more stifling than usual.

"But how certain are they?" Jacob asked. "With a man like Alistair Keeley you have to be one hundred per cent certain, actually *see* the body go into the crematorium."

"We're talking about the Austrian Federal Police, Jacob," Kent said. "They *are* one hundred per cent certain. They scraped his body up off the Grossglockner High Alpine Road, a mountain pass known for its challenging driving conditions. Apparently, he was in a high-impact collision with the lead vehicle of one of these luxury high-performance driving clubs. He was driving a Mercedes into the Tyrol when he crashed head-on with one of these prats speeding in a Porsche. You like cars, don't you?"

"Not that sort of car, sir."

"Hmm. Anyway, the impact was severe and both vehicles were totally wrecked. Both drivers were killed, naturally. I've already requested them to send the file over. They were a little vague about when that might be, but I think we can expect it by the end of the day."

"I presume there are photos?" Jacob asked.

"Of course, there are bloody photos, and from what Oberstleutnant Pichler told me this morning, they're not pleasant viewing."

"I want to see them as soon as they arrive, sir."

"Alistair Keeley is *dead*, Jacob! This is a matter of official record. You have to let go of this obsession you have with the man because he nearly killed Sophie Anderson. I'm sorry about what happened to her, but there it is. What we're dealing with here is a copycat killer and a seriously unhinged one at that. I need you to be clear on this. I need you to be focused on the ball, not chasing ridiculous theories about dead serial killers."

"I'll be happier when I've read the file."

Kent sighed. "You'll get the file as soon as they send it to us, but whoever did this is another man. The method was different. The shroud was wrapped differently, the coins were all wrong and he left a calling card – that black feather. Keeley never did anything like that. If that weren't enough, this time there was violence. All of Keeley's victims were killed by ligature strangulation, and…"

"So was Tansy Babbington."

"Let me finish, Chief Inspector," Kent said with an icy look. "All of Keeley's victims were killed by ligature strangulation but he was very careful not to leave any marks aside from those created by the ligature. Tansy Babbington had bruising on the side of her head. Keeley never roughed them up. Don't you remember the interviews? He kept going on about how he killed them because he loved them, and that he didn't want to hurt them, but Dr Lyon says the blow sustained on Tansy Babbington's temple would have hurt considerably."

"He also said we should wait until the lab report for his final word on the matter."

"Remember what I said about focus, please." Kent shook his head and tossed his pen onto his desk. "As I say, we're looking at a copycat here and that means it could be anyone, so cast your net wide, Chief Inspector. I don't want this getting out of hand like before."

Jacob didn't have to ask Kent what he was talking about. The reference was to Operation Grovely, or as the local and national press dubbed it the Witch-Hunt Murders, a notorious case from several years ago in which the Home Office Pathologist attached to Wiltshire CID, a man named Ethan Spargo, had turned out to be a raving lunatic on a killing spree designed to cover-up multiple murders he had committed decades earlier.

The investigation had centred on an area in the south of Wiltshire called Grovely Wood, a forest with a very ancient and dark past, including a burial site containing the graves of four women accused of being witches several hundred years ago. Jacob had worked well on what turned out to be a complex and harrowing case and brought it to a swift conclusion, but Kent was not happy with his work. Too many people were killed and the nature of the killings generated far too much negative attention in the newspapers. There were even television news crews on the scene with talk of serial killers running wild, which Kent took as a personal rebuke of his competence as the Detective Chief Superintendent heading the investigation.

"It didn't exactly get out of hand, sir," Jacob said, with a hint of defiance in his voice. "It was a very tricky case and we worked it through to a sound conclusion."

"Police marksmen had to shoot someone dead at Stonehenge, Jacob! That's not a sound conclusion in any world. Make sure it doesn't get to that point again."

"Of course," Jacob said with a warm smile. "I'll do my best."

"Hmm. Do we know if this victim was drugged or not?"

The question irritated Jacob as did Kent's habit of firing questions at him out of the blue. It made the man very difficult to predict, which was exactly why he did it. Kent liked to maintain control and keep his juniors on their toes. Anyone engaged in a conversation with DCS Kent could never know what was about to be asked of them next.

"We don't know yet. Not until Dr Lyon has produced the autopsy report."

"And when will that be?"

"He has prioritised the case and he's going to give us a call as soon as it's ready."

Kent was silent for a while, even turning in his seat and looking through the window for a few seconds. Then he swung around and locked eyes on Jacob, like a hawk. "Professor Keeley always used drugs to induce paralysis, did he not?"

"Yes, sir. Post-mortem reports showed he used substantial quantities of gamma-hydroxybutyrate to render his victims quite helpless. He did this before strangling them. Then he slid the coins into their mouths and wrapped them in the shrouds. It's never been clear if the women were dead before being wrapped tightly in the shrouds. The drug he used slows brain activity down to the point where the victim would be conscious but unable to act, even in response to something like being strangled, especially if the correct amount of the drug were used. In other words, the women were aware they were being choked to death but could do absolutely nothing about it. That was how he was able to kill them without leaving any marks. The slang name for the drug is 'coma in a bottle'."

"I'm perfectly well aware of that, but that's not my point. My *point* is that if this drug is not found in the victim then I think we have formally to rule out Keeley."

"Rule out a dead man, sir?" Jacob said

"He's ruled out in my mind, Chief Inspector. I mean ruled out in your mind. Without the drugs, the modus operandi is just too different. The way the sheet is wrapped is different, the coin is different, the feather is new and there was some kind of blunt force trauma to the victim's head. If there is no use of the drug then this has got nothing to do with Keeley. Considering the man is almost certainly dead I want you to draw a line under it and consider it a copycat."

"As you wish, sir," Jacob said, keeping to himself most of his thoughts on the matter for the time being. "I'll bring you the information just as soon as I speak to Dr Lyon."

"He said he was going to give you a call as soon as he's ready," Kent said tapping his forefinger down on his desk. "Are we talking this morning, this afternoon… when?"

"I believe Dr Lyon told me a good preliminary report will be available in the early afternoon, but a full report will have to wait until later due to the time it takes to run certain tests."

Switching subject out of the blue yet again, Kent now leant forward in his chair and focused his eyes on Jacob. "You had better make sure you get to the bottom of this and fast. I don't know what crazy ideas you're entertaining about Keeley rising from the dead so he can kill women and dump them in Malmesbury, but I know this much – this is a deranged copycat who is intent on reigniting the terror and fear that Keeley instilled in thousands of women before he was finally caught. And I think we both know what nearly happened when he was caught."

"Yes, sir. Have you got a cold, by the way?"

Kent looked at him like he was mad. "No. What are you going on about?"

"It just seems rather warm in here."

"Don't talk rubbish, it's a perfect balmy twenty-four degrees." Keeley paused a beat. "How is Dr Anderson?"

"She flew to Italy early this morning. She has an international psychology conference in Rome. She's going to be there until next week. I was planning on flying out to spend some time with her there at the weekend but then something came up."

Kent frowned. "You're one of the best investigators in the county, Jacob. Believe me, I don't enjoy saying that. When the body of a dead woman turns up wrapped in a bloody dustsheet on the grounds of Malmesbury Abbey, I want my best man on it! So, you'll just have to put Rome away for a few days and go and visit it with your girlfriend in a few months instead. I take it that's OK with you?"

"It's more than OK, sir," Jacob said with a smile. "I can think of nothing better to do with my time than catch the man responsible for this egregious and horrifying murder."

"And just make sure that's how you put it when you speak to the press later today."

Jacob felt his heart sink. "The Press? Surely they can't be involved at such an early stage."

"Oh, they'll be involved alright! You can't keep something like this secret for long in a place the size of Malmesbury. We've already taken calls from all of the local rags, and even a couple of the Nationals. For now, we're stalling them, but at some point, they're going to want someone to speak to them and that someone's going be you. Got it?"

"Got it." Jaco's smile faded.

"Good. Then you'd better get on with it. Get out there, Chief Inspector, and find whoever did this before he leaves us another one. Organise the team. Get everyone straightened out so they know what they're doing and get that report from Lyon to me as soon as possible."

"Yes, sir," Jacob said, rising from his seat. "Thank you, sir."

CHAPTER 6

Ten minutes after he met with Kent in his office upstairs, Jacob called a full team briefing in the main conference room. Word had rapidly gone around the station about the major incident up in Malmesbury and the case had already been designated the code name Operation Abbey. The room was chock full of staff from across the station who were there because of the dark rumours circulating about the suspicious death. Jacob had already decided to control that situation very firmly right from the outset to maintain some degree of objectivity in the approach to the case, while at the same time alerting everyone to the possibility that they could be looking at a return of one of Britain's most notorious serial killers.

Jacob now assessed that everyone with a vested interest in the case had arrived and was settling down, so he closed the door and walked to the front, glancing across the packed conference room, and quickly scanning the faces of those in attendance. Standing at the back, he was pleased to see Mia Francis and Anna Mazurek, talking quietly as they took their seats by the window on Jacob's right. Sensing a quiet lull in the frenzied gossip-mongering, Jacob now called everyone in the room to attention and waited for a few seconds for the sound of chatting, whispering and chairs scraping on the floor to come to a close.

"Good morning everyone, and thank you for coming at such short notice," Jacob began, shoving his hands in his pockets and walking towards the front row. "I'm sure by now, you will all have heard about the suspicious death that was phoned in up in Malmesbury earlier today. I've already attended the scene with Mia Francis and Dr Richard Lyon the Home Office pathologist and some other members of my immediate team."

As he spoke several people turned to look at Mia and Anna standing at the back. Jacob immediately called them back to attention.

"The body was discovered this morning by an arborist working at the abbey, elevated in a cherry picker so he was able to be at a certain angle that allowed him to see what turned out to be a body wrapped in a sheet."

An immediate ripple of chitchat moved around the room in response to what Jacob had just said about the sheet.

"Settle down everybody," Jacob said. "I understand why this has caused so much interest, but there is no evidence yet to suggest that this is the work of Alistair Keeley. As some of the more experienced officers will already know, Keeley, or the Ferryman as the press dubbed him during his spree of killing several years ago, was notorious for placing a coin in his victims' mouths and then wrapping them in a shroud. This was motivated by a depraved re-enactment of an ancient Greek ritual involving helping his victims pay for Charon, the original Ferryman to sail them across the River Styx after their deaths. So Keeley was not actually the Ferryman, but helping the women pay the Ferryman to take them into the next world. This subtlety was lost on the press who simply called him the Ferryman. We've all heard of him. We all know what he did. We also all know that he was arrested after a very dangerous and challenging operation involving the work of Dr Sophie Anderson who put herself at great risk to catch this man."

Another ripple of excitement went around the room. There was not a man or woman here who did not know that Jacob and Sophie Anderson lived together.

"Again, back to the settling please," Jacob said. "For younger or newer members on the team who may not be up to date, Keeley notoriously escaped from prison after jumping from a high landing. We believe he must have calculated very carefully that he would break his ankles but cause no further damage. He did this to be transported to the prison hospital from which it was easier to escape. Those of you who like to keep up with events may also know that Keeley was last seen in Austria after being involved in a lethal car accident which killed him and the driver of the other vehicle. Austrian authorities are emailing over the file they created on the accident and once we've seen those, including photographs of Keeley, who was found dead on the scene by a fire rescue crew, we will all be able to put Keeley behind us."

"But not the Ferryman," Inspector Bill Morgan said.

Jacob knew what his old friend and colleague meant. "Sadly no. Not if this is the work of a copycat killer who wants to become the Ferryman all over again, and for now we are going to consider this to be the work of a copycat killer until we hear otherwise about Keeley."

"I don't suppose it makes much difference," somebody at the front called out. "If someone's going to go around killing women, putting coins in their mouths and wrapping them in bloody dustsheets, does it really matter who that is? Whoever it is must be a bloody nutcase!"

"I take the point," Jacob said, "but I think it *does* make a difference. Keeley was an extremely evil and depraved man but he was also blessed or cursed, depending on your point of view, with an extraordinarily high IQ. He was a polymath genius and university scholar, specialising in Greek Underworld myths and the Metropolitan Police in London say he was very difficult to catch. Dr Sophie Anderson nearly lost her life in the process of doing so. Moving on, although at this stage we can't be sure if it's Keeley or a copycat, we can say there were some fundamental differences at the scene of the murder today."

"So, it's definitely being treated as a murder then?" another asked.

"At this time it is being considered a murder informally, but we're expecting that to be formally confirmed by Dr

Richard Lyon later on today after he has conducted his tests in the mortuary."

"So what were these differences then?" a police constable called out.

"They were subtle but significant," Jacob said. "First of all, the dustsheet or so-called 'shroud' had been wrapped differently, according to both Mia Francis and Dr Richard Lyon. They believed it had been wrapped by a left-handed person rather than a right-handed person like Keeley. Second, the coin inside the victim's mouth was a different type of coin from those used by Keeley. Keeley used ancient Greek coins, always silver and always imprinted with the image of a honeybee on them. These were called Charon's Obol, which the ancients used to put in the mouths of the dead so they could pay the Ferryman, as I've just said. But they were a specific type of coin, whereas the one found this morning was an ancient coin but a Roman one and from a slightly different era. It was also bronze and not silver. There were other differences as well. Dr Richard Lyon pointed out bruising on the victim's temple, which indicated violence, but Keeley never used violence. Finally, there was a calling card left at the scene. Whoever killed this woman, left behind one single feather – a black feather which probably belonged to a crow. We're not sure yet. Again, Dr Lyon is looking into that too. It may have some significance depending on what bird it came from."

A woman police constable raised her hand. "So, you reckon because of all of these differences it's a copycat then, sir?"

It was a difficult question to answer, especially in front of practically the entire station. Jacob had been torturing himself with the answer to this in speaking to Kent earlier this morning, and perhaps even earlier since seeing the victim out in the abbey grounds. All the evidence pointed to a copycat killer. The Austrian authorities were one hundred per cent certain that Keeley had died in a road traffic accident several years ago, and then there were all of the mistakes made that he had just pointed out to everyone in the conference room. His head told him this was a copycat killer, but his heart told him that somehow Alastair Keeley was responsible for this murder, that the Ferryman was back and killing innocent women all over again.

"The only way I could answer that, is by saying I'm trying to keep an open mind," Jacob said. "The facts point to this being a copycat killer, and I take the point that someone made earlier about how from the victim's point of view it doesn't make much difference. Although it would make a big difference from our point of view because I believe Keeley would be significantly harder to catch than a random nutcase who wants to copy the method of Keeley's murders. But those are the facts, but in my heart, I can't shake the feeling that somehow Keeley has duped us all and that he's back murdering all over again. For now, I want everyone to pursue this with an open mind, and get back to good policing basics. Go to work everyone. You know what to do."

CHAPTER 7

Jacob escaped from the charged atmosphere of the briefing to the comparative calm of the large open-plan office where he worked with his team, but turned around halfway to his desk to go and get himself a coffee from the machine in the corridor. With the hot cardboard cup of frothy coffee warming his hand, he now stepped back into his office and walked over to his desk. He was just wondering if he still had some custard creams in his deck when he noticed Morgan had got back from the conference room before him and was already sitting at his desk peering into his computer. A delicious savoury smell of meat and cheese grew stronger as Jacob walked over to Morgan's desk and identified the culprit as a sausage, cheese and bean bake from the cafeteria downstairs, fresh off the hot plate and sitting on a plate just inches away from Morgan's mouse mat.

"Blimey, that was quick work," Jacob said, gesturing at the bake. "I only broke up the briefing about five minutes ago."

Morgan beamed. "That's the trick, isn't it? When you're in a briefing room with that many people just right before lunch, you know what's going to happen when the briefing ends, don't you? That is why I flew out of the briefing – so I could be first in the queue and why I'm sitting here with a hot bake while everyone else is standing in a big long line waiting for theirs. You looked very hot and bothered in the briefing by the way. Keeley bothering you?"

"No, I had a meeting in Kent's room."

Morgan shook his head. "How can he stand it that hot? It's like a blast furnace in there!"

"You can say that again."

"His car's even worse," Morgan said, taking a chunky bite of his bake. "I drove down to Salisbury in it with him once. Hotter than a glassblower's arse, it was."

Jacob resisted the imagery. "I take it you're already hard at work on the Malmesbury case?"

"Indeed I am. Not only have I bought myself a delicious hot sausage, cheese and bean bake for lunch, but I have also been a very busy boy here on my computer. While you were shutting down your briefing and getting yourself that rather pathetic-looking coffee, check this out."

"What have you found?"

"I found Meredith Ash's hidey-hole."

"Who says he's hiding?"

"Innes looked into it. She called him on his mobile and got a cryptic voicemail about how he had to go away for a few days to get his head straight. Anyway, I checked out his Instagram and found a little more – another message to his adoring fans about him going to a writer's retreat, where he needed to go and get his ego stroked for a few days. Look here."

Morgan navigated to a new window revealing Meredith Ash's Instagram page. After scrolling through a series of pictures of his large back garden, ostensibly detailing the colour of the autumn foliage beginning to come through on his trees, but clearly there to show the expansive property that he owned, Morgan finally landed on pictures of somewhere different – the interior of a beautiful rustic cottage with exposed stone walls and oak beams and a roaring fireplace. There were even a couple of photographs of a patio area with a beautiful view stretching out across the English countryside on a frosty morning.

"Read what he wrote here," Morgan said. "He says he's having a great time restoring his mental health after he argued with Tansy Babbington. By the looks of previous posts, she would normally reply, but of course, we both know why she hasn't done that today."

"And where is this place?" Jacob asked.

"It's in the Cotswolds Area of Outstanding National Beauty, in between Tetbury and Didmarton, just outside the Westonbirt National Arboretum. Apparently, this is where famous writers go to rough it for a few days."

"I'm sure he won't mind having his thinking time interrupted by a visit from you and Innes."

"You don't fancy going over there and shaking him down, sir? He seems like a right prick to me. Thought you'd enjoy it."

"Maybe in other circumstances, I might enjoy it, Bill, but I just got a message from Richard Lyon telling me his preliminary report is ready."

"I see. Is Innes still up in Malmesbury?" Morgan took another bite of his bake.

"I'll just give her a quick call," Jacob said, ringing Innes. "Innes, how's it going?"

"Not good at all, sir, I'm afraid," Innes replied. "I conducted the door-to-door this morning with a couple of uniformed officers and got absolutely nowhere. No one saw anything else relating to the suspicious death at all. The only thing I have is a security camera in a small shop on the other side of the road to the abbey. I've been in and asked him if I can go through it all, but he got difficult and demanded a warrant."

Jacob sighed and squeezed his temples. "You told him it was for a murder investigation?"

"Yes, sir, but I got the feeling he is a very difficult man all around. He sells pretentious chess pieces."

"All right, we'll organise the warrant then we can go back and get the footage. In the meantime, I want you to meet Bill Morgan at the Westonbirt National Arboretum."

"Does Inspector Morgan fancy taking a break to look at some pretty trees, sir? They are starting to turn after all and there are some lovely colours to be seen."

"Very funny Detective Constable Innes," Jacob said. "But it's even better than that. Inspector Morgan has tracked down the location of Meredith Ash, author of the Poison Pen Instagram posts to Tansy Babbington. Apparently, he has been stressed out by his feud with her to such a degree that he needs to go and meditate at the Woodhaven Writers Retreat just outside the arboretum. You and Morgan can go and ask him a few questions and see if he can shed any light on what happened this morning."

"Be happy to, sir. I'll meet the inspector at the entrance."

Jacob thanked her, hung up and relayed the information to Bill Morgan, who had already derived most of it from Jacob's side of the conversation. The Welshman looked around the office, and seeing no one could hear them, he lowered his voice.

"About this morning's briefing, Jacob. Are you going to tell Sophie?"

Jacob nodded. "I've got to tell her, Bill. How can I not tell her that there's a chance Keeley has started killing again?"

"But there's no evidence that this is him yet," Morgan said, trying to sound more reassuring than he actually did. "For all we know, this is just the work of some deranged copycat."

"That's what Kent thinks and that *could* be true, but we know that Keeley escaped from Wakefield four years ago now. We have to consider him as a possible suspect."

"But why wait four years?" Morgan asked. "That's what I don't understand. We all read the stories about when the bastard broke out of Wakefield. None of us could believe it had happened. Then he just disappeared. Why come back now and start killing again?"

Jacob thought about the Category A prison Wakefield, dubbed the 'Monster Mansion' due to the reputation of some of its prisoners over the years. It wasn't a moniker Jacob agreed with. It gave a certain undeserved cachet to some of those inmates. "He didn't just disappear into thin air, though. The Met looked into it. They had a lead that made them think he'd gone to Austria and then he was found dead there, or so the story goes."

Morgan seemed even more sceptical. "And why would he come back from Austria if he'd successfully escaped there and was free, living a new life? Why would he risk coming right back to this country and start doing it all over again? It just doesn't make any sense. I never thought I'd say it, but I'm with Kent. This has got to be a copycat. I'm surprised we've not had one sooner if I'm being honest."

Jacob shook his head slowly, still thinking about the woman hideously wrapped in the shroud. "This is him, Bill. I just know it. I have to tell Sophie and prepare her for the worst. Don't forget Keeley held a serious grudge against her after she helped to put him away in the first place – and don't forget his reach. He had someone leave one of his damned coins on Sophie's pillow at the conference she went to in Devon. We're going to need to move her somewhere when she gets back from Italy, somewhere new and with no links to her and I'm going to want a uniformed presence there around the clock until we've caught him."

Morgan gave a low whistle. "It's gonna have a hell of an impact on her. You know that."

"I know it will," Jacob said. "It hit her really hard the first time around. It was so traumatic for her, that she wondered if she would ever work in psychology again. She posed as one of his students and allowed him to get very close to her, to form a bond. Then she posed as one of his victims – you know, played along with him."

"Which was very brave of her."

"It was stupid," Jacob said. "I would never have let her do it. He nearly strangled her to death!"

"What was his MO again – manual strangulation?"

Jacob shook his head. "Homicidal ligature asphyxiation."

"Less common."

"Right," Jacob said. "Usually in cases of strangling, it's manual, done with the hands after an explosive outburst, a catastrophic failure to control temper. Keeley was a sadist, always carefully planning his attacks and executing them in perfection to the last detail, or that was how he saw it. I won't let anything happen to her, Bill."

"I know you won't. None of us will. But please remember there's no evidence it was him – just the opposite! Everything points to a copycat."

Morgan glanced at his watch. "I'd better get going. You think Mr Ash will enjoy us interrupting him in his special thinking spot?" Morgan asked with a devilish grin.

"Indubitably," Jacob said. "Anyway, have a lovely time with your pretty trees."

"And you have a lovely time with your corpse."

CHAPTER 8

Morgan was pleasantly surprised to see that the Woodhaven Writers Retreat was so close to the arboretum that it could almost have been a part of it. It was certainly as beautiful as the arboretum, with an enormous variety of oak, ash, maple and sycamore in various shades of autumnal colours although many were still fairly green. By the time he pulled up at the entrance to the retreat, Innes was already parked up in her car waiting for him. She flashed her lights at him to show him where she was parked but he had already seen. He now pulled up beside her, climbed out of his car, closed and locked the door and walked over to her as she emerged into the dull overcast day.

"You made good time, sir," she said, looking at her watch.

"And I kept to the speed limit all the way, as well," Morgan said with a grin. His reputation for flagrantly ignoring the speed limit preceded him, but he had recently decided to take things a little more easily after receiving a gentle rebuke for his driving, especially some of his cornering, by Detective Sergeant Anna Mazurek, after he had driven her out to an interview concerning a case in Marlborough.

"That was very good of you."

"I thought so, but you'd better do the driving inside the retreat. Go on and get back behind the wheel. There's no sense taking two cars down there."

Morgan climbed into the passenger seat and Innes climbed back in, switched on the engine and drove through the gate. They followed a beautiful sweeping avenue which slowly climbed in elevation until the trees flanking them eventually thinned out to reveal exposed ground on either side of the car. There was no longer any mist in the air, the day was flat and dull but there was a breathtaking vista of the gentle rolling Cotswold hills stretching out to the horizon. Up on the brow of a hill, Morgan spied a beautiful Georgian mansion, built of honey-coloured stone. Beautiful bay windows looked out across the sweeping gravel drive as they pulled up and came to a stop, staring at them like suspicious eyes.

They climbed out of the car and made their way through to the retreat's reception area where a bubbly young woman with spiky blonde hair had been working, or at least pretending to work, Morgan mused, behind a desk. She looked up at them and gave them a beaming smile.

"Good afternoon!" she said jovially. "How can I help?"

Morgan pulled his police warrant card out of his pocket and showed it to her.

"I'm Detective Inspector Morgan and this is Detective Constable Innes from Wiltshire CID. We're here to speak to someone who is currently residing at the retreat."

"Ah, well that could be a problem," she said with a gentle and understanding nod of her head, the kind of smile and nod that suggested everything she was about to say was going to be very difficult and not at all helpful. "You see, Woodhaven has a strict policy of not allowing any of our residential writers to be disturbed by the outside world while they are here. We believe in creating an environment of total peace and calm, a place where they can unwind and allow themselves to be restored by the beauty of the nature surrounding us."

"That's too bad because this is a murder investigation," Morgan said in his usual blunt manner. "So, you'll be telling me where to find Meredith Ash right now. Thanks ever so much."

The woman's smile faded away into her round face. "Oh, I see. In that case, I think you'd better wait here while I get the owner."

She shuffled away through a door behind the desk and Morgan met Innes's eyes and saw she now had to look away to give herself time to suppress a smile before the owner arrived. The woman who returned beside the receptionist was stick-thin, with a perfectly cut, dark brown bob of hair, and thin maroon lips. Her eyes were a watery grey colour and when she spoke it was in severely clipped and brief sentences as if there had been a heavy tax levied on words themselves.

"I'm Mrs Hacket, the owner."

"As I was explaining to your colleague here," Morgan went on, "We are detectives from Wiltshire CID conducting a very important murder investigation and we want to speak to someone who is staying here at your retreat."

"As I think you've already been told, we have a very strict policy here at the retreat. We do not allow any incursion made by the outside world to come in and breach the inner peace of our retreat or its residents."

"It would be very unpleasant for your writer's retreat, I'm sure if you were to be charged with obstructing a police officer, Mrs Hacket."

The thin lips got even thinner. "Obstructing a police officer? What on earth are you talking about?"

"It's perfectly simple," Morgan continued. "I need to talk to Meredith Ash in connection with the murder of a woman whose body was discovered this morning in another part of the county. If you are obstructing me from talking to him, then you are preventing me from carrying out my duties or making it much more difficult for me to do so. That's correct, isn't it, Detective Constable?"

"I believe it is, sir. I think it's Section 89, Part 2 of the Police Act 1996."

Morgan jabbed a thumb at Innes while still fixing his eye on Mrs Hacket. "You see what they're like these days? They know every paragraph, they know it all chapter and verse, the way I know the Bible. Worrying, isn't it?"

Mrs Hacket grew anxious. "I don't know about this. I don't think it can be obstructing a police officer. I mean these are private premises! We've made a contractual promise to our guests that we won't allow them to be disturbed."

"Mrs Hacket, what you are doing is wilful obstruction and I'm going to arrest you for it if you don't let me speak to Meredith Ash. That's your last warning."

Mrs Hacket shared a glance of concern with the other woman behind the reception desk, but she was no support, offering only a vague shoulder shrug.

"Very well then, but if I get into any trouble and Mr Ash decides to sue me, I shall turn around and sue you as well!"

"You knock yourself out, Mrs Hacket. Now, where can we find Mr Ash?"

"He's down in the Constable Lodge," she said as if the words had been pulled out of her with pliers.

"Constable Lodge?" Morgan said. "That's rather ironic given the circumstances, isn't it?"

"Our lodges are named after famous English artists and composers Inspector Morgan. You'll find the Constable Lodge at the far west of the property. If you drive around the back of the main house here, you'll see a signposted lane leading down to where the lodges are. It's the furthest one away, directly ahead of you."

Morgan smiled. "You've been too kind, Mrs Hacket."

*

The drive down to the lodges was even more beautiful than the drive up to the main house. They followed the road as directed by Mrs Hacket around the house to the signposted lane and then back down the other side of a slope until they were once again surrounded by trees. The lane grew narrower and Innes slowed because she didn't want chips flicking up and damaging her new car. Trees flanked the lane on either side and Morgan peered through them and could see no end through their trunks. Gazing up through the windscreen, the thick canopies met over the top of the lane and gave the impression they were driving down a green leafy tunnel. They passed by half a dozen lodges: Turner, Elgar, Shakespeare, Wordsworth, Shelley and then finally Constable.

Innes pulled up out the front beside a brand new Black Range Rover Evoque with the number plate MA1 R1TR.

"Do you think we've got the right place?" Morgan asked with a smile.

"I think we might, sir, yes." She was staring at the ostentatious vehicle as she unbuckled her seatbelt.

They climbed out of the car and walked towards the lodge. This was a modest, white-painted cottage nestled in the forest like something out of a Hansel and Gretel poem, with a green front door sheltered by an intricately carved wooden porch. In the summer, Morgan could see roses would bloom around the door and part of the cottage on the far right seemed to have a wisteria growing on it. Morgan knocked on the door and waited.

Meredith Ash swung the door open with a face like thunder. He was a very tall, thin man in his sixties with a thick head of silver hair and wire-rimmed spectacles. He wore a frayed hoodie with the name of an American baseball team written on it, stone-washed blue jeans, and a pair of scuffed, canvas yachting daps.

"Who the fuck are you?" he snapped.

"Are you Meredith Ash?" Innes asked.

"You know what you've done?" Ash continued. "Do you know what you have fucking done? I'm in the middle of one of the most difficult scenes of my entire life and I'm just beginning to understand it and make sense of it and then someone knocks on the fucking door!"

Morgan had already known he would not like Mr Ash after reading his Instagram page, the Evoque with the personalised ego plate was the next clue, but even he had been slightly taken back by the welcome he had just received from one of Britain's premier romance writers. Being a policeman with many years' experience, Bill Morgan showed none of his surprise, and keeping an entirely calm and straight-faced demeanour, he reached into his pocket and pulled out the magic wallet. Casually flicking it open with one hand and raising it right up a few inches from Mr Ash's spectacled eyes, he spoke in quiet almost hushed tones.

"Good morning, Mr Ash. My name is Detective Inspector Morgan and I am from Wiltshire CID. This lady to my right is Detective Constable Innes. She is my colleague. We are both here to talk to you this morning about Tansy Babbington."

Ash changed colour. He seemed to be having some kind of breakdown. "I'm sorry. Is this for real? That cow has sent the sodding police out to harass me in the middle of one of my most important books! That's just typical of her, isn't it? That talentless little bitch can't write a bloody word without ripping it off from someone else, and then spends all bloody day long banging on about how amazing she is and how people steal from her – from her! Who the hell would steal her garbage? It's not as if any of it is even *hers* in the first place. If you rip her off you don't know *who* you're ripping off. And if they're not plagiarised they're bloody ghostwritten? Everyone knows that! I suppose she sent you out here because of our little argument we had the other day on the internet when I set her straight on a few things? Well, you can tell her to get fucked."

Before Morgan could speak, Ash slammed the door in their faces.

Morgan and Innes exchanged an amused look before Morgan knocked on the door again. He was sliding his wallet back into his pocket when it swung open to reveal a very red-faced Meredith Ash standing in the doorway, yet somehow looking smaller than before.

"You'd better get out of here! I'm not even kidding. I'll be on the telephone to my lawyer just like that." He underlined his threat with a click of his fingers, which sadly he slightly mistimed so instead of a satisfying crisp click there was more of a dull slap. "You hear me?"

"I'm afraid we won't be able to pass on your kind message to Mrs Babbington," Morgan said.

"Maybe you won't pass that message on but you can tell her that if she doesn't stop harassing me, I'll have my lawyer on her. You can tell her I'll expose all of her plagiarism and ghostwriting to the entire bloody world. She's a filthy fraud."

"I won't be able to tell her anything, Mr Ash," Morgan patiently said. "Because unfortunately…"

"Whyever not?" Ash spluttered. "Has she done a runner? She finally found her ethics and did a bunk!"

"No, sir. I won't be able to tell Tansy Babbington any of those things, because she was found brutally murdered this morning and we'd like to have a word with you about it, if that's ok."

Ash shrunk even smaller and now turned the colour of a sun-bleached putty. "God. I see. You'd better come in."

CHAPTER 9

Jacob found himself suffering from a severe case of déjà vu as he stood outside the Great Western Hospital in Swindon waiting for Anna to finish smoking her cigarette before going in to speak to Dr Richard Lyon about the post-mortem. It was Anna's custom always to smoke what she called her pre-post-mortem cigarette before any meeting with the Home Office pathologist, and it was a custom she intended to maintain for as long as she was a police officer. After she had crushed out the cigarette butt and dropped it into the bin, she exhaled a large cloud of smoke into the cold air and met Jacob's eyes.

"All ready for the horror show, sir?" she said.

Jacob and Anna each opened one of the two swing doors at the front of the hospital and began the long journey to the mortuary. Jacob had endured more than his fair share of places like this and hated hospitals even at the best of times, so he was not in the best mood as he followed the long disinfectant-smelling corridors to their final destination. It was a journey that they had become sadly familiar with, and now they descended several short flights of stairs and continued along another corridor until they were finally faced with a set of metal double doors.

Jacob and Anna stepped into the mortuary, where they found Dr Richard Lyon leaning over a desk and swinging his hips to a 1980s synth hit. Seeing them, he stopped what he was doing, which appeared to Jacob to be writing some kind of a report, and stood up to his full height and gave a cheery wave. Richard Lyon was a very short, plump man with thin, silver hair which he always kept shaved down very close to his scalp, giving him the appearance of being slightly younger than he really was.

"Hello chaps, great to see you again," Richard said.

The gloomy windowless mortuary tucked way down in the hospital's basement was not exactly conducive to a convivial atmosphere, but Jacob managed to summon up enough casual pleasantness to offer Richard a smile in return.

"I'd say it's great to be here, Richard, but that would be a lie."

Richard laughed and walked over to the elephant in the room, or in this case, the corpse of the woman found earlier, now covered in a surgical sheet and lying cold and motionless on a stainless steel gurney in the middle of the room beneath a very bright arc light.

"That is *exactly* what she would say if she could talk," Richard said, slowly lifting the sheet away from the dead woman. "But she has definitely spoken her last words, and I would say around thirty-six to forty hours ago."

Jacob was immediately intrigued. "She was killed on Tuesday afternoon then?"

"I should think so yes," Richard said. "The difficulty is, the further death gets in time, the harder it is to pinpoint it very accurately. Eventually, it all starts to blur into one, if you catch my drift. In this case, I can be fairly certain. It has been quite cold overnight these past few days so I have taken account of that. I also spoke with Dr Summer, a forensic entomologist I know and it's our opinion that it's probably somewhere between thirty-six and forty hours ago."

"So that would put the time of death at some point around the *late* afternoon or *early* evening on Tuesday?"

Richard nodded. "Yes, I would think so."

"She must have been stored somewhere after he murdered her," Anna said.

"That's exactly what I was thinking," Jacob said. "We know that the body wasn't dumped in the abbey grounds between the time of the murder to Wednesday afternoon because the entire area was mown on Wednesday afternoon and Hendricks the groundskeeper saw nothing."

"So the bastard must have killed her and then kept her stored somewhere," Anna said. "But why? I don't understand."

"There must be a reason for it," Jacob said. "But I agree with you – it doesn't make immediate sense. The thing foremost in the mind of most killers is getting rid of all evidence, especially the body."

Jacob saw from the look on Anna's face that they were both thinking the same thing.

"Any evidence of pre or post-mortem sexual assault?" Jacob asked Richard.

"Yes, I see where you're going with that, which is a rather disgusting thought but I'm pleased to be able to say that there's absolutely no evidence of that whatsoever. She would have suffered a fairly painless death and then that was the end of the matter."

Jacob frowned. "You just said painless, but earlier you said the injury to her head was substantial and would have hurt."

"The headwound is post-mortem, Jacob."

"Why would he do that?" Anna asked.

Jacob stared at the gash on the body's head. "He hit her head by accident when he was carrying her to where he dumped her. Probably on one of the gravestones."

Lyon clicked his fingers. "That's been driving me mad. Good man."

Jacob asked, "Formal cause of death please, Richard?"

It was the question that Jacob was most nervous to ask, but it was important and unavoidable that he knew how this woman had died.

Richard left a dramatic pause worthy of Pinter, as he slowly put on a pair of latex gloves and gently pulled the dead woman's hair away. "Yes, I thought you'd get around to asking that pretty sharpish. This woman was first administered with a large dose of gamma-hydroxybutyrate, and I would say quite enough to drug a much heavier man. Its slang name is…"

'Coma in a bottle,' Jacob said, finishing Richard's sentence for him.

A grim silence filled the room.

"Yes, that's correct Chief Inspector."

"Then what?" Jacob asked.

"After the drug was administered, she suffered a compression of the neck with a ligature which led to suffocation, I would say she probably retained consciousness throughout, but in a very drugged up and delirious state. The rest I think you already know. She was wrapped in a shroud, which I believe Mia Francis is doing some work on for you, but I'll tell you now it was a normal white bed sheet obtained from any department store or online, and the coin was a bronze coin from late Roman Antiquity."

Jacob shoved his hands in his pockets and walked to the end of the mortuary and back, deep in thought and absent-mindedly stroking his chin. He turned and fixed his eyes on Richard.

"The feather that she was holding. What about the feather?"

"A raven's feather," Richard said immediately. "I'd like to be able to tell you that I derived that information from some clever molecular technique or isotope analysis, but the bottom line is that I was a bit of a nerd as a younger man and a bird spotter. I was a twitcher. Still am from time to time – when I can get away from this bloody place."

"How do you know it's not a crow's feather?" Anna asked.

"There are some fundamental differences between the feathers of ravens and crows and there is no doubt that this is a raven's feather. Ravens have longer primary feathers and also longer tail feathers than crows. They have differently shaped tails entirely. I might not know that music has moved on since 1985, but I do know my Corvidae!"

He laughed loudly.

Jacob nodded, staring at the corpse. "I see."

"I have more," Richard said. "This is a wing feather from an adult male raven. One can tell by the size of the 'finger' at the wing's tip. All very rudimentary for a twitcher. I let Mia take it along with the shroud and coin. Is there a significance to any of it?"

"If it's a calling card, there might be," Jacob said.

Richard let the sentence hang in the air for a long time until the atmosphere became quite heavy and intense again. "You're thinking about the Ferryman?"

Jacob nodded but said nothing.

"We're all thinking about the Ferryman," Anna said.

Richard squinted. "But he never left a calling card, did he?"

Jacob shook his head. "No, he didn't. I've read all of the reports compiled by the Metropolitan Police and there were never any calling cards unless you count the coins he put in their mouths, but that was always seen differently. The coins were intimately connected to the ritual of their deaths, rather than about Kelley leaving a signature behind. That's just how they saw it at the time and I can't find a way to disagree with that."

"I can see what they're driving at there," Richard said, slowly peeling the gloves off. "I have not read any of the postmortem reports about Keeley, but I did read what was in the press at the time. Either way, this raven's feather was left in the woman's right hand and then her arms were brought up to cross over one another over her breasts. As if she was holding the feather in a perfectly normal way."

"It can't be Keeley," Anna said.

"Why can't it be him?" Richard asked. "He's in prison isn't he?"

"No, he escaped from prison a few years ago," Jacob said. "He fled to Europe and was killed in a car crash in Austria."

Richard said, "Forgive me for not keeping up with these things, but in my spare time I enjoy listening to music, drinking wine, watching sunsets and occasionally twitching. I keep meaning to stay more up-to-date with the lives and times of depraved serial killers, but I just can't seem to get around to it. For me that would be a bit of a busman's holiday, you see. Har har!"

"Yes, I see what you mean," Jacob said. "And you're certain about the administration of the gamma-hydroxybutyrate and the ligature asphyxiation?"

Richard looked like he was mildly offended. "Of course, I'm certain, Chief Inspector. You can clearly see evidence of sustained compression around her windpipe, and this has been affected by the use of a ligature of some kind, crushing the trachea and the larynx and causing suffocation which has consequently induced this woman's death. This was done while she was suffering delirium caused by the administration of gamma-hydroxybutyrate. It's obviously murder, but I'm formally telling you now for the avoidance of doubt: it's murder."

"And you're equally certain about the temple injury being caused postmortem?"

"Surely I don't have to defend my honour and experience all over again?"

"I'm sorry Richard," Jacob said. "It's just that this is a very delicate business right now. Keeley never punched or struck any of his victims. There was the administration of the drug, then after they slid down into a delirium he would slowly choke them. Then the business with the coins and shrouds was probably all postmortem. If this wound on her temple had been delivered while she was still alive it would give me a small bit of hope that it wasn't Keeley."

"Perhaps he's changed his act over the years. Hang on, didn't you just say he was dead?"

"Yes, I did," Jacob said. "But with a man like Keeley, you don't believe he's dead until you're staring down at his corpse."

"If he died in Austria in a car crash there would be some kind of postmortem records," Richard said. "It would have gone through the police. There would be photographs."

"There are photographs," Jacob said. "And they're being sent over to us as soon as possible, at least they are according to Kent."

"Oh, dear. Marcus Kent. I had hoped for your sake that he might have retired by now."

"Sadly no," Anna said, her phone ringing. She stepped away to take the call.

Jacob decided they had got all they were going to get out of Richard for now. "Okay, thanks, Richard."

"Quite all right, old chap."

Anna now stepped back over to them, her phone still in her hand. "That was Innes, sir. They just got a report of a missing woman."

Jacob felt his heart sink. "Details."

"Jennifer Stanley, 46 year-old. Lives in Charlton. A neighbour went around to her house to take her some cake, and when she got there she found the door open and the entire place smashed up. No sign of Jennifer Stanley."

"When?"

"She went round with the cake today, but she said she hasn't spoken to her since Monday evening. She could have been missing since then."

"Job? Family?"

"Not clear, yet. Could be our copycat."

"It could be anything. Get some uniforms out asking questions in Charlton and try and find some next of kin or close friends."

"Sir."

"Looks like you've got your work cut out for you, Jacob," Richard said. "One dead on a gurney and another one vanished into thin air. Perhaps it's time you revisited your theory about Keeley being dead."

"That's not my theory," Jacob said. "It's Marcus Kent's. The more I learn about this case, the more I think that the Ferryman has come back across the river and started work all over again."

CHAPTER 10

Meredith Ash was looking distinctly calmer by the time he had led the two detectives through to the cottage's living room. It was supposed to relay cosy nook vibes, but to Morgan's eye was somehow artificial, despite the genuine old age of the building. He supposed it had something to do with how expensive the interior décor obviously was, which was incongruous to a building of this era.

Ash took up a position in the middle of the room, just in front of a crackling fire he had clearly been tending with much love and patience. Morgan took up a position in the centre of the room, and throwing a glance over his shoulder, saw the view outside through the window was a wall of trees, and nothing like the expansive vista Ash had posted on his Instagram page, claiming it to be the view from his window.

"The trees certainly grow very fast around here," Morgan said, nudging his chin to the window.

"I don't know what you're talking about," Ash said.

"It's just that I was looking at your Instagram page today and I noticed that lovely view you said you had from your living room. Would that be this living room, Mr Ash?"

"Have you been stalking my Instagram page, Inspector?"

"I know you're a writer of romance fiction, but don't you think that's embellishing things a little too much?"

"I took the picture from the main house if you must know. So what, if I gave the impression it was the view from my retreat? I don't see what harm that does anyone."

Morgan watched Meredith Ash turn to look around the room for no reason other than to evade eye contact. The look on his face had changed completely from the incensed rage of a few moments ago to someone looking very much on the defensive. This was not an unusual transition for Morgan. As a senior policeman for many years, he was more than familiar with the way people changed behaviour when confronted with two plainclothes detectives standing right in front of them in an enclosed space.

"Look, I'm sorry for how I behaved at the front door," Ash said. "And I never meant any of those things I said about poor Tansy. She could give as good as she got, believe me, but no one deserves this. Anyway, can I get you anything? Perhaps a cup of tea?"

"No thank you, sir," Morgan said. "I'd like to get straight down to business if that's all right with you."

"Yeah, straight down to business, of course." Ash's eyes once again began to crawl all over the room, settling now on the carpet which he seemed to be analysing every square inch before finally returning his gaze to Morgan. "Yes, terrible business, I can't quite believe it actually."

"I quite agree," Morgan said. "And if you don't mind, I'd like to ask you a few questions relating to the matter – now we've all settled down and we're nice and calm."

Ash wrung his hands. "Yes, of course. Please ask anything you like."

Morgan took a second to consider what he knew about Meredith Ash concerning his relationship with Tansy Babbington. He had done this on purpose because it meant another few seconds of long, tense silence for Ash to continue stewing. Ash like Tansy, was a writer of fiction, although they were at different publishing houses. They were both, by anyone's standards, very successful authors, and both had large publics hanging on their every word, although Ash's star was waning. Innes's research revealed they both sold large numbers of their books both upon publication and each had strong backlist sales. There were substantial advertising budgets poured into both authors by their respective publishing houses. Innes had gleaned this information from telephone calls to each publishing house. As for why a man like Ash would want to kill Tansy remained to be seen, but Ash would have to account for his whereabouts at the time of the murder because he had been engaged in a long and vicious online feud with the victim.

"Where were you on Tuesday afternoon?" Morgan asked.

"Tuesday afternoon? I thought you said she was found dead this morning?"

"That is correct, but we believe she was murdered on Tuesday afternoon or early evening. I would like you to account for yourself during that time, please."

Meredith Ash became flustered all over again. "I arrived at the writing retreat yesterday morning. Everyone here can back me up. And they'll know that I haven't left because my car hasn't passed through the front gate – there are security cameras."

"Yes, but you seem to be talking about Wednesday. We need to know where you were on the Tuesday."

"I was at home, writing."

Morgan now pulled his notepad from his pocket, took out a pencil stub and began making some notes. "You were at home all day Tuesday and you didn't leave the house at all?"

"No, I didn't leave the house at all, not for a minute. That's because I knew I was coming here the next day so I wanted to get as much work done as possible in preparation for the big scene I'm writing. I decided to book myself into the retreat for a few days to get away from my normal writing environment as I find it sometimes helps me find the muse."

"I see." Morgan wrote the word *muse* and underlined it three times. "So there's no one to account for your movements on Tuesday at all?"

"I live alone – well there's Aristotle of course."

"Aristotle?" Innes asked.

"My cat," Ash said with some kind of an attempt at a laugh.

"Unfortunately, your cat cannot help back up your alibi," Morgan said.

"Sadly, no."

"You seem to be very angry with Tansy Babbington if your Instagram page is anything to go by," Morgan said.

"Oh, that was nothing," Ash said, dismissing the feud with a simple wave of his hand. "Tansy and I often went a few rounds. Look, the truth is she was a real bitch and she wound me up and sometimes I responded to that."

"I see," said Morgan. "Here, just after you accused her of – and I quote – 'ripping off an American TV detection series', you said that 'you'll get what's coming to you, your sort always do.' Care to expand on that?"

"Come on! That was just the heat of the moment stuff! I was angry with her because she lifted an entire scene from *Russotto*."

Innes frowned. "Russotto? Isn't that some kind of Italian rice dish?"

"No, that's *risotto*, constable. *Russotto* was one of the greatest American crime dramas ever to be broadcast on television. It ran from 1965 to 1974. Of course, its cancellation was a complete disgrace. The writing was some of the best done for television. One of my favourite scenes is in Series 1, Episode 7. It's quite intricate, quite involved and complex. It involves Lieutenant Russotto luring the killer into a trap by switching chess pieces during a game, but without the killer knowing about it. It's absolutely ingenious. You can read that same scene in one of Tansy Babbington's repugnant little bodice-rippers! I mean the same scene, *exactly*!"

"I think I remember that scene," Innes said. "From Book 4, *The Holy and the Damned*."

"Exactly!" Ash went on. "All she does is pretty much change the names of the characters. And then she goes on her bloody social media and has the nerve to accuse other people of stealing from her. I can tell you, I'd had a few drinks and I just lost it. I know a lot of people in the writing community who were bloody glad that I said it. Understand this Inspector Morgan, this doesn't mean that I murdered her and dumped her on the grounds of an abbey this morning!"

"But you still cannot account for your whereabouts during the time we believe she was murdered though."

"I can account for them perfectly well – I've already told you this. The problem is that nobody can back me up."

"That is a bit of a problem, isn't it?" Morgan said.

Ash sighed. "Seriously, you can't honestly believe this was me? Isn't there some kind of forensic evidence or something that can rule me out?"

"As one of the suspects in the case," Morgan said, "I must ask you if you would mind giving us a DNA sample and also a set of fingerprints?"

Ash became defensive again, his anger returning. Morgan watched his face, noting a spark of genuine fear in his eyes when he asked this question. He enjoyed watching him trying to keep his temper under control and had to fight back a smile. Mr Calm n' Casual seemed to have disappeared very easily and Morgan wondered if this man could lose his temper just as easily when arguing with Tansy Babbington.

"I don't have to give you those things! That would constitute an unlawful search. You have to formally arrest me and charge me before you can get that out of me."

"There's really no need for us to go that far, but if it would help to eliminate you from our inquiries, I would have thought you would jump at the chance."

Ash calmed down again. "All right, I'll think about it. I'm going to speak to my lawyer first."

Morgan folded his notebook away, put it in his pocket and got to his feet. Innes joined him and the two made their way past the fire to the door. "That will be all for now, I think. How many more days are you here at the retreat?"

"Just another two and then I'll be returning home to Cirencester."

"If you wouldn't mind staying in the vicinity please," Morgan said. "Just in case we need to get hold of you. And do let us know what your lawyer says about helping us out with the DNA and fingerprints. If you're happy to do so, call into the station and we can send some uniformed officers around." Morgan didn't want to tell him about the dearth of forensic evidence found at the scene this morning but knew the more samples on file, the better.

"I have nothing to worry about," Ash said.

"I'm sure you haven't," Morgan said.

"And I do feel bad that somebody killed her, Inspector. Her writing was awful and she had a very sour personality, but strangely I enjoyed the rivalry, I enjoyed the competition and even sometimes the online fights. Who will I have to cross swords with now?"

Morgan turned to walk down the corridor to the front door. "Well, not Tansy Babbington," he said. "That's for sure."

Ash closed his door and the two detectives went back to Innes's car.

"What did you make of that, sir?"

"That I need something to eat." Morgan opened the passenger door. "Take me up to my car and then follow me into Devizes. I'll buy you a late lunch."

*

Nestled deep in the heartland of Wiltshire, Devizes was built around a motte-and-bailey castle established by Osmund, a Norman nobleman and Bishop of Salisbury, in 1080. Besieged during the notorious 12th Century 'Anarchy' and again during the Battle of Roundway Down in the English Civil War, four hundred years later, the town had a long and bloody history. Today, its endless listed buildings, ancient churches and a village green rested more peacefully, surrounded by the beautiful Vale of Pewsey. There was order here, Morgan thought, as he pulled into the Market Place car park and cut the engine.

Order and peace.

Usually, but not today, he thought with a frown as he slammed the car door shut and blipped the locks with the little keyring. Today the order and peace of this quiet, safe place was gone. It had vanished the moment Tansy Babbington was brutally and ritualistically murdered just up the road. He let out a long sigh, then joined up with Innes and the two of them crossed the road by the Bear Hotel and made their way along the pavement towards their destination.

With Devizes Castle visible at the end of Castle Road just behind it, Pontin's Pie Shop had been on St. John Street for hundreds of years. Famed for its local pies and other treats, all sourced from local ingredients, the shop was usually packed with people buying something for lunch or dinner and today was no exception. As they edged their way over to one of the counters, Innes pointed at the local delicacy made from veal, pork tongue and boiled eggs.

"Devizes Pie, sir?"

"Not for me, no," he said with a frown. "I've got more of a sweet tooth."

He perused the fine selection, finding Wiltshire Tatties, Marlborough Cake and a solid-looking affair full of apple and mead and assorted spices.

Seeing him looking at it, Innes said. "A slice of Druid's cake, sir?"

The Welshman frowned. "I think I'll give that a miss, too."

"Or some Malmesbury Pudding?"

Morgan gave her a look, not knowing how to take Innes's notoriously oblique sense of humour. "Perhaps another day, constable."

The search passed over the Wiltshire Buttermilk Cake and ended on a thick slice of spiced bread glazed and sparkling under the counter lights.

"I'll take one of the lardy cakes," he said with a beaming smile.

Innes looked at him, eyebrows raised. "Really?"

"Sure, why not?"

"That and cigars, sir?"

"Your point?"

"Talk about throwing caution to the wind."

He laughed. "It's a good job I like you, DC Innes. Now then, are you paying, or shall I?"

She looked at the rendered lard cake and winced. "Something tells me that whoever buys them, you're going to pay for this one, sir."

Stepping outside of the pie shop, Morgan finally spoke about the Ash interview. "You asked me what I made of it, and the sad truth is I think Ash is totally innocent of everything except being a little prick."

Innes was pulling her car keys from her bag. "What makes you say that, sir?"

"Instinct, experience. The way he held eye contact. His body language. I dunno. I still want all of his statements gone over and get hold of the CCTV to see who went in and out of the retreat on Tuesday, but I'm sure the bastard's innocent."

"Which means the search goes on if you're right."

Morgan used the remote to open his car's locks, then swung his door open. Leaning on the top of his door, he turned to Innes who was approaching her own car.

"I'm right. You can bet on it."

CHAPTER 11

At the same moment Morgan and Innes were buying a late lunch in town, Jacob was in Mia Francis's office talking about the forensic techniques she had employed at the crime scene and on the sheet, coin and feather looking for trace evidence. Unfortunately for Jacob, she had found nothing at the scene in terms of footprints because the killer had stayed on the freshly cut grass to place the body where they had found it, and the sheet turned out to be a run-of-the-mill white bed sheet with zero transfer evidence on it.

"Nothing at *all* on it?" Jacob asked.

"Other than evidence relating to the victim, then nothing at all," Mia said. "No traces of any odd types of soil or anyone else's hair or skin cell – absolutely nothing. It's a new bed sheet and I can tell you that it hasn't been used or washed. The label was cut off so nothing there. It could have been bought absolutely anywhere at any time. You're in more luck with the coin though."

Jacob suddenly felt a ray of hope breaking through an otherwise cloudy sky. "What makes you say that Mia? You got a fingerprint or something from it?"

Mia laughed. "Nothing quite so convenient as that, Jacob, sorry. I performed a microscopic examination on the coin looking for anything of interest – you'd be surprised what kind of fascinating particulate matter can be found on something like a coin that is completely invisible to the naked eye, but sadly this one had been rubbed clean with alcohol and presumably a clean cloth before being inserted in the victim's mouth."

"So how does that put me more in luck than with the sheet?"

"Because this is a very unusual coin, but as you know, not the same coin that was used by your Ferryman. I'm sure you will recall the late Professor Keeley used a very particular type of silver coin from ancient Greece stamped with the image of a honeybee. I believe there were ritualistic reasons for his use of these coins, and as you saw at the abbey, this is a different type of coin entirely made of bronze and from Roman late antiquity. This particular coin was minted during the reign of the Emperor

Constantine The Great, who ruled from 306 AD to 337 AD."

"You like making me wait to the very end before you deliver the good news, don't you Mia?"

"Indeed I do, Jacob, indeed I do. Obviously, you're not going to get one of these coins in your change down at the local supermarket, so I had a quick look on eBay and made a list of everybody who was selling these coins, which are not quite as many as you might think. I found a fair number of traders on there, but looking through their past histories I wasn't able to find anybody who had sold any of these particular coins or indeed this *exact* coin. However, if our killer is as clever as Keeley was, he of course would avoid the internet as much as possible when in the commission of a crime, especially one as foul as murder. That's when it occurred to me that he might have bought the coin 'old school'."

"There are such things as ancient coin shops?"

"There are such things as ancient coin shops and also auction houses and so on. Not only that but there happened to be several within an hour's drive from Malmesbury. I appreciate the killer could have done his business in any part of the United Kingdom and driven for a very long time before dumping the body there, but I think we both appreciate that it's a wise idea to start in reasonably close vicinity to the location of the body and work our way out. At least in the absence of any other evidence pointing to it having been committed further afield."

Jacob nodded. "Agreed."

"This cut down the number of possible traders considerably, and after a series of phone calls, I located a shop which sold three of these coins in Marlborough last week."

"Mia," Jacob said. "If I wasn't engaged to be married to Sophie, I'd get down on my knees right now and pop the question."

"Really Jacob, I don't think there's any reason to make threats like that, especially not after all the help I've just given you."

Jacob smiled broadly. "And they sold these coins?"

"They sold three coins of this era, and I can tell you now that I believe the coin found in the mouth was bought at that shop, to almost a one hundred per cent certainty."

"How so?"

"Come hither."

Jacob gave her a look and moved closer. "Go on."

"Look here, Chief Inspector. Here is a photograph taken of the coin in question through the microscope, and you'll notice this very specific scratch running across the face of the Emperor. Now look over here."

Mia paused for a moment before bringing up the website of the coin trader in Marlborough and clicking on a page of recently sold coins. Using the scroll wheel on her mouse and the control key on her keyboard she now zoomed in on the picture of one of the three coins. Jacob saw exactly the same scratch running across the Emperor's face.

"It's the same coin. Got to be." Jacob said.

"I think so and that's my professional opinion, but I think just about any layman would be able to tell you that. The coin is a very rare one to start with, so it's highly unlikely that you're ever going to come across more than a handful, throw in such a specific mark in such a specific place and I think this is almost one hundred per cent the same coin. The small area of doubt is it's possible someone deliberately made the scratch on purpose on another coin. That's as unlikely as Bill Morgan ever asking Anna Mazurek out."

Jacob smiled. "You heard those rumours, too?"

"Yes."

"That's Bill." Jacob nodded, then switched back to business. "But Keeley would never make a mistake like that. Not only would he use a different coin, but he would never leave a trail like that. I mean talk about breadcrumbs! This is as if there's a bright red neon arrow pointing to the killer."

"Have I given you more problems than help?" Mia said.

"You might have yes," he said with a long sigh. "I don't believe Keeley would have made a mistake like this. Making the scratch on purpose is more his style. This makes Kent right about the copycat killer and makes me wrong about Keeley still being alive. And not only that, but I have a very bad feeling about that shop selling *three* of those coins."

"I wondered about that. If this really is a copycat killer, he may be intent on showing everybody that he's every bit as dangerous as Keeley by killing more than once."

"I didn't want to say that part out loud, but that's exactly what I was thinking. Why buy three if that wasn't your intention?"

"That's over to you I'm afraid, Jacob. I've done all I can do for now. I'll get the official report on your desk by the end of the day, but the summary is quite simple. There was nothing to be found at the scene in terms of forensic evidence, the sheet yielded nothing and neither did the feather, which is a simple male raven's feather. I ran an isotope analysis on it. All you've really got by way of a lead is this coin and what we've just discussed."

"Thanks, Mia," Jacob said, his head already racing with thoughts. "You might have rejected my marriage proposal, but I owe you a drink one night."

"I'm free right now."

"Sorry, I've already got a date."

"I thought Sophie was in Rome?"

"She is. This date is with the press."

"Lucky you."

"Yes indeed," Jacob said, pushing open the door. "Lucky me."

*

As a watery sun sank towards the western horizon, Jacob pushed his way through the doors of the same conference room he had used earlier to brief his team, only this time he was met with a sea of much less friendly faces. Marcus Kent had become concerned by online rumours and theories getting out of hand, so he had arranged a formal press briefing in which Jacob had firm instructions to pour cold water on these rumours and theories, particularly any involving the Ferryman. Jacob would have preferred to maintain silence for a while longer until some more progress had been made in the case, but that wasn't Kent's way. The DCS was very much a 'get out in front' type who liked to manage public relations as much as possible. Jacob's preference was to divert as much of his time to solving murders.

"Thank you everyone," Jacob said. "Please settle down. I'll read a short statement about the case and then open the floor to questions."

Jacob waited a moment longer for the shuffling and rustling to die down and then he began.

"Early this morning, Wiltshire Constabulary was contacted by a member of the public concerning a body that was found on the grounds of Malmesbury Abbey. The scene was attended by both uniformed and CID officers. We made the decision early on to treat the case as a suspicious death and since then we have escalated it to a full-scale murder enquiry. We are already working hard to track down the person responsible for this terrible crime and bring justice to the victim's loved ones."

"Is there any truth to the rumours the body was wrapped in a shroud?" a reporter shouted.

"At this time, I am unable to comment on that."

The same reporter called out again, her voice cutting through the groans of disappointment emanating from the TV and press journalists in the room. "Rumours are circulating online that the body was found wrapped in a shroud with a coin in her mouth. Does this mean the Ferryman isn't dead after all and is back on the rampage?"

Rampage. Jacob knew how Kent would be responding to that sort of language. "There were some similarities found at the scene to those connected with the Alaistair Keeley murders, but we have strong reason to believe this murder was not committed by Keeley. And let me remind people that Professor Keeley was killed in a car accident in Europe some time ago."

"So this is a copycat killer?" shouted another reporter.

"It's possible. We're too early into the case to form that sort of judgment."

"Do you have any leads?" another yelled.

"Wiltshire CID is pursuing several lines of enquiry and we are entirely confident we can bring whoever did this to justice."

"If this is a copycat killer, trying to emulate the Ferryman, isn't it likely that he will kill again?"

"There is no evidence that is the case, although we ask people to remain calm and vigilant."

A man holding a microphone stood up. "Are you fit to lead the investigation after the bloodbath that was the Witch-Hunt murders?"

Jacob looked at him for a moment, then turned to the sea of faces. "Next question."

The journalists shouted at him, all raising their hands. "Answer the question!"

Jacob now looked into one of the TV cameras at the end of the room. "The man behind the Witch-Hunt murders thought he was very clever. He was very clever, but that didn't stop me from finding him. And whoever is behind this murder should know this: you're not that clever either and I'm already on your trail. There is nowhere you can hide from me in this world and I will find you wherever you go."

Jacob stood up, shoved his hands into his pockets and walked out of the room, leaving uproarious outrage behind him. *Now*, he thought, *all I have to do is catch a killer.*

CHAPTER 12

After the press briefing, Jacob and Anna drove to Marlborough, pulling into the beautiful old town via Bath Road on its western approach before turning left at the roundabout and making their way slowly up the High Street. He drove past the Rick Stein pub on the south side of the street, causing Anna to tap on the window with her fingernail as she recalled a recent memory.

"I had crab linguini in there once, with chilli, garlic, parsley and olive oil."

"Any good?" Jacob asked.

"Absolutely bloody delish, if I'm being honest."

"I should hope as a detective sergeant you're always honest."

She looked at him with a devilish smirk. "Moi? But of course."

"I've seen him on the TV," Jacob said as he drove the old Alvis past the pub and signalled right to drive down

Figgins Lane. "Food always looks pretty good, but you never know what post-production magic they do."

"How dare you say that about Rick? Take it back."

"I take it back."

"His food is absolutely lovely, I can vouch for it. I went into his Cornish place once and it was just as nice down there."

"Someone has a little Rick crush, I see."

"Might go in there again," she said, completely ignoring Jacob's last comment. "I remember there being some kind of French sausage dish with a caper and shallot salad. Damn it, I've made myself hungry now."

Jacob smiled as he pulled over to the side of the lane, parked up and killed the engine. "I'm sure you can get some lovely beans on toast when you go home."

"Don't judge others by your own standards, sir."

"As a matter of fact, they really *are* my standards, at least they are this week. I enjoy doing a bit of cooking from time to time, but with Sophie being in Italy and us being so busy on the case, I suppose tonight it really might be some beans on toast."

"Then call it 'a rich bean cassoulet served on crispy garlic bruschetta'."

"I'll stick with beans on toast, but thanks."

Anna smiled as the two of them walked along the pavement, pulling up outside Walton's Coins and Ancient Artefacts. They stopped to take a few moments looking in the window, where a beautiful display of finely arranged coins and banknotes was arranged for passers-by. Jacob noticed from the prices that perhaps not every passerby would have business inside.

"Should we go and have a chat with Mr Walton?" Anna said.

"Nothing I would enjoy more."

They stepped through a low doorway, Jacob having to dip his head so he didn't bang it on the head jamb. A small brass bell tinkled, alerting the owner of the shop to their arrival on his premises. The shop was unattended, then a tall and very thin, old man appeared in the doorway behind the counter. He was wearing a single-breasted grey suit with a white shirt and a conservative blue-striped tie and had the air of a happily retired bank manager.

"Good morning, how may I help? Are we in the market for some coins today?"

Jacob smiled and produced his police identification, holding it up in the little black wallet for the man to read as he reeled off the usual introduction.

"Good morning, sir. I'm Detective Chief Inspector Jacob and this is my colleague Detective Sergeant Mazurek. We've driven up from Wiltshire CID to have a chat with you concerning a recent sale you have made."

The man did not move a muscle, and the inscrutable expression on his face did not change for an instant. "And what sale would that be regarding?"

"Specifically the sale of three coins of late Roman antiquity bearing the image of the Emperor Constantine."

As Jacob spoke, Anna pulled a piece of folded paper from her suit pocket and unfolded it revealing a colour photograph of the three coins that she had printed off from the coin shop's own website before driving over to them. Now the man took the piece of paper and spent a few seconds studying it.

"As you will see," Jacob continued, "the picture of these three coins was printed from your website this morning. You'll see the three coins that I have just spoken to you about. We found them on your website in the section of recently sold coins."

"Yes, that's right," Mr Walton said. "I sold them last week to someone. A man."

"And what can you tell me about this man?"

"He's not the sort I normally get in the shop, I have to say. I was a little surprised when he came in here."

"What do you mean by that?" Jacob asked.

Walton paused for a moment, scrunching up his face as he tried to recall the man to whom he had sold the coins. "He was a little rough around the edges if you see what I mean. Most collectors of antiquities, including coins or old or precious banknotes, are usually fairly well-educated people."

"What are you saying?" Anna asked. "That this man was no historian so he was in here looking for a way to make money trading coins?"

"Contrary to popular belief, there's not a huge amount of money in this business. If you get really lucky and find something exceptionally rare then a large amount of money can be made – in fact, sometimes fortunes have been made. But I've been in this business a long time and that's never happened to me. Any collection of coins being sold, whether in a shop like this or online, attracts the attention of people who know the business. It's not possible to fool them into thinking a coin is worth more than it really is."

"So you say this man was a little rough around the edges," Jacob asked. "Would you care to elaborate on that, please?"

"He pulled up in a pickup truck and parked it outside the shop, which is wrong for a start because you'll notice we have double yellow lines outside the shop. He didn't seem to care about that one bit. He was quite short and abrasive and asked if I had three coins that were all the same. He was very insistent that they had to be the same. Now you'll appreciate that when you're dealing with coins that are hundreds or even thousands of years old, it's often not that common to have several that are all the same. Some are more common than others, but as it happens I did have four of the Emperor Constantine coins here in the shop at the same time."

"Four of them?" Jacob asked.

"Yes, I had four but he was very specific that he only wanted three. And he bought three and then left. And without a 'thank you' I might add. Seemed that he was some sort of tradesman perhaps – he had the air of someone like that about him. A red plaid shirt."

Jacob noted that Walton said this as if it was the worst thing he'd ever seen.

"Could you give us a description of this man, beyond the one you've already given? Age, height, any unusual features."

"I can do better than that, Chief Inspector." The man now paused and pointed over Jacob's shoulder.

Jacob turned to see a small camera lens bubble in the corner of the shop.

"We had a robbery in here two years ago and I had these cameras set up. Luckily, I was fully insured but it would have been a hell of a lot quicker to organise and make the claim if we'd had security cameras… plus the police would have had something to go on. As it was, they never found the perpetrators, or my coins again."

"I think I'd like to see the footage, please," Jacob asked.

The man led them through the door behind the counter and they walked to a small room that also functioned as a tea-making facility. There was a small sink, the kind you find in camper vans, set up and plumbed in the corner, and a little plastic kettle beside a brass tin which presumably held the tea bags. A miniature refrigerator was keeping milk cool beside a microwave oven. On the other side of the room was a computer connected to the security system. The man sat at the computer and after a few moments called up the correct piece of footage.

"Of course, I can have all of this beamed directly to my telephone these days, thanks to the marvels of modern technology, but you can see what you need to see right here."

Jacob watched as the man in the plaid shirt walked into the shop. It was colour footage and the plaid shirt was black and red. The man was in his fifties with messy, greasy hair and he had several days of hair growth on his face. It was a silvery stubble that caught the light coming in through the front window. He had a hard, weathered face, the sign of a life spent outdoors and was absolutely not Alastair Keeley.

"How did he pay?" Jacob asked.

"Not with a card, if that's what you're hoping. He paid in cash. Getting rarer and rarer these days, of course. They want everyone to pay with cards and phones these days, so everything can be tracked."

Jacob was tempted to tell this man that if he had paid with a card or phone, it would help him track him down and if he was a murderer that would surely be a good thing.

Instead, he asked the man if he had any outside CCTV footage.

"As a matter of fact I do," Walton said. "In a manner of speaking. It's actually fitted inside the window on the floor above the shop looking down on the street. If you're after the man's pickup then I should be able to get it for you right away."

Jacob and Anna exchanged a hopeful glance as the man fiddled around clicking his mouse. A few moments later, he tapped on the screen with his finger at the picture of a bright red pickup truck. It was old, battered and dented and had some rust running around the tailgate. Unfortunately for Jacob, the angle of the camera only caught half of the registration number.

"Does it get any more of that number when it drives away?" Anna asked.

"No, that's as good as it gets I'm afraid. You can tell from the angle of the camera in the window that when they drive away it just moves out of sight."

"OK, that's good enough for now I think," Jacob said. He made a note of the partial registration number in his notebook and slid it back down into his pocket.

"Have to solve an important crime, Chief Inspector?"

"I'm afraid I'm not allowed to divulge any details outside of those already made public, sir, but I'd like to thank you very much for your time today. Hopefully, we will not need to get back in touch but we know where to find you if we do."

"Are you sure you don't want to look at some of the coins before you go? I could sell you that fourth Emperor Constantine one for an absolute bargain."

"No thanks," Jacob said. Given his history with Keeley, the very last thing he wanted to collect was ancient coins.

Outside, they walked back to the Alvis and the night was drawing in.

"Any plans for tonight, Sergeant?" Jacob asked.

"Just a long soak in a hot tub and then an early night," she said, opening the passenger door and sliding onto the soft, leather upholstery. "You?"

"Work," he said, turning the ignition on. "Always more work."

CHAPTER 13

Anna Mazurek shook her dressing gown off her shoulders and let it slip down onto the tufted pile bathmat. Studiously avoiding the mirror above the sink, she stepped out of the gown piled on the floor and into the old chipped rolltop bath, sinking slowly down into the bubbles. She wasn't the type to have candles in a bathroom, but she could run to the occasional luxury bubble bath. Tonight, she was trying out a new jasmine and rose milk brand she had received as a gift at Christmas.

She closed her eyes and let the warm, scented water wash over her. For a fleeting moment, there were no problems in the world, but that moment soon passed and real life piled up in her mind. Long hours and stress at work. Rising rent and no chance of a decent mortgage and now a copycat murder in the style of a long-deceased serial killer, the Ferryman.

And then there was always Declan Taylor.

She and her ex-husband had gone their separate ways during his trial when he had been found guilty of armed robbery. That was fourteen years ago. Back then she was a uniformed police constable on the beat in Swindon and Dex was struggling to get his car repair business off the ground. She respected him for the long hours he put in. She loved him. She had no idea he was planning a heist to pay off massive gambling debts and didn't find out until after the raid.

That was the learning curve from hell; everything changed after that day.

Dex grew more possessive and controlling and this culminated when he almost tried to kidnap her after a case she had worked on down in Salisbury, but Jacob had organised a restraining order. After that, Dex had faded away but she always knew he was out there somewhere, lurking in the shadows,

Her thoughts turned to Bill Morgan. He was a good man but she knew he had a long and winding past, including his commando work he never talked about and then his greatest challenge, his ex – Leanne. Was there any way she could see herself with him? Lots of ways, she mused, but somehow she felt no rush. He was dependable, rational, brave, and like a rock, always there for her. Maybe one day when the time was right, they might get together and —

"Enjoying your bath?"

She turned fast, sloshing water up over the sides of the ceramic rolltop. Her blood turned icy in her veins when she saw the grizzled, unshaven face of Dex appear in the open doorway. Older now, and bearing a scar he'd earned in a bar fight, he looked more like a perfect stranger than the man she had married all those years ago.

"Oh my god, Dex!"

He moved in his usual casual, relaxed way, arms hanging at his sides and stepped further into the steamy bathroom.

"Hello, Ania."

She felt his eyes crawling all over her and sank into the bath to cover herself with more of the soft white bubbles. "Get out."

He laughed and threw a towel. "Here, preserve your modesty."

She grabbed the towel off the side of the bath and pulled it up around her. It was just a towel, but it gave her more confidence.

"I'm not scared of you, Dex," she lied. "So leave me alone and get the hell out of my house."

He tutted, wandered over to the toilet, slammed the lid down and sat on top of it. Now she saw his filthy boots had left mud all over her mats. "Is that any way to speak to the love of your life?"

She had forgotten how much she loved the way his voice sounded when he spoke quietly, focusing so strongly on her she felt like the only person in the world. That had been part of his charm, but now she was older and knew better.

"Get out of here now or I'll—"

"Or you'll what?" he sneered. "Call the cops? You are the cops."

Yeah, she thought, *but I was going to call a commando.*

"This isn't going to achieve anything," she said. "All the stupid texts and taking pictures of me you did all those years ago achieved nothing except getting a restraining order put on you, which you are now breaking by the way. It's still in force, Dex. You're breaking the law. Coming near me is just going to mean more jail time. You don't want that, do you?"

He ran his fingers along the towel rail until his hand reached the curtains. "These are nice. Very pretty, just like you. You still look pretty even after all these years."

She felt her skin crawl and tightened her grip on the towel. The nearest phone was her mobile, on the small table beside her bed. She had to stay calm and strong and show him she wasn't scared.

"That's a nice thing to say, but it doesn't change anything."

He flicked the curtains back and turned his cold blue eyes on her. "That bloke you're seeing looks like a bit of a dick."

Her heart quickened. "If you mean Bill Morgan, I'm not seeing him at all, so just leave him out of it, Dex. He's got nothing to do with you. Neither have I, not anymore. I moved on a long time ago, and so have you."

Without warning, Dex leapt to his feet and swiped all of her ornaments off the windowsill, smashing them all over the floor. His eyes were wide now, bulging slightly just like the veins in his neck. "Don't you damn well tell me whether I moved on or not!"

She gasped and moved back in the bath, sending more of the tepid water sloshing over the side onto the mat. He was angry now, just the way she remembered him in those last few months when they were an item – a nasty, raging beast with a wild temper and hard fists. She remembered how those fists felt on her face and felt a sudden wave of nausea rising deep inside her.

"Please, Dex, just take it easy."

"Take it easy?" he said, producing a switchblade knife and flicking the blade out. It glinted in the bathroom light. "You ain't seen nothing yet. Get dressed. We're going for a drive."

*

At exactly the same time, several miles southwest of Anna's house in Swindon, Jacob had finished securing the doors and windows of the Old Watermill and was sitting down in his leather wingchair by a crackling fire. He held a glass of single malt whisky in his hand and was viewing his laptop on the table beside him.

Work. Always more work.

After sifting through various unimportant email messages and spam, he finally found what he was looking for – a message sent to him by Detective Chief Superintendent Marcus Kent attaching the full Austrian police report of the road traffic accident in which Keeley had been killed.

Kent's note was written in his usual short and clipped style with no niceties or pleasantries. It simply summarised the report which was written in German and made it clear to Jacob that Professor Alastair Keeley was dead and that he would proceed from this point forward in the investigation on the understanding that their killer was a copycat and a highly dangerous one.

Jacob then went on to scroll through the scanned pages of the report and use what little he could remember of his secondary school German to help him understand what had been written about the accident. He had to type a few sentences into a translation engine on the internet to get the full understanding, but it didn't take Sherlock Holmes to see that Marcus Kent had been right all along and that Alistair Keeley was brutally killed in a high-speed road traffic accident in an Austrian mountain pass several years ago. The clincher for Jacob was a series of photographs taken at the scene of the accident, several of which were close-up images of Keeley slumped forward dead in his car seat with his face covered in blood.

Jacob continued to trawl through Keeley's other files, including various newspaper cuttings he had scanned and kept on his laptop. The first was one in *The Telegraph*:

"The Metropolitan Police arrested a man today in connection with the notorious Ferryman murders that have triggered widespread panic across London. The man, as yet unnamed, is in his forties and was arrested at his home following one of the largest investigations in the Met's history."

Then, later, Keeley's escape was reported in *The Times*:

"Police urge caution tonight as they report Alistair Keeley, the notorious serial killer also known as The Ferryman has escaped from HMP Wakefield, a Category A Prison in Yorkshire. Police are advising people to remain at home until Keeley is caught and have unleashed the biggest manhunt in British history to track him down."

Jacob returned to the Austrian report and finished off with a cursory scan of some of the technical details concerning the accident, then closed down his email and shut the laptop lid. He took a sip of his whisky. Then, his mobile buzzed, alerting him to a new message. It was from Innes, reporting that the woman who visited Julian Squires at the abbey was called Eliza Richardson, a local cakemaker from Malmesbury. After some grilling, she confessed to having an affair with Squires behind her husband's back. The alibis checked out. Jacob read it without emotion and made a note. His phone buzzed again presuming it was Innes again, he was pleasantly surprised when he saw Sophie had written a short message to him telling him that all was well and that Rome was as beautiful as ever and that she wished he was there. She also said she was looking forward to him arriving on the last day of the conference so they could see the city together and had included a selfie of herself standing in front of the Colosseum at sunset.

Jacob replied that he'd never seen anything so beautiful in his entire life and that Sophie didn't look too bad either, before signing off with a wink emoji and then he set his mobile down and took another sip of the whisky. He stared into the fire but all he saw was the dead face of Alastair Keeley slumped forward in the seat of his Mercedes, with his dead staring eyes and blood running down his face from a cut on his forehead. Maybe it was true what they said about Karma. He played with the thought for a while then he considered how the information impacted the case. The good news was, that it was highly unlikely the copycat would be as intelligent as Professor Keeley. They had already seen evidence of that with several slip-ups the killer seemed to have made. The bad news was, in terms of a suspect, they were pretty much no closer to when they started and now the field was wide open. Without Keeley to consider, their killer was no more than a ghost.

And the problem with that was he thought, he did not know how to catch a ghost.

He was startled by a knock at the door. He and Drifter got up and walked down the corridor to the front of the house and Jacob opened the door. Vincent, the neighbour who sometimes walked Drifter was standing in the rain with wet, bedraggled hair and holding a plastic carrier bag.

"Vincent? What's going on?"

"Well that's the thing, Mr Jacob. I wanted to talk to you about this."

Vincent lifted the bag.

"That's the thing, Mr Jacob, it's a dead bird. I found it on your doorstep this morning when I brought Drifter back from his walk."

Drifter went forward, sniffed Vincent and then toddled back down to the sitting room, probably to lie beside the fire again.

Jacob felt his blood turn cold when he looked inside the bag and saw a raven with one of its wings torn off. "Good God."

"It can't have been accidental, not from where it was positioned. I think someone put it there on purpose."

"All right, thanks, Vincent."

"What do you want to do with it?"

"Throw it away, and thanks again."

"Is everything all right?"

Jacob sighed. "It's nothing for you to worry about. You did the right thing telling me."

"Goodnight then."

Jacob watched Vincent walk across the drive and out through his gates, then closed the door and headed straight up to the spare room where he kept Jess's old things. She was his fiancée when he lived in Oxford. She had studied medicine at Oxford and worked at the Royal London Hospital before being killed by a thug trying to get to Jacob. He held himself responsible for her death. Now, as he rummaged through her things, he felt the same raw sorrow he had felt on the night of the fire that killed her. When he finally found what he was looking for – her old copy of *The Tragedy of Hamlet* from school – he wasted no time in flicking through it. As soon as the raven feather came up, something had started to nag him, something Jess told him once about Shakespeare and ravens and now he had worked it out. In Act Three, Hamlet and Ophelia are talking when he says: 'the croaking raven doth bellow for revenge'.

Jacob closed the book and stared out through the window at the rain falling on the river at the end of the garden. So, that was what this was all about.

Revenge.

CHAPTER 14

Jacob woke with a start. His phone was ringing.

He fumbled for it and nearly knocked it off the nightstand before snatching it up and taking the call. He'd already seen it was from Marcus Kent and that could only mean one thing coming at this time in the morning.

"Morning, sir. This is Jacob. Please don't tell me what you're about to tell me."

"Don't tell you what, Chief Inspector? Tell you that another woman wrapped in a shroud has been found on our turf? Too bad, because she has. And she has a coin in her mouth and a bloody feather in her hand."

"Oh my God."

"I told you to keep a lid on this, Jacob. I told you to get after this copycat. Please don't tell me you still think this is Keeley?"

"No, sir. Not anymore."

"Thank goodness for that. Now get your arse down to Old Wardour Castle. That's where she was found. Now."

THE FERRYMAN

*

The journey from Devizes down to Old Wardour Castle was a little over thirty miles, and Jacob made the journey in three-quarters of an hour. He pulled off the main road and slowed down to crawl for a short while on an unsealed road, before pulling up and parking under some trees. He saw the castle and Innes walking over to him on the path ahead.

He slammed his door shut. "Morning, Constable."

"Morning, sir. Got another one, unfortunately."

"So I hear."

Jacob walked with her to the castle, and along the way, she regaled him with some history of the place after having researched it on her phone. Jacob allowed his mind to wander to what he had read last night about the raven in Hamlet; as much as he enjoyed learning about the castle's original construction in 1390, its role in the English Civil War, and its use by Sting as a photograph on his most-famous album cover, he was more than hoping the lecture would come to an end.

The walk from the car park to the castle was a short, paved pedestrian walkway leading to a series of metal gates built into the original castle wall, which after so many hundreds of years was not much more than a crumbling ruin. Two uniformed police officers were standing in front of the gate, both of whom now gave Jacob a respectful nod as they stepped out of the way and opened the gate, allowing him to walk through without hindrance.

The castle itself was an enormous stone structure that was no more than a skeleton, apart from its eastern façade which still bore some resemblance to the original building and contained several complete windows looking out across an expansive lawn and beautifully maintained parkland. Most of the buildings behind this façade were crumbling ruins covered in moss and lichen and other plant life growing out through the cracks and nooks and crannies in the ancient stonework.

They approached it from the north, and Jacob could see through the open arched doorways dotted around the ground floor of the ancient building a flurry of activity within its ancient stone walls. A forensics tent had been erected inside the building, several uniformed officers were walking around with notebooks. Mia Francis and her team were already busy at work taking evidence from around the scene.

"Over there on those steps, sir," Innes said. "That's where Sting was photographed for the album Ten Summoner's Tales."

"Thank you for that," Jacob said. "Perhaps we can save the album artwork tour for later when we've got the rest of this day behind us."

"Just trying to be helpful," Innes said.

Inside the castle, Jacob made directly for Holloway who was standing just outside the forensic tent with a grim look on his face. Holloway noticed the tall chief inspector striding towards him and made a gesture with his hand, acknowledging his arrival.

"What's the story?" Jacob asked. "Although I'm not sure I really want to know."

"No surprises, I'm afraid, sir," Holloway said. "It's exactly the same as last time. The body was discovered earlier this morning by an estate worker. She reported an unusual bundle of what she thought were clothes wrapped up but when she came closer, she realised it was almost certainly a body. As you'll see in a moment, the body is wrapped in the same shroud, in exactly the same way and I already authorised Mia to unwrap the shroud, and I'm afraid we've been paid another visit by Emperor Constantine."

"I know, Bill. Kent told me when he called me."

"I can't believe it."

Jacob shook his head from side to side, still unable to process the information the last two days had presented him with.

"So, our killer has dumped another body and still desperately wants us to believe he's the Ferryman."

"You definitely don't think it's Keeley anymore, then?"

"I don't think so. Not since I saw the CCTV footage of the man who bought these coins in the shop in Marlborough yesterday. That, on top of the report we received from the Austrian police yesterday and, including images which were quite obviously a dead Alastair Keeley, means I think we have to swallow our pride and admit Marcus Kent was right all along."

"Oh no, sir. Anything but that!"

"I know how you feel," Jacob said with a shrug of his shoulders. "But the old bugger has got a lot of experience and I suppose he was just being more objective than I was.

It's just because of Sophie and everything… I couldn't help it."

"Even if it *is* a copycat, and for what it's worth sir, I'm starting to think so as well, we've still got a major problem on our hands. Our killer has now murdered and dumped two women, posing as the Ferryman. Don't forget you said how the bloke in the coin shop had told you the man in the plaid shirt had bought *three* coins. He clearly intends on killing another time!"

Jacob threw a glance back over to the tent and the bustling figure of Mia Francis as she moved around inside in her white Tyvek coverall. In the opposite direction, through the open arched doorway, he caught sight of a woman being comforted by a female police officer.

"Is that the woman who found the body?"

"Yeah, that's it. Her name is Barbara McGee. She's an estate worker here and she discovered the body about an hour ago. She's in a terrible state as you can see. I've already interviewed her and got all of her details."

"Good work. Anything I should know?"

"Not really. Nothing to be of any bloody help to us, anyway."

"I suppose I'd better go in and have a chat with Mia, then."

Jacob made his way over to the tent and stepped inside, where he found Mia on her knees beside the body scouring everything inside with a powerful magnifying glass.

"Morning Mia."

"Morning Jacob," Mia rose to her feet and turned to face him, the polypropylene forensic suit crinkling and rustling as she put her hands on her hips and shook her head.

"I'm sorry to tell you this, but I think it's pretty much exactly the same as the first one. I can't comment on the cause of death and Richard is running late apparently, but what I can say is that we have a woman in her fifties, with no sign of violence, wrapped in a shroud, raven feather in her hand and I found another coin featuring our friend Emperor Constantine in her mouth."

"This just keeps on getting better and better."

Jacob wondered if he should have told Sophie about the two murders, given the link to Keeley, because now with a second corpse on his hands, it was starting to look like the perpetrator might be a serial killer, and if he knew that much about Keeley, he would also know about the role

Sophie Anderson played in his arrest. A shiver ran up Jacob's spine when he considered how the killer might consider murdering Sophie as the ultimate form of honouring Keeley's legacy. For the first time, he was beginning to think she could be in real danger but was temporarily calmed by the knowledge she was hundreds of miles away in Italy.

"I don't suppose there's any sign of a murder weapon anywhere?"

"Like a ligature?" Mia shook her head. "No, nothing, sorry. Just like last time. But I don't think I'm taking a big risk by telling you that this person was probably killed in the same place as the first one, stored there for a day or so and then dumped here."

Jacob turned and took in the entire scene once again through the open tent doors, thanked Mia and then stepped back outside into the main hall of the castle. He paused to stare up at the leaden sky and the clouds scudding speedily above him. It almost gave him the impression that the castle was moving and not the clouds, it made him feel for a moment even less in control than he really was.

Then he saw Holloway's face, ashen white, from across the other side of the hall. He had been outside on the lawn talking to some uniformed police officers but now he was walking through the Gothic arched doorway quickly towards Jacob. His phone was in his hand and he did not look happy.

"What's the problem, Holloway?" Jacob asked.

"It's Sergeant Mazurek," Holloway said. "Something's up."

Jacob saw the concern in Holloway's eyes. "What makes you say that?"

"A call just came through. Something about her going missing. There's some confusion."

"There must be a mistake," Jacob said. "Let me talk to them."

Jacob walked across the lawn to his car, his brow furrowed with confusion as he snatched the two-way radio out and held it to his mouth. "This is DCI Jacob. What's this about Sergeant Mazurek?"

"I repeat, sir," the uniformed constable said. "One of DS Mazurek's neighbours has called into the station and reported that she is missing. She noticed that her front door was wide open when she woke up this morning and when she went around to see if everything was okay, she found signs of a struggle in the hallway and no response when she called out to DS Mazurek."

Jacob and Holloway exchanged a glance. "That doesn't sound right, sir."

The older detective ignored the comment and thumbed the push-to-talk key. "There was no response when she called out to her?"

They waited patiently for a few seconds as radio static filled the air. "No, sir."

Jacob slammed his hand down on the steering wheel. "Did she go inside the house?"

"No, sir. She came away and called it in."

Jacob's mind raced as he put together another strategic plan. "We're at least an hour away from Swindon. Tell DI Morgan to get over there right now. He's SIO on that case now."

"Sir."

"And no one else goes inside until I get there. Only Morgan."

"Sir."

"Holloway, get over there and tell Innes and Mia to stick around and brief Richard Lyon on everything going on here. You're coming with me to Swindon. Now."

CHAPTER 15

In the Covingham area of east Swindon, Jacob raced along Merlin Way until he saw the row of terraces where Anna lived and then screeched the Alvis to a stop outside her house. There was already a marked police car parked up on the pavement at the end of her front garden and a uniformed constable standing outside her open front door. Jacob recognised an unmarked Audi A4 as one of their fleet and knew Morgan was already on the scene, as he had expected him to be.

Jacob's heart pounded in his chest as he slammed his door and marched up the path. Holloway was only a few steps behind. Anna's home was towards the middle of the terrace and nosy neighbours on either side of her property were cautiously peering out from behind their curtains as he approached the PC and showed him his warrant card. It was unnecessary due to the powder-blue soft-top that he had just climbed out of; everyone in the county on the force knew who owned this car, but he showed it out of respect.

Jacob looked over the young man's shoulder into Anna's hallway, shocked by the devastation he was seeing inside her home. The telephone table was tipped over and the phone ripped out of the wall, its disconnected cable strewn all over the carpet. Some of her pictures were on the floor, their glass smashed, others still on the wall but knocked at an odd angle.

"Anyone been inside?"

"Only Inspector Morgan, sir."

Jacob and Holloway went inside. Morgan was standing in the kitchen and now gave his old friend a helpless shrug. "Anna's neighbour called the police. She said she heard some kind of an altercation in the house last night but didn't think much of it as it ended so fast. Then she went to bed and this morning she went outside and realised that Anna's front door was open. She peered in and saw that furniture had been tipped upside down in the hall and it looked like there'd been a fight in the front room. I've been upstairs and there's a hell of a mess in the bathroom. I think that's where she was. No one else around here saw or heard anything else, and her car was in the garage block around the corner, all locked up. Her phone is upstairs on her nightstand. I think Dex has got her, Jacob."

Jacob understood why Morgan thought this. Declan Taylor, Anna's former husband, had threatened to snatch her on so many occasions that Jacob had seen to it that a substantial restraining order was put on him. At the time, it seemed to have cooled the situation. Then, Declan disappeared from Anna's life and no one heard anything from him. Anna had once confided to Jacob that she had almost forgotten about the threats Dex had made to her.

Jacob noticed Morgan's hands were balled into tight fists. He knew what he was thinking.

"Just take it easy, Bill."

"It's got to be Dex."

"Take it easy. Think things through. I'll get Mia to get over here as soon as she is finished down at the castle and she'll go through the place like a dose of salts. In the meantime, we need to get back to HQ and get a full briefing organised. That's the best way we can help her."

"You're right, but when I get my hands on Dex, I'll swing for him."

CHAPTER 16

When Jacob got back to his desk, he saw a yellow Post-It note stuck right in the middle of his computer screen. It read: CALL DCS KENT.

He sighed and tore the little piece of sticky paper off the screen as he picked up his phone. Briefing his boss about the situation was inevitable but that didn't mean he had to like it. Seconds later Kent snatched up the phone and barked into the receiver.

"DCS Kent."

"It's me, sir."

"I'm most unhappy about this, Jacob."

Despite the early hour, Jacob suddenly wished the extra-large cup of very strong coffee in front of him was a triple whisky.

"Of course, sir. We all are."

"What happened, man?"

"I was down at Old Wardour Castle dealing with the second copycat murder when we got a call from dispatch alerting us to the possible kidnapping of DS Mazurek from her home in east Swindon. I was with Holloway and we drove to Swindon immediately."

After a long pause, Kent sighed long and loudly down the phone. It was the sound of a headache looming on the horizon. "And what did you find there?"

"She's gone, sir."

"Christ almighty."

"There were signs of a struggle upstairs in the bathroom. The bath was filled three-quarters and a lot of water on the mats and floor. Also, mud all over the mats."

"My God, you can't mean he dragged her out of the bath?"

Jacob gave himself a moment to gather his thoughts and shake the brutal image Kent had just conjured in his mind. "Looks that way, sir."

The older man went quiet as he processed the information. Jacob's primary concern was the wellbeing of his friend and colleague but he had already guessed what Kent was going to say next.

"This could damage the force, Jacob. If it gets out that we can't even look after one of our own, we're going to look like a clown show and if anything serious happens to her, a total shit show."

"My focus is on bringing DS Mazurek back safe and sound to her family and friends, sir. Not our public image."

"Yes," he said with brisk detachment. "Of course, DS Mazurek comes first. I'm simply saying to you that as Detective Chief Superintendent there are wider implications I must consider."

Got out of that one nicely, Jacob thought. "Yes, sir."

"Not in the press yet, is it?"

"No, sir. Neither is the second copycat killing, yet."

"Good, good. Very good."

Jacob looked at his watch. "If that's all, sir…"

"No, it is not all, *sir*," he snapped. "I want to know how you are approaching all of this."

He swallowed his sigh and kept his voice calm and level. Professional. "I've called a major team briefing which is about to start now, sir. I'm staying on the copycat killings and I'm putting DI Morgan on the search for DS Mazurek. I'll be kicking things off by opening Anna's ex-husband's case files."

"Yes, that's right," Kent purred. "He's an old lag."

"Armed robbery and ABH, sir."

"I remember now. It's got to be him, hasn't it?"

"He has form, but at this time we have no real evidence linking him to the kidnapping."

Jacob heard his boss drumming his fingers on the table.

"Fine, get started and bring her home."

"Yes, sir."

"And make it cleaner than Grovely and Avebury, Jacob. Thanks to those cases we've already had enough corpses to last the county for a century. The last thing we need now is another omnishambles."

Jacob ground his teeth down and felt his neck muscles tightening.

Think happy thoughts, he said, visualizing Sophie safe in Italy. That was a happy thought.

"You still there, man?"

"Yes, sir."

"It's all riding on you, Chief Inspector. Don't let us down."

Before he could reply, Jacob heard Kent slam the phone down hard in the cradle. Kent was a bastard but he was also usually right. It was all riding on him, and this time it was personal.

*

The Wiltshire Criminal Investigation Department operated out of three central hubs in Swindon, Salisbury and Melksham. Due to its position in the heart of the county, the central police headquarters were in Devizes and when Jacob walked into its main briefing room everyone felt the tension rise. When he had officially declared Detective Sergeant Anna Mazurek as missing, a wave of disbelief washed over the staff and this morning everyone who could make it was now sitting and waiting for him to start.

He paced over to the front of the noisy room. Dumping several files on the desk in front of the whiteboard he picked up a thick black marker pen and wrote OPERATION MERLIN in large letters up on the board.

Anna was well-known across the force as a good-humoured, hard-working colleague with an excellent arrest record. She was also sociable and had great fun on nights out; the news of her kidnapping had shocked everyone and rumours about the culprit being her ex-husband were already doing the rounds. For now, and only for now, there were no reports of the crime in the press but they all knew that would change soon enough.

"All right, quiet down everyone!"

The chatter hushed in seconds until you could hear a pin drop. In the front row, Matt Holloway was already keenly waiting for the tall detective to start work.

"As you all know by now, DS Mazurek was taken from her home at some point between arriving home last night and when her neighbour found her front door open this morning. The same neighbour heard some kind of altercation inside Anna's home around nine last night but wasn't concerned by it as it ended quickly. This is also the woman who called us this morning when she noticed DS Mazurek's front door was wide open with no sign of anyone in the house."

"What time was that call, sir?" a constable asked.

"The call came into the station less than an hour ago while I was down at Old Wardour Castle attending what we believe is another copycat murder."

Holloway wiggled his pen to get Jacob's attention. "Do we have reason to believe the two incidents are related, sir?"

"Not at this stage, no," Jacob said. "But anyone who knows me at all knows I don't believe in coincidences. Murder is rare in Wiltshire, and so is kidnapping. The fact we have a detective sergeant taken from her home in the same week that we have two ritual killings is ringing major alarm bells in my mind. Also, I have reason to believe the ritual murders have something to do with revenge, but I'll go into that later when I know more."

"And it's definitely Declan Taylor?" Holloway asked.

Jacob blew out a deep breath. "We all get threats from people we've arrested and had put away. That's part of the job. Declan Taylor made many serious threats against Anna. Sometimes they are serious threats, but they rarely come to anything. Most of it's just hot air. Given this, and the character of Declan Taylor, the most logical assumption right now is that he is responsible for taking her."

"Then we're officially naming him as the suspect in the kidnapping?" Holloway asked.

"Yes."

"Do we have a motive for the kidnapping, sir?"

"Yes and no," Jacob said. "By that, I mean there is no formal motive at this time but DS Mazurek has mentioned to me on occasion, personally, not professionally, that Declan Taylor is a very possessive man and blamed her for the break-up of their marriage. For now, that's all we have."

"Do we know what his endgame is, sir?" someone asked.

Jacob shook his head. "Not at all. Taylor has form for armed robbery and is a violent man. He does not have form for murder, and that's a very different kettle of fish. We cannot at this time know what his intentions are. Maybe he's trying to scare her, maybe he's having some sort of breakdown and thinks they can get back together. I have no idea, but he's not in charge of this situation. We are, and we're going to get her back, and fast. I'm making DI Morgan the SIO on Operation Merlin and I will continue to lead Operation Abbey.

Jacob searched the sombre audience to gauge the mood and found what he expected to see. Every face in the briefing room was etched with a mix of anger and fear. Someone with a very serious criminal record and a personal vendetta against a much-loved colleague had walked right into the middle of their patch and taken her from right under their noses. They all knew it was up to them to get her back before Declan Taylor decided to up the ante.

As Morgan stepped up to talk tactics and allocate jobs, Jacob gestured for Innes to come with him and they left the conference room.

"What now, sir?" she asked.

"Now we go to Charlton and see if Jennifer Stanley's home can tell us anything."

CHAPTER 17

Jennifer Stanley's small cottage in Charlton was a rundown, crumbling affair made of Cotswold Stone, with a heavily weathered slate roof. There was nowhere to park along the narrow lane so Jacob asked Innes to hop out and then he pulled the car over as far to the left as he could. He climbed out of the car and walked around to the little gate, which had once been painted red but was now no more than a sad, faded reflection of its former glorious self with flakes of paint peeling off and rusty hinges. He opened it and walked up the stone path to the house where he performed almost exactly the same routine he had done at Tansy Babbington's mansion. Using a rock he found in the garden, he put out the frosted glass window in the door, reached inside, unhooked the chain and turned the lock, opening the door and allowing the two of them to step inside.

The property could not have been any more different than Tansy's. It was messy and dirty and damp, with mould spores on the hallway wall, and pieces of underwear hanging over the bannister rails to dry. Beneath the stairs, a cheap electric fire was positioned to expedite the drying process. It was precariously plugged into an outlet on the opposite side of the stairs.

"Trip hazard," Jacob said.

"What is that smell?" Innes asked.

Jacob pointed in the kitchen where he saw stacks of plates full of cold food on the drainer, some empty crisp packets and other mess all over the sideboard. They moved through into the kitchen and took in the detritus.

"Okay, same as before, Innes," Jacob said. "Go through everything, try and find phones or computers."

Innes went upstairs once again and Jacob went around the tiny ground floor which comprised the kitchen, a small living front room, a back room that doubled as a dining room and study. He looked outside and saw overgrown grass and damp cardboard boxes collapsing in on themselves stacked up against the back fence. After finding nothing that might help them, he heard Innes walking down the creaky stairs and the two of them met in the kitchen.

"Nothing," she said.

"That doesn't surprise me."

"What I don't understand is how completely different this place is from Tansy's."

"Not completely different," Jacob said.

She looked at him confused. "What do you mean, sir?"

"There's one thing both properties have in common. This place hasn't got any personal photographs or pictures of family or friends anywhere in it either. I think we're going to find out that Jennifer Stanley was a very isolated and lonely woman, just like Tansy Babbington."

"Good point, sir. I hadn't noticed that."

"It's the dog that barked in the nighttime, Innes."

"Sorry, sir I'm not following you."

"I think you need to brush up on your Sherlock Holmes."

Jacob heard someone calling through the front door and turned to the younger detective.

"C'mon, let's go."

Jacob led Innes through the kitchen door, over the trip hazard, which he now pulled free and rested the wire over the top of the electric heater, and went to the front door. They were met by an elderly man wearing a tweed jacket over a shirt and tie. He was in his eighties but had a clear, inquisitive eye and now those eyes narrowed as he stared at the two strangers in the front hall.

"May I ask just what it is you think you're doing?" he asked.

Jacob produced his identification and introduced himself and Innes. The man immediately folded and began wringing his hands.

"I see. How can I help?"

"Your name please, sir."

"Harry Jeffs."

"Are you the neighbour who called this in today?" Jacob asked.

"I am, yes. That's why I'm keeping an eye on the place."

"Then you might be able to help," Jacob said. "You say you're a neighbour of Mrs Stanley?"

"Yes, I live next door. And it's Miss Stanley – she wasn't married."

No surprises there, Jacob thought.

"Has something happened to Jenny?" the old man asked feebly.

"I'm afraid to tell you that she was found dead this morning by a member of the public."

The man's face visibly crumpled and became paler. His mouth opened slightly and his eyebrows raised half an inch. "Oh no, I don't believe it."

"I'm sorry, but we believe it was murder and we're conducting a formal murder investigation."

"Murder? I don't believe it! Jenny couldn't be involved in anything like that."

Jacob wasn't sure what the old man meant by that but understood people said silly things when confronted with news like this. "When was the last time you saw Miss Stanley?"

"I suppose it would have been three or four days ago. I'm not sure really. We just waved at each other in the street and that sort of thing. Sometimes we'd call over the back fence and have a chat and I sometimes brought her a cake around. I was a cook in the army, you know. Anyway, she never let me into her house." As he spoke, he peered over Jacob's shoulder.

Jacob and Innes now drew together, blocking Mr Jeffs's view of the hall.

"Can you tell us if Miss Stanley was seeing anybody recently?" Innes asked.

The old man tried to recall. "Well, she's usually a very private person, she keeps herself to herself."

"What was her job?" Jacob asked.

"No job. She used to get money from the government. You know, like long-term benefits or whatever you call it."

Jacob made a note on his pad writing the words *benefits, mental health, disability?*

He looked back up at Jeffs. "You were saying something about Miss Stanley's private life."

"She never had any friends round here, or at least I never saw anyone come round here. And she never went out really, neither. She got her food delivered in one of those vans that come round – you know, they make it happen on the computer, don't they?"

"And you saw no one unusual coming to the house in the last few days?" Jacob asked.

"That's a funny thing because I *did* see outside a few days ago which is quite unusual as I say. But I didn't see it pull up and I didn't see it pull away. I noticed it was there and then got about my business. The next time I looked out there, it was gone."

"And can you describe the car? Its make, its colour, its registration number?"

"No, none of that. I stopped paying attention to cars when they all started looking the same about forty years ago. I can tell you the colour though – it was one of those new blue metallic colours. But I couldn't tell you what it was or the registration number because you can't see that from my front window. It's all behind the hedge."

"And how long would you say this car was parked there?"

"I don't know, maybe an hour. Not long."

"And you didn't hear anything in the house where the car was here, no shouting or arguments or anything like that?" Innes asked.

Jeffs shook his head. "Nothing like that. It's always very quiet around here."

Jacob felt another ripple of disappointment as he realised he had exhausted Jeffs's knowledge of Jennifer Stanley in a matter of minutes. Once again, just as with Tansy Babbington, there was nothing here but a series of dead ends. No family, no friends, no significant other. No job, no work colleagues. No one ever saw this woman come and go, and no one reported her missing until her neighbour saw the open front door and became concerned.

Jacob wrote a note on his pad, it read – *chooses isolated lonely women*.

He snapped the notepad shut and fixed Mr Jeff's firmly in the eye. "Thank you very much, Mr Jeffs. You've been very helpful today. I'm going to close this door and put some police barrier tape up in front of it. I would appreciate it if nobody came in here, please. We'll send a contractor around to mend the front door."

"I wouldn't be going in there. I've never set foot in there in my life. I'm not a suspect, am I?"

Jacob looked at the man, thin and frail probably approaching ninety. "No sir, I don't believe you are a suspect. You've been very helpful though and hopefully what you've given us will help us apprehend the man responsible for her death."

Jeffs shuffled down the path, opened the rusty gate, which protested its lack of oil with an ear-bending squeak, turned left and went out of view. Jacob sent Innes down to the Alvis where there was some barrier tape in the glove compartment. Jacob took it everywhere with him, including several other indispensable items such as nitrile gloves, leather gloves, a Maglite, and a retractable telescopic truncheon. Innes returned with the tape and the two of them secured the entrance before returning to the Alvis.

"Nothing but dead ends again," Jacob said, turning the ignition. "Wherever we go, there's nothing but dead ends."

Innes buckled her seatbelt and looked over at him. "On purpose, or did our killer get lucky?"

"Oh, it's quite by design," Jacob said, pulling away. "Quite by design."

CHAPTER 18

Anna Mazurek was floating in darkness. For a moment she felt something like bliss; a strange weightless sensation almost like being underwater, except she was flying. Why was everything so dark? She felt so light. She felt like a feather.

She felt someone slapping her cheek.

She woke up with a start, opening her eyes wide and gasping as she realized she had been unconscious and in some kind of dream. Now she had woken from a dream into a nightmare and Declan Taylor was leaning over her with a grimace on his face.

"Wakey, wakey."

She shook her head, trying to clear her thoughts. She struggled to focus her eyes and she felt cold all over her body. Then she realized her hands and legs were tied to a rocking chair. As she squirmed to try and break through her bonds, her ex-husband gave an icy laugh.

"You're wasting your time, Ania. You're stuck to that chair with duct tape. You're not going anywhere, darlin'."

His voice echoed in the darkness surrounding her and then he turned his back on her and walked over to another chair. He had placed it ten feet away, facing her. Beside it was the bright white LED glow of a plastic camping lantern.

She blinked and brought her eyes back into focus. Searching the space around her, she saw they were in a room in some kind of old stone house. The walls were large blocks of grey stone and the window was covered by an old, faded curtain, tattered and shredded along the hem. Wherever they were, looked like it hadn't been lived in for a long time.

Anna swallowed and worked hard to keep control. "Where are we?"

"You're too used to asking questions."

"Just tell me where I am."

"Shut up."

"What did you drug me with?"

"That's another question. I don't like questions."

She started to consider all the places she could be. Obviously, this was some sort of abandoned house, judging by its age probably a farmhouse or a tithe cottage, but she had no way of knowing how long she had been unconscious. Had he knocked her out for an hour? Two hours? They could be almost anywhere. Declan leaned against the back of his chair and crossed his arms over his chest, surveying his prize.

"You always were a good-looking woman, Ania."

"Stop calling me that."

"Even now in here, all trussed up like a spring chicken, you're still a knockout."

He uncrossed his arms and reached down into a canvas bag. He pulled out a can of beer and cracked it open, taking a long sip and then smacking his lips.

"That's good stuff."

Anna tried to stay calm. "I can't believe you're actually enjoying this."

He took another long swig and wiped his mouth with the back of his hand. She watched his shoulders start to slope down a little. He was starting to relax, she thought. The beer was already working.

"Don't get much good beer these days, Ania. Trying to get fit. Start a new life."

Anna said nothing.

"I sometimes dream of good, cold beer like this, and now I've got one. You couldn't begin to imagine how good it tastes."

"I'm sorry about what happened," she said, trying to pacify him.

He broke up, laughing. "You're sorry for what happened?"

"Yes."

"Oh no, no." He lifted the can and waved it in her face at arm's length. "You don't get to be sorry for what happened, Ania. You cut me loose. You dumped me. I got down and depressed and fell in with some real scumbags. My life fell apart. You don't get to be sorry. That ship has sailed. As far as apologies go this is the day after the fair, darlin'."

"Please…"

He took a long swig and belched. Then he crumpled the can and threw it over his shoulder. "No more please, no more sorry."

He got out of the chair and went over to her until she could feel his breath on her face, then he raised his arms in the air and screamed at her. "No more sorries, Ania!"

She winced at the ear-piercing scream so close to her ear and pulled her head away from him as much as she could. Struggling to pull her arms and legs free from the rocking chair only made him laugh again.

"Duct tape, bitch. Two rolls. You've got more chance of levitating out of here than getting off that chair."

Anna fought hard to keep the tears back.

*

Sophie had been right in her text message to Jacob. Even in November, Rome was warm enough to walk outside with just her shirt sleeves on. Now she was walking along the Piazza de St Eustachio with her friend and fellow psychologist Louise Markham and Kit Bailey, one of the world's most famous and cited criminal psychologists, after having just visited the pantheon. Bailey had become something of a mentor to Sophie over the past few years and she respected his professional opinion a great deal. He was also an experienced traveller who had spent much of his life in various Mediterranean countries, so she now deferred to him on the subject of where they should eat lunch today.

Kit pointed to a small pizza restaurant on the side of the square, with the usual array of outside tables underneath square patio umbrellas and jumbles of chairs here and there. They walked through a line of parked Vespas and stepped inside the restaurant where Bailey spoke in Italian to a waitress behind the counter. The waitress replied in Italian and then Bailey turned to Sophie and Louise. "Would you like to eat inside or outside this evening, ladies?"

They exchanged a quick look and both agreed that outside would be lovely, given how warm the city was this evening.

Bailey relayed this information back to the woman in Italian and moments later they were shown to one of the tables outside. The three of them took their seats and by the time Sophie had got herself comfortable, the waitress had reappeared with some menus, which she now handed out to them. There was another short Italian conversation between the waitress and Bailey, and then the waitress disappeared inside and Bailey explained that she was bringing some water out before they made their choices from the menu.

Sophie checked her phone to see if Jacob had messaged her and saw he had. It asked her to call him urgently when she got the next chance. The message was less than an hour old. She excused herself and walked away from the table to make the call.

"Soph, thank God," Jacob said.

"What's the matter, Tom?"

"I take it you haven't seen the British news?"

"I've been deliberately avoiding it. Why?"

"It's about the suspicious death I was called to attend yesterday morning."

"What about it?"

Jacob paused. "Don't panic, Soph, but the body was wrapped in a shroud and the killer had left a coin in its mouth."

Sophie felt the ground give way beneath her. "What did you say?"

"I understand this is a shock, but there's no need to jump to conclusions."

"No need to…" she threw a glance at her friends at the table and realised they were looking at her. Now she lowered her voice. "No need to jump to conclusions? What else am I supposed to do? I thought that bastard was supposed to be dead?"

"Kent thinks it's a copycat."

Sophie felt the warm air "And what do you think?"

"I think there's a possibility he's right."

"But there's a possibility it could be Keeley?"

"We have to allow for that possibility, but all the evidence points to Keeley being dead. I saw the Austrian police reports with my own eyes. I saw his body at the scene of the crash. Not only that but there's other evidence pointing this to a copycat. The shroud was wrapped differently, and the wrong coin was left in their mouths."

"Their mouths? I thought only one body was found."

Jacob sighed. "Another body was dumped today."

"My God."

"Just try and stay calm."

"Even if this is a copycat, he would know about me, and how Keeley felt about me. I could be a target."

"I think there's a possibility of this, but whoever he is, he's here in Wiltshire. He's killed two women in the last forty-eight hours and there's something else."

"What else?"

"Anna Mazurek has been kidnapped."

Sophie felt a chill run up her back. "Anna was taken? By him?"

"We don't know, but we believe it was Declan Taylor."

"How do you know?"

"We're looking into it, Sophie. Trust us."

Sophie looked around her, seeing nothing but tourists and local Romans enjoying the warm, sunny day. Inside, she felt sick. "I don't like this, Tom. What if it's Keeley? What if he comes for me?"

"It's not going to come to that," Jacob said. "Just stay in Italy with your friends, enjoy the conference and if I can get on top of the case by the end of the week, I'll try and fly out and join you. If not, then I'll meet you at Bristol Airport when you come home. We'll be together, whatever happens."

After the call, Sophie didn't know which way to turn. Was the Ferryman back, somehow risen from the grave and intent on killing her? Was Anna safe? She took a walk around the piazza, taking some deep breaths and then returned to her table where the wine was already flowing. She sat down, confused and angry. She understood Jacob was busily engaged in the hunt for whoever was doing these crimes – she prayed it was a copycat killer, but even then she knew she could be at risk from a deranged maniac stalking Wiltshire and murdering women in the same bizarre ritualistic style that Professor Alastair Keeley had done so many years ago, the very same man who had almost strangled Sophie to death. She shook the image from her mind but gave silent thanks that Keeley was dead. She considered that whoever the copycat was, he might consider her to be the main prize, but no one knew she was in Italy apart from the people at the conference and Jacob and his team. She felt safe here in Rome but would sleep a lot better when she returned to England when Jacob had caught and locked up the deranged copycat killer.

She heard Louise laughing in her usual dizzy way and looked up to join the conversation, sliding her phone back into her bag and placing it down under her chair.

"What's so funny?" she asked.

"Oh, not much," Louise said. "Kit was just telling me a story about the first time he came to Rome and accidentally ordered some kind of seafood dish that he was allergic to."

"Sorry I missed it," Sophie said. "I was just talking to Tom. He says there have been two murders in Wiltshire now, each one wrapped in a shroud, just like Keeley did."

"Two murders?" Bailey said. "The news only reported one."

"You saw it on the news?" Sophie asked.

Bailey nodded grimly. "I didn't bring it up because I guessed you'd seen it and didn't want to talk about it, what with you and Tom Jacob being together and what you went through with Keeley. I'm sorry about it all."

"Me too," Louise said, reaching out and touching her hand. "It's horrible."

Sophie got her phone out and checked the British news for the first time since landing in Rome. After browsing for a few seconds she saw that news of the murders had been reported in both local and national newspapers and there had even been a news report on the main national news on the BBC about the two murders – the second murder having broken only recently. This was understandable. Murders were a rare occurrence in Wiltshire, and for two of them to have happened in as many days was completely unprecedented. Adding to that the copycat nature of the killings and the huge impact that Professor Keeley's murders had made on the nation when he had stalked London all those years ago, Sophie was only surprised that it had taken the press this long to get hold of the story. Kit and Louise were now looking at her with faces painted with sympathy.

"It'll be OK, Sophie," Bailey said. "Jacob will catch him."

"I don't want to talk about it if that's OK," Sophie said, picking up her menu. "I'm here and that means I'm safe and I want to enjoy myself."

Bailey and Louise got the message and also started perusing their menus. Sophie was grateful that she could hide behind her menu for a few moments and compose herself. She was grateful for Bailey's voiced support, but she really didn't want to talk about it. The whole business terrified her and that was the truth. Luckily, she felt completely safe here in Rome.

CHAPTER 19

Jacob had to force himself not to think about Anna's disappearance. It was naturally occupying a large part of his mind, but he had to put it to one side and trust Bill Morgan to handle the situation while he remained focused on the copycat killings. He couldn't think of a better detective to find Anna, or one more motivated, than Inspector Bill Morgan, so he filed the matter away and continued to put all his efforts into finding whoever was copying the Ferryman's murders across Wiltshire, but what he had found in Charlton earlier today had not filled him with confidence. His efforts to remain solely focused on the case were bolstered when Detective Constable Laura Innes walked over to his desk in the busy open-plan office with a beaming smile on her face.

"I think I've got something, sir," she said.

Jacob looked at her with some hope. "Please, go ahead. Make my day."

"It's the partial number plate that you and DS Mazurek found on the CCTV footage at the coin shop over in Marlborough. I think I might have found the vehicle we're looking for."

Jacob tossed his pen on the desk and leaned back in his seat. "It's about time we had some good news, Innes. What exactly have you found?"

"There are several cars with those first three letters, sir, but there were only three that the DVLA have records of as belonging to a red pickup truck. One of them is registered to an address in Snowdonia, another one of them is registered to an address in Devon, and the third one is registered to an address in Gloucestershire."

"OK, that sounds promising," Jacob said, trying not to get his hopes up too high. "Whereabouts in Gloucestershire?"

"It's registered to an address in Tetbury, which is only a couple of miles north of Westonbirt Arboretum."

"Isn't that where you and Inspector Morgan went to talk to that author – what was his name?"

"His name is Meredith Ash, sir. He was an extremely nasty little man. And yes, that is where we went this morning. The writers' retreat is just outside the arboretum on the north side of the road up to Tetbury. A bit of a coincidence, wouldn't you say?"

Jacob didn't believe in coincidences, because it was not a very clever way for a detective to behave. In fact, Jacob had never met a good detective who believed in coincidences in his entire career. On the other hand, it was a small world, so he was prepared to give Innes's burgeoning theory linking Meredith Ash to the red pickup a wide berth for the time being.

"I think we need to go out to Tetbury at once and visit this address," he said. "I've got a printout of the man who drove the pickup truck to the coin shop, which I'll bring with us, but I can remember his face anyway. I'll know him if I see him again."

"Should we take like an armed team or something, sir?" Innes asked.

Jacob wanted to smile at her innocence but kept things professional. "I don't think we need an armed response team to go and interview a suspect in a murder inquiry, Innes, especially since the case hasn't had any firearms involvement at all."

"But, sir! If this guy with the pickup is the copycat killer, he's completely insane!"

"I'm not a mental health professional, Innes and neither are you, so we'll leave out the insanity diagnosis if you don't mind. We don't know if this man is the killer or not, but we do know that the killer takes his victims' lives by administering a heavy quantity of drugs and then choking them slowly to death. He does not attack his victims with brute force such as punches or kicks, he does not use knives and he certainly does not use guns. Guns are quite hard to come by in this country, as I think you'll agree. I can't justify putting in a request to deploy an armed response unit to go and interview a man who may or may not be our suspect or our killer, plus it will slow us down – a lot."

"Sorry, sir," she said. "I understand now."

"You're young," Jacob said, easily recalling his days as a young detective. He had many memories of silly or embarrassing things he had said and done when acting impetuously or talking without thinking over the years. Luckily that sort of thing reduced *almost* to zero with age but it never completely vanished. He respected Innes, she was competent and brave, but she had still much to learn about the business of murder investigations.

Jacob rose to his feet and snatched his car keys off the desk.

"Right, it looks like the two of us are driving up to Tetbury."

*

Holloway had driven Morgan to the nearest petrol station to Anna's Covingham address, which the young man had assured the Welsh inspector was festooned with security cameras. When Holloway pulled up in the unmarked Audi on the forecourt of the petrol station, Morgan saw that while he had exaggerated slightly, the place seemed to be well-fitted with a quality security system. Everyone on the team agreed that whoever snatched Anna would have done it in a car to make a quick and clean getaway, and Holloway had also been correct in suggesting that the car that snatched Anna would almost certainly have had to drive past the station. Now, the two detectives climbed out of the Audi and made their way across the forecourt to the petrol station's main building.

"Bloody hell!" Holloway said. "Would you look at the prices of this fuel? Daylight robbery."

Morgan huffed out a bitter laugh. "I can see that you've never been to West Wales. We have to pay *much* more than this, believe me."

"I'm surprised anyone can even afford to get to work and back on prices like this," the young man said, shaking his head wistfully. "You know, one of my cousins actually had to quit his job because he couldn't afford to drive there and back every day. Daylight robbery."

"We all have our cross to bear."

"It's all bloody tax, you realise that, don't you?"

"I am thirty years older than you, Holloway, so I *do* realise that it's nearly all tax."

Morgan wanted to smile at Holloway's comment as he pushed through the door, but Anna's disappearance was still too fresh in his mind. The young man followed him into the station and the two of them approached the front desk where Morgan showed his identification.

"Good morning. I am Detective Inspector Morgan and this is Detective Constable Holloway. We're from Wiltshire CID and we would like to have a look at your CCTV cameras today, if at all possible, as a matter of urgency."

Morgan was more than well aware that looking at the security footage constituted a search in law and that they could not force the petrol station staff to show them the footage without a warrant. He had come across many difficult people over the years who had insisted on this technicality being observed before allowing them not only to see security footage they had wanted to see but even things as little as demanding identification, especially back when he was a uniformed constable out on the beat. Most people did not realise that when they were out in public they were not obliged to give the police any identification with the two exceptions of if they are driving a car on a public highway, or if they are under arrest. Morgan, like most young police constables, had invariably forgotten to inform people of their rights when getting information out of them such as names and addresses, but those days were a thing of the past. He had reached an age where if he didn't play fair he didn't want to play at all, But as it turned out, the manager of the petrol station was more than happy to oblige and a minute later they were in the back office going through the CCTV array fitted around the station. There were so many cameras and so many angles and so many cars driving past and in and out, that the two detectives were sat scouring through the footage for nearly thirty minutes before Holloway's keen young eyes saw a blue

Honda pull up in one of the parking bays away from the pumps, before the unmistakable image of Declan Taylor climbed out of the car and walked into the petrol station.

"Bloody hell, would you look at that!" Holloway said. "It's Taylor!"

It was a strange sensation, but Morgan felt a soft wave of relief. Declan Taylor was a nasty piece of work and had been physically abusive to Anna back when they were together, but at the back of his mind had been the horrible idea that perhaps he was wrong and that Taylor had not got Anna and that instead she had been kidnapped by the copycat killer. Taylor was small fry compared with that.

"Yes, it does indeed appear to be Declan Taylor," Morgan said.

"The question is: why is DS Mazurek waiting in the car so peacefully like that?"

"That's what I'm worrying about," Morgan said.

From the angle of the camera, he could clearly see a woman sitting in Declan's Honda, he could not see the face to confirm it was Anna but he was prepared to assume the other evidence of the morning. What bothered him more than that, was why she was sitting in the car and not trying to get out.

"Aren't some of these new cars impossible to get out of if somebody locks them from the outside?" Holloway asked.

"I think there's usually some sort of way of opening them," Morgan said. "Besides the indicators didn't flash when he walked away, so I don't think he locked it."

"That just doesn't make any sense, sir! Why would the Sarge just sit in the car when she has a great opportunity to escape?"

"Well, that's what we're going to have to find out, isn't it, Holloway?"

He turned to the petrol station manager, who had been loitering behind them rubbing his hands together while they were watching through the tapes.

"I want copies of all of this."

"No trouble at all, Inspector. I can get it all on a flash drive immediately."

"The wonders of modern technology, sir," Holloway said with a smile.

Morgan stared at the image of Anna sitting completely still in the Honda out on the forecourt and felt distinctly uneasy. "The wonders of modern technology indeed,

Holloway." He turned to the station manager. "Close in on the number plate will you?"

The petrol station manager zoomed in on the number plate and now it was perfectly legible, allowing Morgan to make a note of it.

"What did he buy when he came in here?" Morgan asked. "Because he wasn't here to get petrol."

The manager peered at Declan's face. "Just some bottled water I think."

Morgan stared at the freeze-frame of Declan Taylor for a long time. Then, he got to his feet, thanked the manager, took the flash drive and he and Holloway made their way back out through the shop area and outside to the forecourt. Walking back over to their Audi, Morgan glanced at the now empty parking bay where Declan Taylor had parked up in the Honda and thought once again about the creepy image of Anna sitting perfectly still inside the car.

Morgan climbed back inside the Audi, immediately snatched at the two-way radio and called back into the station. "I want a check done on a number plate, please. Immediately. It's a blue Honda." Morgan reeled off the number plate to the police constable on the other end of the phone and moments later he got an answer, but not the one he was looking for.

"The car was reported stolen this morning, sir," the police constable said. "It was stolen from an address in Penhill in Swindon."

"Oh, that's bloody fantastic," Holloway said.

The older more experienced detective felt the same way but did not feel the need to express it. "And it hasn't turned up anywhere yet?"

"It might have, sir."

Morgan sighed. "Don't mess me around, constable! What the hell does that mean?"

"We've had a report of a burnt-out car out at Ravensroost Wood."

"What's that?" Holloway asked.

"It's a small nature reserve in between Swindon and Malmesbury," Morgan said.

Then he turned back to the man on the radio. "All right. Thanks very much. We're gonna drive over there now and see what we can see."

Morgan looked at Holloway. "Well, you heard me! Turn the bloody engine on and get us out to Ravensroost. It's time to let the dog see the rabbit."

CHAPTER 20

Anna Mazurek felt a strange mixture of contempt, pity and fear when she looked at Declan Taylor pacing up and down in the gloom a few yards in front of her. She was still lashed tightly to a heavy wooden chair, a rocking chair, so she was unable to tip it over. Looking at Declan closer, she realised there was something else she saw as well – he was nervous.

"Why have you done this to me, Declan?"

"You never called me Declan," he said sulkily. "You always called me Dex."

"I called you Dex when I was in love with you, now you're holding me hostage in an abandoned farmhouse. What do you expect me to call you?"

He exploded in a sudden fit of rage she had entirely not expected. "You just shut your fucking mouth! It's you that's got me in all this shit! The only one responsible for all this fucking mess is you!"

Anna recoiled as far as she could, trying to push herself back into the chair and turning her head to look away from the red-faced monster Declan Taylor had so quickly become when she had provoked him only in the slightest way. Seeing him spitting with rage as he shouted at her told her two things. First, he was even more violent and dangerous now than he had been during their marriage and second, he had to be confident no one could hear him if he shouted that loudly, telling her this place must be fairly remote. She certainly had heard no cars or other vehicles or any other sounds of civilization since being in here. But then Declan Taylor was never stupid, she thought grimly.

"What do you mean when you say it's me that's got you in all of this?" she asked, deliberately softening her voice to a more caring tone so as not to wake the monster a second time.

"It doesn't matter. It doesn't matter and you shouldn't ask."

"This isn't your idea, is it, Dex?" She had used the abbreviated version of his name on purpose to soothe him further and she saw now that it seemed to have worked.

"What are you talking about?" When he spoke, it was in a normal speaking tone. The rage had almost completely disappeared and instead, he once again appeared to be slightly nervous.

"I know we had our moments over the years, Dex," she continued softly, "but you were abusive to me. You hurt me sometimes – you know that, don't you?"

She watched his face fall and he began pacing up and down again, squeezing his hands into tight fists and then releasing them with tight outstretched fingers, something he used to do whenever he was stressed or nervous.

She continued. "I couldn't stand it when you hurt me because I used to love you, but this isn't you, not now. You wouldn't do something like this, I just know you wouldn't. Domestic violence is a very serious offence Dex, but kidnapping a police officer takes you up a whole other level. This will mean proper jail time."

He exploded with rage all over again, his hands now balled into tight fists. "Well, that'll be your fucking fault, won't it? If I go to prison, it'll be your fucking fault!"

Anna let him walk away and cool off again. "I don't understand how it can be my fault, Dex. I'm not the one who hit you, I'm not the one who kidnapped you. You used to beat me. You are the one who snatched me from my house last night and drove me out here. You're the one who injected me with whatever the hell it was, to sedate me when I was in the car."

"I had to do it or you would have escaped, especially when I went to buy water. I was supposed to get the water first. I was stupid! Stupid! Stupid!" He walked in a circle now, smacking his forehead with his hand every time he said the word 'stupid'.

I was supposed to get the water first, Anna noted.

"But you don't understand things like injections, Dex." She had been circling but now she wanted to pounce. It was her police training and her detective experience kicking in. "You're a clever guy, Dex, but you wouldn't know about things like that."

He walked over to her now and towered above her, craning in until his face was just inches from her and she could smell cheap whisky on his breath. "How do *you* know?"

She fought the urge to gag; she desperately wanted fresh air to breathe. "Come on, Dex! I know you better than anyone. You hate anything to do with medicine and drugs and doctors and hospitals. And I know you wouldn't want to kill me, and yet that could happen if you got the wrong dose. You were told to inject me with that, weren't you? I think I know who told you."

Declan now walked around behind her and began nudging the rocking chair so she started rocking backwards and forwards. Her lack of control over the chair's movement induced a wave of nausea in her.

"You always were too clever by half, Ania," he said, using the Polish version of her name. "Yeah, always too clever by half… the great big wonderful perfect Sergeant Mazurek."

"But, I'm right though aren't I? Just be truthful with me, Dex. I can help you. I can help you if you're honest with me. Just let me go and the two of us will go to a café and talk. Who told you to do this to me?"

"*Him.*"

The way he said that one word sent a shiver down Anna's spine. She already knew who he meant but she still had to ask.

"Who do you mean, Dex?"

"The man with the coins."

Anna wasn't sure what to do next. She had to tread carefully. It was already obvious to her now that Declan was being manipulated or threatened in some way and had been forced to kidnap her, although she wasn't sure why.

One thing she was sure of was who had forced Declan to do it.

"You mean the Ferryman?"

"Yes, I mean the Ferryman."

"He frightens you, doesn't he?" Anna saw his face become shaded and dark. "It's OK, Dex. He frightens everyone."

"You're going to die, Ania. You're going to be the next one he sends over the river, he told me."

"He told you that?"

"He told me he's ready to kill again, and soon."

"When did he tell you this?" Anna asked, her mouth as dry as sand.

"I don't wanna talk about this anymore. You just sit there and be quiet or I'll gag you again."

Before she could say another word, Declan stormed out of the room and slammed the door behind him, causing a large chunk of plaster to fall off the wall from above the door and crash down onto the scratched, filthy floorboards. Anna wasn't sure how to take what Declan had just told her about the Ferryman. He was clearly terrified of him, as was she. Had he ordered Declan to kidnap her so she could be his next victim? She felt nauseous at the thought. Surely Declan would never do anything like that. Sure he would never even *agree* to do anything like that. She knew he was angry with her, but this was on a whole other level.

She slumped down in the chair, the tape still sticking her wrists and ankles to the wooden framework of the rocking chair. It was so tight, its edges were biting into her skin and making it red and raw. She was a strong woman but when she closed her eyes she began to cry.

*

Sophie decided tonight's pizza was the best she had ever eaten, but then she said that about every type of food she bought in Rome. The ice cream she had earlier that day when they had lunch near the Pantheon was also the best she'd ever eaten. Maybe it was the atmosphere, maybe it was how exotic everything was, or maybe it really was better. She had ordered a Florentine pizza, with mozzarella cheese and spinach and an egg cracked into the centre and cooked beautifully and she had already made a mental note to try and cook one for Jacob when she got back to England.

Thinking of Jacob back there now, probably sitting up working on the case after work, made her mind leap with thoughts of the Ferryman and she felt sick all over again. She had only just got over her lunchtime telephone call with Jacob, using the afternoon conference session to take her mind away from it all. It didn't seem fair, watching Kit and Louise enjoying themselves so easily and with no worries when she would never be able to fully remove the memory of Keeley slowly choking her to death. She had come so close to dying that night that she still had recurring nightmares about it, nightmares she had not been able to resolve, even with all of her understanding of psychology. She was dimly aware of Louise talking to her and now she turned to see her friend smiling and pointing at the dessert menu.

"Are you going to have anything, Soph?"

Sophie shook her head. "No, I don't think so, not after that massive lunch today and all the wine we had with the pizza tonight. I'll have to hit the gym when I get back to England."

"Spoilsport!"

Kit Bailey laughed but ultimately came down on the side of Sophie, claiming that he felt completely stuffed and wanted a light walk through the streets of Rome back to their hotel.

"After all," he said, "we have a very busy day at the conference tomorrow. I'm giving my keynote speech, for one thing!"

Louise laughed very easily again, but Sophie was tired and wanted to go to bed. She pushed back her chair, fished her bag out from underneath it and slung it over her shoulder. Shall we go then?"

Sophie noticed Louise give the dessert menu one last sad glance and then she also got up and stood beside her as Kit rose to his feet and put his hands in his pockets.

"If we go north, it's a beautiful walk and we'll end up at the River Tiber," Bailey said. "Believe me, it's just wonderful to stroll along the river here in Rome at this time of day, and it's on our way back to the hotel as well."

Sophie thought that was a wonderful idea, and now the three of them paid for their food and wine and began to stroll gently north to the river. Rome was alive and buzzing with people and excitement as it always was, especially in the early evening, and she felt more alive just for being here. She also felt safe in the company of so many strangers who didn't know who she was.

All except one man who had been sitting at a table outside a café on the opposite side of the street, staring at her from over the top of his newspaper the entire time she had been eating. He didn't bother following her now and when she moved out of sight, he simply folded the newspaper, got to his feet, put the paper under his arm and strolled in the opposite direction. Rome was a beautiful city, he knew. It was also an ancient city, whose history was stained by hundreds of years of murder and blood going back to Julius Caesar and far earlier.

Tonight, this man also had murder on his mind.

CHAPTER 21

In the late afternoon, Jacob and Innes drove into Tetbury, approaching from the south and headed towards the address where the red pickup truck was registered in the small town's east. They drove past the Tetbury Town Football Club and then turned right on the Cirencester Road and found themselves driving along a long narrow unsealed track. The vintage car's ageing suspension handled the job well enough and they soon found themselves pulling up to an isolated and fairly rundown cottage about half a mile east of the town, situated in front of a narrow band of woodland which divided the town from a large swathe of agricultural land.

Jacob climbed out of the car, closed the door behind him and walked to the front door with Innes beside him. The door was no more inviting than the rest of the building, with large flakes of paint peeling from it and putty crumbling away from a frosted glass window set into its upper half. Jacob rang the bell and then looked around him one more time as he waited for someone to open the door. There was a roll of rusty barbed wire dumped carelessly in the front garden, which was overgrown and hadn't seen a lawn mower for many months. Jacob could see that the barbed wire had been bought to repair a section of fence that was missing on the property's northern boundary but must have been sitting out in the rain for a long time to get into such a decrepit state.

Seeing no one had come to the door, Jacob now leaned his tall frame towards it once again and this time knocked on it hard several times. A dog barked from inside the property and then they saw its black blurry form through the frosted grass as it ran to the front door and began barking and snapping and snarling at them as they stood on the doorstep.

"Why do houses that look like this always have dogs that sound like that?" Innes asked.

Jacob thought this was a good question but not one that deserved a detailed response. "I'll ask Sophie when she gets back from Italy. She's the psychologist."

He leaned back towards the door and hammered on it one more time, this time with the heel of his hand and banging the wood as hard as possible. This set the dog off all over again who now began turning in circles and growling and barking even louder. Then Jacob heard a man's voice calling out but not from inside the property. The voice was coming from outside, somewhere around the back.

"Alright, alright, I'm coming! Keep your hair on!"

Jacob heard the voice again and determined it was coming from the side of the house where the barbed wire fence was broken down, to the north. He turned and began to walk towards the corner of the house hoping to meet the man halfway, which he did. As soon as he saw the man's face he knew instantly that this was the person who had bought the coins in Marlborough. There was no doubt about it. Not only was his face identical, but so was the hair and he was wearing the same red plaid shirt.

The man now pulled up to a stop around the side of the house and stared at them with deeply suspicious eyes. "What are you two doing round here? I ain't got no truck with Jehovah's Witnesses so you can just fuck off right now."

Jacob stopped himself from smiling and pulled his identification wallet from his pocket. He now took two or three long strides towards the man, their new proximity to one another highlighting Jacob's height as he showed the man his police identification warrant card. "I am Detective Chief Inspector Jacob and this is Detective Constable Innes from Wiltshire CID. Your name, please?"

"I'm Matt Tanner."

"We'd like to ask you a few questions about your activities over the past few days."

"What on earth do you mean by that?" The man said, his eyes suddenly crawling anywhere and everywhere except Jacob and Innes. "I ain't done nothing."

"Perhaps we could go inside and have a conversation in there, where it's a little more private?"

Tanner laughed and looked over to the fields beyond the broken fence. "There ain't no one around here, not within earshot anyway. I'd rather talk outside in the fresh air if that's ok with you."

"Makes no difference to me," Jacob said, gesturing to the red pickup. "I take it that's your vehicle over there?"

Tanner grew more furtive. "Yeah, that's my old truck. Why would anybody else be parked up here?"

"You confirm it's your vehicle then?"

"That's what I just said, Chief Inspector."

"Have you got an interest in antiquity, Mr Tanner?"

The man's face scrunched up in confusion. "I don't get what you're talking about. You mean stuff like old chairs and antiques and whatnot? If so, then the answer is no, not really. My brother used to do some trading in old furniture but we found there wasn't much money in it. Just bought a load of old rubbish and after time couldn't get rid of it so it sat around his house and garage for months."

"No I don't mean old furniture, Mr Tanner," Jacob persisted. "I'm talking about old coins."

Tanner looked away from Jacob and found something interesting to look at over near the barbed wire roll. "I might have bought some old coins recently as a matter of fact. I didn't know that was against the law."

"It's not against the law, but murdering people and putting those coins in their mouths is."

Tanner now turned white. "I read about that on the news and when they started talking about coins, I couldn't believe what I was hearing. I didn't have nothing to do with it – you have to believe me!"

"I don't have to believe you at all," Jacob said. "Right now I don't believe anything you say. What were you doing on Tuesday between midday and midnight?"

The man suddenly looked relieved. "This Tuesday just gone past?"

Jacob nodded.

"Let me think… I was over at my brother's place just outside Gloucester. I was there with him and his wife and their eldest. We spent the whole day together and I slept over because I had too much to drink. Thinking about giving the bottle up, but now I'm bloody glad I didn't."

"Why are you bloody glad you didn't?" Innes asked.

"Because if I hadn't been drinking, I'd have driven back over here and I wouldn't have an alibi!"

"We'll be checking that alibi in good time," Jacob said. "Give the name and address of your brother to Detective Constable Innes here, please."

"Certainly, it's John Tanner…" Tanner said, reeling off the address in Gloucester. As Innes made a note of it on her phone, Jacob scanned the property once again. Inside, the dog had finally stopped barking and a strange heavy sort of peace seemed to be laying over the cottage.

"If you were with your brother and his family all day Tuesday, that doesn't necessarily get you entirely off the hook," Jacob said. "We know the women were murdered on the Tuesday but that doesn't mean to say that the coins weren't put in their mouths until the moment they were dumped. You could have done that easily enough when you dumped the bodies."

"Now you look here, Chief Inspector! I never had nothing to do with those bodies, I swear it up and down."

Jacob said suddenly, "Who told you to buy the coins then, Matt?"

"A buddy of mine if you must know. Things have been a bit tight lately and he promised me a couple of hundred quid if I did him a job. When he told me all it was involved was going over to that place in Marlborough and buying the coins and leaving them out in the woods, I jumped at the chance."

"Woods?" Jacob asked.

"Ravensroost."

Jacob resisted the urge to meet Innes's eyes, which he could feel crawling all over him. Ravensroost was where Morgan and Holloway were attending the scene of a burnt-out car believed to have been stolen by Declan Taylor.

"So," Jacob continued. "You're telling me that your buddy called you up, and offered you two hundred pounds to buy three coins, whose value is twenty pounds each, or sixty pounds for all three. Did your buddy pay for the coins or did you have to take that out of the two hundred?"

"No, he paid for that too. He gave me two hundred and sixty in full. Sixty for the coins and two hundred for my time and petrol."

"And then you're telling me that you were to leave these coins in Ravensroost forest for someone to collect?"

"He didn't actually tell me that someone was going to collect them, but that was sort of presumed. Why would you buy three ancient coins and leave them hidden under a tree in the forest unless someone was going to come and collect them?"

"Why indeed. Did any of this strike you as suspicious at all?" Innes asked.

Tanner shrugged. "I thought it was a bit odd if you must know, but as I said, two hundred quid for less than an hour's work? I jumped at the chance."

Jacob was making notes. "And you've no idea who was supposed to be collecting these coins?"

"No idea at all. Nobody told me nothing more than I just told you. I got the coins from Marlborough, drove them out to Ravensroost, put them exactly where he told me to put them and then I drove home and that was the end of it."

"Until you heard about the murders on the news?" Innes asked.

Tanner's countenance changed once again, now a genuine sadness seemed to appear on his face. "I got to admit I wasn't too happy when I heard that. I was out with the old dog in the shed listening to the radio and then it came on the news that this murdered woman was found dead over at Malmesbury, which is close to Ravensroost. I thought that was odd enough as it was, but then they started talking about her being wrapped in a shroud and the coin was left in her mouth. I got to tell you I went inside and got myself a stiff drink. When they said it was a Roman coin I knew I was in a spot of bother, but I thought I'd keep a low profile and hope it blew over."

"How civic-minded of you," Innes said.

"And now it turns out you're right in the middle of the storm," Jacob said.

"I guess it looks that way yes, Chief Inspector, but everything I've told you today is God's own truth I swear it."

"Where's your buddy live?" Jacob asked. "The one who told you to go and buy the coins."

"He lives at His Majesty's Pleasure. Over at HMP Leyhill. In between Gloucester and Bristol."

"And why is he serving time at His Majesty's Pleasure, may I ask?" Innes asked.

"He got involved with a bit of armed robbery in Newcastle a few years ago."

"A Cat D for armed robbery?" Innes asked.

"He started in Whitemoor but got moved to Leyhill after a few years of good behaviour, to be nearer his family. He's an old mate of mine from school. He was always out on the edge, was old Ted."

"Full name?"

"Edward Curtis."

"How did he pay you this two hundred if he's in prison?" Jacob asked.

"He told me to pick the money up from his sister Emma."

"All right, I think that'll be all for now, Mr Tanner," Jacob said. "We'll be looking into everything you've said today, and speaking to everyone who can back your alibi up. Thank you for your time."

"At least it wasn't another dead end," Innes said as they walked back to the car.

"Let's hope not," Jacob said, checking his watch. "I think there's just time to speak to Mr Curtis before Leyhill tucks everyone up for the night."

CHAPTER 22

His Majesty's Prison Leyhill was nestled deep in the Gloucestershire countryside, roughly equidistant between Gloucester and Bristol. It was the usual jumble of modern single-story red brick buildings that were so common at the time it was built and its security was fairly relaxed owing to its Category D status. Originally billed as a United States military hospital in the Second World War, it was converted into its present-day use as a prison in 1946 and underwent a substantial redevelopment in the 1970s and 1980s. Today, there was a reasonably relaxed atmosphere at Leyhill, compared with other prisons and the Category D adult male prisoners spent their time gardening or working on City and Guilds qualifications. There were other training programmes for employment following release from the prison such as driving forklift trucks or tractors, and gardening on its 140-acre site, which included formal gardens and an arboretum. After signing in at the main visitors centre, it was here among the trees in the arboretum that Jacob and Innes found the man they were looking for, pushing a wheelbarrow full of soil with a pitchfork laid across the top of it.

"Ted Curtis?" Jacob asked, producing his identification card.

The man who had been pushing the wheelbarrow stopped and rubbed his hands on his trousers as if he were going to shake hands. That never happened.

"That's me, yes."

"I am Detective Chief Inspector Jacob and this is Detective Constable Innes. We're from Wiltshire CID and we'd like to talk to you about your business transaction with Matt Tanner over the last day or so."

Curtis nodded as if in some silent reproach to himself; he knew this moment was always going to come. "I've been expecting you."

"Why have you been expecting us?" Innes asked.

"Since word went round the prison about the Ferryman killing again."

Jacob asked, "And why would that concern you, safely tucked up in here?"

"Don't be coy with me, Chief Inspector. You've not driven out here from Devizes to piss about in the bush. If you've talked to Matt Tanner then you already know about our little business deal and you've come here to ask me why I asked him to buy the coins. I don't think that would qualify me as some kind of mind reader would it now?"

Jacob put his wallet away and shoved his hands in his pockets. He had spoken to many criminals over the years, including much harder and nastier old lags than Ted Curtis. He wasn't about to be intimidated, thrown off the scent or belittled by a man like this.

"So why did you ask him to buy the coins then? You can't possibly have had anything to do with those murders."

"What makes you say that? We can walk in and out of here just about any time we please. We're not locked in our pads at night."

"But there's good security cameras here at the prison, Ted. And I called ahead to the prison and I've already made an investigation into whether or not anyone left here without approval or supervision during the timeframe in question and the answer is they did not, not even you. You were here when those women were murdered and you were here when the bodies were dumped. Now I want to know who rattled your cage and got you to organise someone to buy those coins."

"Well, not the Ferryman, if that's what you're getting at."

"I'm not getting at anything except the truth and I intend to get there as fast as possible." A cold gust of air blew through the arboretum, rattling the leaves on the trees and sending a shiver down Jacob's spine. He pulled his collar up and fixed his eyes on Curtis. "So, who asked you to get hold of those coins?"

"An old mate of mine, from way back when."

"Another old lag?"

Curtis nodded. "Yeah, he spent a lot of time at Frankland."

"Why didn't he get the coins himself?" Innes asked.

"I don't know what goes on inside another man's mind, Constable. "All I know is, he asked me if I knew anyone that could do a job for him. I said I might be able to help him out."

"Why didn't he ask Matt Tanner directly?"

"As I say, I don't know other people's minds. But my mate from Frankland ain't from around here and he don't know no one round here. He knows I'm local with a lot of contacts so he came to ask me if I knew anyone who could help."

"More like he didn't want to be caught on CCTV camera in a coin shop," Innes said.

"That's for you to decide," Curtis said.

"You're saying this mate of yours has a bit of a phobia about CCTV," Jacob said. "He gets in touch with you and he asks you if you know anyone unsavoury around here to do a job for a couple of hundred quid. You say, yes my mate Matt Tanner and then Tanner goes into the coin shop, buys the coins and delivers them to Ravensroost. Why did your Frankland friend want them dropped in Ravensroost woods?"

Another shrug from Curtis. "You're asking the wrong man. He asked me if I knew anyone who could get the coins, and I said yes I did. He was very specific about what type of coins and then he told me that they had to be dumped at a particular place over at Ravensroost. I passed the message on to Matt Tanner and gave him the money. He did the job and that's the end of it."

"Only it's not the end of it is it," Innes said. "The end of it was the tragic brutal murder of two innocent women."

Curtis seemed to recoil a little now, finding it easier to look away from the two detectives and stare out at the trees blowing in the wind. When he spoke again his voice was softer and frailer.

"I didn't know anything like that was going to happen, did I? Like everyone else in the nation, of course, I've heard of the Ferryman. I knew some people who served time with him in Frankland. He was kept isolated most of the time. I never met him and I never knew him and now he's dead! So when all these years later my mate says he wants someone to go and pick up some coins for him, I did not immediately think of a bloody serial killer like the Ferryman, but when I heard on the radio about those women turning up, then it all started to come together. I'm sorry if I played any part in that. Since I got out of Whitemore, life's not been too bad for me and there's even talk of parole. I wouldn't want to jeopardise that for anything. I want to go straight. There's nothing illegal about being asked to find a mate to go and buy some coins. It wasn't a job, it wasn't a hold-up."

Jacob considered carefully everything that Curtis was telling him. He had spoken to hundreds of criminals over the years and had learned to look out for subtle body language signs as well as verbal cues that often gave them away. His general reading of Ted Curtis was that he was uncomfortable but telling the truth. Better than that, he thought he might even have given him another lead that could take him closer to the copycat killer.

"I'm going to need the name of this mate of yours," Jacob said. "The old lag that used to live in Frankland. I'm sure that's going to be alright with you, especially if you don't want anyone to rock the boat here at Leyhill."

Jacob saw from Curtis's expression that he understood at once what was being threatened.

"I'm ready to give you his name; I'm not gonna have my life crapped up just because he's got involved with a nutcase like the Ferryman, or whoever it is. You need to speak to a man called Kevin Philips."

Jacob heard the name and a bell rang somewhere in his mind, especially as it had come connected with the word Frankland. "That's Kevin Phillips, as in the leader of the Byker Gang?"

"The very same. I'm not surprised you've heard of him."

"I've heard of him, all right."

"Sir?" Innes asked.

"The Byker Gang were one of the most notorious armed robbery gangs to have been imprisoned in Britain in the last twenty years, having successfully raided over two dozen banks and building societies in the northeast of England. Kevin Phillips had served somewhere around ten or fifteen years for his part as the getaway driver."

"And where does Mr Phillips reside these days?" Innes asked.

"As I said," Curtis said. "He doesn't come from round here, he comes from Northumberland so he doesn't know anyone local, like. He told me he's been staying at the Travelodge in Cirencester."

Jacob snapped his notebook shut. "Thank you, Mr Curtis. I hope we don't have to speak again and in the meantime, if we never see each other again, please refrain from helping old mates out especially if it involves antique coins."

*

Jacob said nothing as he and Innes signed out of the prison and made their way back to the Alvis parked up at the end of the car park under an enormous horse chestnut tree. He unlocked his old car and slid down into the soft leather seat, finding the beautiful scent of the worn leather and wooden interior of the car beautifully relaxing after the last half hour talking with Curtis. Pushing back in the seat, he waited until Innes had climbed in and closed her door before saying anything.

"Do you believe any of that, sir?"

Jacob was staring out through the windscreen at the prison ornamental gardens just beneath the canopy of the chestnut tree over the car. Some people would work hard their entire lives, always staying on the right side of the law and sometimes being exploited in the workplace, overworked and underpaid, hammering themselves into an early grave, and could not live in an environment as beautiful as this. He stopped his mind from wandering when he realised Innes was waiting for an answer.

"I believe every word of what he said. Bastards like Curtis know when they're onto a good thing. You heard what he said. He's trying to keep his nose clean. He doesn't mind getting on the wrong side of an old lag like Phillips if it means sucking up to us and keeping on the right side of the system. All he's thinking about is getting released from here and then he's going to disappear somewhere, never to be seen or heard of again. He's got no reason to lie to us. I can make his life an absolute misery if I want to and he knows that."

"So, you think this Phillips is the copycat killer then?"

Jacob sighed. "It's possible, but something about it doesn't sit right with me. I can't remember every last detail of the case, but I know Kevin Phillips was a getaway driver for the Byker Gang. I knew that as soon as he said his name – it all came flooding back. The thing is, I remember from the trial that he was always a bit of a weasel but other members of the gang were really nasty pieces of work. I have a hard time imagining men like that committing crimes like this. They're the scum of the Earth, holding up post offices and building societies and banks with sawn-off shotguns, but they never actually harmed anyone, at least aside from the psychological trauma they inflicted. And they were the tough end of the gang. Phillips was just sitting outside in a bloody Transit van. Why would he be asking men like Curtis to find some local scrote to go and buy coins that wind up in the mouths of murdered women?"

Innes shrugged. "I don't know, sir. This whole case is just getting too complicated."

"Someone's making it complicated on purpose," Jacob said. "That's what I think."

"So what do we do now?"

Jacob checked the car was in neutral, dipped the clutch and turned on the ignition. The powerful vintage engine roared to life as he selected reverse and gently swung the car around until its nose was pointing at the car park's exit. Then he selected first gear and cruised the car to the exit, paused to check the road was clear and then swung out to the north, settling down for the long drive back to HQ in Devizes.

"For now we have to hope that we can get hold of Kevin Phillips and persuade him to tell us what his part in all of this is."

"You mean like put the frighteners on him?"

Jacob couldn't help but smile as he glanced at the young detective constable sitting beside him, her long red hair bouncing up and down as they drove over a pothole.

"I don't think we put it quite like that anymore, Innes. We're not in an episode of *The Sweeney*. Having said that, yeah… we'll put the frighteners on him and hope we can get something out of him."

Innes went quiet for a mile or so. Then she said, "Do you think Sergeant Mazurek is OK?"

Jacob had been so preoccupied with talking to Tanner and Curtis that the kidnapping of Anna Mazurek had been pushed to the back of his mind. Now Innes mentioning her name brought it all flooding back.

"I don't know whether she's alright or not, but I do know that Bill Morgan is one of the best detectives I've ever worked with. Not only that, he cares a great deal about Anna. He's going to put his everything into finding her, and Holloway is a damn good detective as well. They'll find her."

"But what if Declan Taylor has already done something to her? I mean hurt her or worse."

Jacob didn't want to go there, but he knew he had to do something to calm the junior detective sitting on his left.

"Listen, Bill Morgan has already established that it was Declan Taylor who kidnapped her. They're on her trail and they're going to find her. I know Declan only through what Anna's told me, but I believe I know him. He's got no form at all beyond domestic violence. I don't think there'll be an escalation to murder."

The word murder hung in the car for a very long time.

CHAPTER 23

Jacob woke to the sound of his telephone ringing. It was only a quarter to eight on Saturday morning, and he was hoping for a quiet hour or so in the Old Watermill to recharge his batteries before going back to work on the copycat killer case. Looking at the screen on his phone, he saw the call was coming from Detective Constable Innes.

"Good morning Constable. I know this can't be good news."

"You can say that again, sir," Innes said. "We've just had a call about another body being found. This time it's out at an abandoned farmhouse not far from Malmesbury."

Jacob squeezed his temples, rubbed his eyes and reached for the lamp beside his bed, switching it on and illuminating the room. He blinked several times to try and adjust his eyesight to the light and then swung his legs out of the bed, sitting on the edge of it.

"Please don't tell me this body is wrapped in a shroud?"

"I'm afraid so. It was found by a man walking his dog this morning. The body was visible from a path used by dog walkers in the morning, quite visible. This lines up with the other two bodies being left out deliberately so they could be seen."

"He wanted someone to find it," Jacob said.

"Looks that way, sir."

"This dog walker called the police and some uniforms went up there, is that right?"

"That's about the size of it. They saw the shroud, confirmed there was a body, and called me - I was already in HQ working on the case, so now I'm calling you."

"Already in HQ at this time?"

"Keen to get a result, sir."

Jacob was quietly impressed. "So no one's been up there except these uniformed officers and the dog walker?"

"That's right, sir."

"You interview the dog walker?"

"Yes, sir. Nothing to be had, unfortunately. What do you want me to do?"

Jacob was now fully awake. He stood up from the bed and walked over to the window, pulling the curtain open to see a dark grey, overcast morning. There was also a drizzle covering his garden, almost making the river beyond almost impossible to see. It was difficult to believe this was the same garden he looked out on in high summer, a place of sunlight sparkling on the river, long shadows across his walled garden and his wildflower meadow alive with butterflies – Harebell, Saxifrage, Adonis Blue, Chalkhill Blue, Marsh Fritillary. By November, the year was getting colder and dark and he'd have to wait another long winter before enjoying these things again next year. He looked down at the foot of the bed where Drifter was still asleep.

It's alright for some, he thought.

"I'm going to get dressed and drive up there immediately. I also want you to call Mia Francis and get her entire team up there."

"Yes, sir. Did she get back to you about the properties of the two victims?"

"She emailed me last night. Nothing in either property, as we all thought. All very clean and very surgical."

"What about Inspector Morgan, sir? Should I call him in?"

"No, leave Bill Morgan out of it," Jacob said. "He's busy working on the Anna Mazurek kidnapping."

As soon as he said this, he knew they were both thinking the same thing – was the third victim Anna Mazurek?

"So, if I get there first, do you want me to unwrap the shroud?" she asked nervously.

He could tell that was the last thing in the world she wanted to do.

"No, don't do that, Innes," Jacob said, fearing the worst. "Just wait until I get there. I'll probably be arriving around the same time as Mia Francis and her CSI team. In the meantime, you and the uniformed officers are to search the property at once."

Jacob felt his heart quickening and his mouth go slightly dry. It was easy to conjure an image in his mind of arriving and unwrapping the shroud and seeing the dead face of Anna Mazurek staring back at him. She had been missing now for over a day and while Declan Taylor was incapable of killing her, or so Jacob thought, he had also to entertain the idea that Taylor was being used as a puppet by the copycat killer. Perhaps Declan Taylor had been paid or bribed or threatened to kidnap Anna and deliver her to the copycat killer, in which case Jacob knew there would be a very good chance that he would find his colleague and friend dead this morning.

Jacob thanked Innes and told her to stand guard with uniformed officers until he arrived. Then he got dressed into his suit, slipped on his watch, patted a sleepy Drifter on the head and told him that he would be back by lunchtime. Then he went downstairs straight through the front door, locked it behind him and walked over to the Alvis, parked on the gravel drive in the drizzle. Firing the old engine up, his heart was heavy at the thought of what he might find up in Malmesbury.

*

The shrouded figure was no different to the other two Jacob had already seen this week. It was lying outside a crumbling, abandoned farmhouse a mile or so outside of Malmesbury, on the front lawn, perfectly visible from a public right of way used by locals to access a dog walking field. Wrapped tightly in the white shroud, it was on its back facing the sky. Standing a few yards away from the body, Jacob now saw it had been clearly laid out to be as visible as possible so someone would discover it this morning while walking their dog and call it in to the police.

He walked over to Innes who was standing out of the drizzle in the farmhouse's covered porch. The two uniformed police officers had gone back to sit in their cars.

"I take it there's been no further problems since our call?" Jacob said without preamble.

"Nothing, sir," Innes said. "Apart from the dog walking field, you can see this place is pretty isolated."

"The kind of place you'd bring a kidnapped police sergeant," Jacob said out loud, but wished he hadn't. "I see Mia is still not here."

"She called in and said she would be slightly delayed because of traffic. I think she should be here in the next fifteen to twenty minutes. Are we going to wait for her until we unwrap… it?"

Unwrap it, Jacob thought, the words making him feel instantly nauseous. "No, I'm going to do it now. If it's Anna then there's no point delaying it by a few minutes."

Jacob walked over to the body, and halfway to reaching it he noticed both the uniformed officers suddenly appear out of their police cars where they had been sheltering from the rain and wander over behind him. Innes was also there now, close beside him in the drizzle. The small group of four sad figures stood around the shrouded corpse dumped out on the damp grass.

"All right, I'm unwrapping it," Jacob said.

CHAPTER 24

"It's not Anna," Jacob said.

Innes stared at the cold face with the complexion of putty. "Thank God."

"It's Declan Taylor, her ex."

Innes took a longer look. "Bloody hell. It is, isn't it? I never knew him but Anna has shown me plenty of photographs. What does this mean, sir?"

"It means whoever was pulling Declan's strings decided he was no longer of any use and it was time to take him out of the equation."

"The copycat killer?"

Jacob nodded vaguely, pulled on a pair of surgical nitrile gloves and gently opened Declan's mouth, pulling out the third coin featuring Emperor Constantine. He rose to his feet and held the coin up between his finger and thumb in the light for him and Innes to be able to get a much better look at it. The Emperor's cold, impassive profile looked away from him as if in disgust at his failure to stop the killing. "This is the work of the copycat killer for sure. He was using Declan just as I had started to theorise, and for whatever reason he decided he had now passed his sell-by date."

"But what about Anna? I don't understand. Where could she be?"

Jacob looked around the abandoned farm building and shook his head from side to side as he silently took in the isolated cottage. "The place was completely and thoroughly searched, like I ordered, yes?"

"Completely sir," Innes said. "There was no sign of Anna at all. Maybe Mia Francis or the CSI team will pick up some forensic evidence of her being here."

"She was here all right," Jacob said, looking down at the body in the shroud. "This bastard brought her here. The question is where is she now?"

"The copycat has her."

"Not necessarily."

Innes now looked from Declan up to Jacob in horror. "You can't mean…?"

"It's possible the copycat has already killed Anna, or he had Declan kill Anna and dumper her body somewhere else, then he killed Declan. She could be dead, Innes. We need to understand that."

As Jacob stared down at the unnerving spectacle of Declan Taylor, choked to death, a coin inserted into his mouth, wrapped in a shroud and dumped, he paused to consider the implications of the case. This was another hammer in the nail of his Keeley theory, because Alistair Keeley, the serial killer who had given the Metropolitan Police such a run for their money had never killed a man. All of the victims during his reign of terror had been women. For Jacob, this was the biggest single piece of evidence that they were absolutely dealing with a copycat killer and not Keeley. The evidence was now overwhelming and he was able to gratefully push thoughts of Keeley permanently out of his mind.

He stared down at Declan Taylor's body, a grisly sight with just his face protruding from the section of the shroud that he had unwrapped, the wild cold glazed staring eyes seeing nothing, and was struck by a depressing sense of how many times he had been forced to look down into the faces of the deceased, the poor tortured souls who had been victims of some of the most deranged killers in Britain.

And the lack of other material evidence was very frustrating. Yet again, there was nothing tangible for anyone to get hold of and use as a lead, at least not to the naked eye. His hopes rose when he saw Mia Francis's Volvo pulling into view and parking a few yards away. She climbed out and changed into her polypropylene suit and forensic slip-on shoes before even waving to him, and then finally made her way over to him and Innes and the uniformed constables standing like silent sentinels around the corpse of Declan Taylor.

"Is that Anna's ex-husband?" Mia asked.

Jacob nodded, a cold wind scratching across his face as he replied. "It's Declan Taylor. The current hypothesis is that he was working for our copycat killer and finally stopped being useful."

"Because Keeley never killed men, did he?" Mia said.

"That's right," Jacob replied, unwrapping the shroud until he found what he was looking for – a single, blue-black raven's feather being held in Declan's cold, white hand. He watched Mia's CSI team pull up behind her in the van and slowly begin unloading their equipment from the back. Soon they would go through this entire property and its surrounding grounds executing the most invasive forensic search imaginable, he could only pray that they would find something leading them to the killer.

"Same M.O.?" Mia asked looking down at the corpse.

"I think so yes," Jacob replied. "You see the shroud and I found this in his mouth,"

He handed Mia the coin and she stared down at the fat face of Emperor Constantine and winced. "Oh yes, it really does look like the same M.O., doesn't it?"

"The body will be going to Richard Lyon just to make sure. But I think we can make an educated guess at this time that he was killed by our great admirer of Professor Keeley, whoever the hell he is."

Mia sighed. "I'm just grateful it wasn't Anna lying dead if I'm being honest. It's not a good thing that Declan Taylor is dead, but he was a real bastard to her, made her life an absolute misery. I have to say that on the drive over here, I was seriously worried about what I was going to find. I take it there's no sign of Anna here at the property?"

"Not at all," Jacob said. "Not to the naked eye anyway but then that's why you're here. Innes says there's a rocking chair inside, but there's no evidence of any rope or cord or anything that might have been used to tie her to it. I'd start there if I were you."

Mia drew her lips tight and nodded. "You're the SIO, Jacob. If that's what you want me to start then that's where I'll start."

"That's where I want you to start inside the property, Mia. But first I want you to get a tent up around this body. This is now the third victim of this nutcase and was reported by a member of the public walking his dog. Detective Constable Innes here interviewed him and I don't think we can get anything more out of him but she sent him home. Just since I've been standing here, I've observed several people trying to get through with their dogs down at the stile. For now, they're being stopped by a couple of uniformed officers I have down there, but it can't be long before this gets through to the press and then they're going to have a field day with it."

"I'm sure it's gonna make Marcus Kent a very happy man," Mia said.

Jacob nodded. "Yeah, you could say that and when Detective Chief Superintendent Kent feels an emotion, I get to feel it as well. Lucky me."

"You're doing all you can, sir," Innes said.

Jacob not for the first time was wondering if that was true. Declan Taylor was not a good man, but he didn't deserve to die like this and neither did the two other victims of the copycat over the past few days. Yet again he felt a deep sense of frustration as the case seemed to be running away from him, once again spinning out of control just like the Witch-Hunt Murders that started back at Grovely Wood, during Christmas 2018.

"OK, Mia. You and your team can get to work and hopefully, you'll find something besides traces of Declan Taylor. In the meantime, I'm going to call Bill Morgan and call him off the search and tell him that we found Declan Taylor. That's going to make his job a hell of a lot more difficult because up until now Declan was his main lead in the hunt for Anna. Now that lead just dried up completely and he's going to have to start all over again. At least now we'll be able to work together because finding Declan Taylor like this is a good indication he was wrapped up with the copycat killer and so the two cases of the two investigations have become one."

"Wrapped up?" Mia said, looking down at the corpse in the shroud. "Was that a deliberate pun Chief Inspector, or merely a Freudian slip?"

Jacob was not in the mood for humour. "Just get your team inside and start working please, Mia."

"OK, Jacob. I'll send you my report just as soon as I have it. Is that young Holloway?"

Jacob saw Holloway now pulling up in an unmarked car. He got out, held his hand out, cursed at the drizzle, and then began to walk over to them.

Jacob watched Mia make her way into the crumbling cottage in her white polypropylene suit and disappear out of sight. She was followed moments later by a couple of members of her team carrying large cases and a metal box.

"I've got to make a call to Inspector Morgan," he said at last. "I'm going to let him know that our two cases seem to have conjoined, but that might simplify things for us and help us out a little bit with resources, especially as we're already a man down."

"A woman down, surely, sir," Innes said.

Jacob gave her a look. "I'll also ask him to come up here and oversee operations. A murder scene like this will require a senior officer present. Until he arrives you're in charge. I want you to oversee what goes on here at this property. You're in charge until everything is finished and when Mia and her team have finished, I want the place secured with barrier tape and a couple of uniforms kept up here as well, until further notice. We've had three victims already and something tells me that our killer hasn't finished yet."

Jacob turned and stomped back to his car, meeting Holloway halfway.

"Morning, sir. I heard Declan Taylor bought the farm, no pun intended."

"Funny. Now come with me. We're going to Cirencester."

"What about my car?"

"It's not your car, it's the station's car. One of the uniforms will return it."

"Sir." Holloway turned as if on a sixpence and caught Jacob up. "What's at Cirencester?"

"Hopefully the solution to this entire nightmare."

CHAPTER 25

Jacob raced north to Cirencester in the Alvis, his mind was whirring almost out of control. Flooded with thoughts, ideas and hypotheses, he barely knew where to start. Morgan had been less than happy with the news Declan Taylor was found dead this morning out at the abandoned empty cottage in between Malmesbury and Ravensroost Woods. He had expressed a mildly tasteless note of celebration, but that was due to his closeness to Anna Mazurek, his disappointment and unhappiness were centred on the fact that now Anna was simply missing again, and all leads he had been using to find her were connected with Declan Taylor.

Jacob quietly hoped Mia Francis would find something at the cottage that would enable them to track her down before it was too late if that weren't already the case. Jacob was certain the copycat killer would have moved Anna to another secure location after killing Declan Taylor if that is what had happened because he could hardly believe he would be dragging her around with him as he stalked and murdered more women. The other working hypothesis which he had mentioned back at the farmhouse to Innes, was that the copycat had already murdered Anna and they would find her body next. He did not want to go there and preferred the other option.

"You think this Kevin Phillips is the copycat, sir?" Holloway asked.

Jacob momentarily glanced at the keen young detective beside him in the Alvis's passenger seat and saw a look of determination on his face that matched the note of excitement in his voice. Something Jacob had not felt during a murder investigation probably for over twenty years.

"I'm doubting it very strongly Holloway, but he doesn't fit the personality profile of a killer, least of all someone who would kill in a very deranged and ritualistic style like this. He was small fry for a bank robbery gang in Northumberland a long time ago. Most of these old lags know each other from their criminal activities or from the time they spend with each other in prison. I'm betting that our copycat is maybe someone he met in prison, or maybe someone he's met since he left prison, but either way, I don't think it's Phillips. Hopefully, we'll get some information out of him today that will lead us to the copycat. And right now I think it's the only chance we've got."

After a pause, Holloway said, "Nice part of the country around here, sir. I wouldn't mind living around here."

"Well, that's a noble aspiration, Holloway."

"You're talking about the prices?"

"I'm talking about the prices. Even when I was young this place was outrageously expensive, God knows what it's like now."

"I can imagine somewhere in between completely unaffordable and absolutely bloody ridiculous, sir."

Having reached Cirencester, Jacob made his way through the quaint old Roman town to the Burford Road roundabout where he turned left, cruised past the petrol station and then pulled up in the car park of the Travelodge Cirencester.

"Think we'll find the little oik, sir?"

"He's not a little oik, Holloway."

"I'm sorry, sir. I didn't mean to be offensive about a person of interest to the investigation."

Jacob smiled at his sarcasm. "No, you'll see what I mean when we get in there."

Jacob and Holloway walked away from the car and joined the path up to the main reception area. Holloway pushed open the door and held it open for his senior officer, allowing Jacob to stroll through into the hallway and pull his ID wallet once again from his inside suit pocket. Jacob presented it to the woman behind the desk and made the introductions.

"So, we'd like to know which room Mr Phillips is staying in please."

"Don't you need a search warrant or something?"

"I do not need a search warrant, I merely need to speak to Mr Phillips, but thank you for your concern about the law."

She became flustered. "I need to speak to my manager. It's very irregular."

"Perhaps you should try some bran flakes," Holloway said under his breath.

Jacob darted his eyes, giving him a look and Holloway bobbed back down again, as the woman behind the desk walked off to an office out of sight. A moment later she returned with a young man with spiky, gelled hair wearing a bright silver suit and a very obnoxious and loud yellow tie emblazoned with trumpets.

"My colleague says you're police officers?"

"Yes, I'm Detective Chief Inspector Jacob and this is my colleague Detective Constable Holloway from Wiltshire CID."

"I don't suppose you have any identification on you?"

"We've already done that bit," Holloway said.

Jacob had already produced his wallet out of his pocket for the second time before Holloway had finished his sentence and now he presented it to the manager, who now scrunched his nose up as he looked at it.

"I can see from your little name tag that your first name is Darren," Jacob said. "What might your last name be?"

"My name is Darren Peters and I'm the manager of the Travelodge Cirencester."

"I'm very pleased for you," Jacob said. "Now I want to speak to a man called Kevin Phillips in connection to a murder inquiry I'm conducting and I want to speak to him now. What room is he in?"

"A murder inquiry?" Darren said. "Goodness, that *is* exciting."

"Not to the victims or their loved ones, it isn't," Jacob said. "What room is Mr Phillips staying in?"

"If you'll come this way. I'll take you to him. It's Room 13."

"I think we can find our own way to Room 13."

Jacob gave Darren a vague nod of gratitude and walked off to the left of the reception desk where he had already seen a sign pointing the way to Rooms 1 to 20.

"He was a jolly nice chap, sir," Holloway said as they walked down the plush carpeted corridor.

"Wasn't he just," Jacob said, pulling up outside Room 13 and banging on the door."

The door swung open to reveal an enormous man, probably close to thirty stone. He was mostly bald with wispy blond hair and wore very small, silver-rimmed spectacles that enlarged the width of his face even more than his eating habits had done.

"Yes?" He spoke in a very faint, hoarse voice that seemed ridiculously small for a man of such size.

"I'm Detective Chief Inspector Jacob this is my colleague Detective Constable Holloway. I'd like to speak with you Kevin if that's alright?"

Kevin Phillips seemed to deflate the moment Jacob's finished his sentence.

"I knew you'd come," he said in his hoarse voice. "You'd better come inside."

"Well, that's very kind of you Kevin," Jacob said. "Don't mind if I do."

They stepped inside the motel room, of which the large man seemed to occupy at least half. When they were all inside, Holloway clicked the door shut and Kevin Phillips sat down on the side of the bed, making it creak and groan until Jacob was sure he was going to snap one of the legs off of it.

"Staying here long?" Holloway asked.

"As a matter of fact, no. I'm back off to Northumberland today. Just came down to see an old friend."

"I didn't know you'd gone into the business of antique coins, Kevin?" Jacob said, shoving his hands in his pockets and strolling over to the window. They were on the ground floor and he was able to get a good view of the Alvis parked out the front, which looked beautiful to his eye even on an overcast day. As he admired the contours of its classic design of the coachwork, he was aware of Kevin Phillips beginning to ramble behind him.

"Thing is like, Chief Inspector, I'm not really involved in the antique coins business, but the thing is, well the thing is…"

"What is the *thing*?" Jacob asked with emphasis. Meanwhile, Holloway was going through the drawers of the unit at the foot of the bed.

"Well the *thing* is that you know how it is, Mr Jacob. When you're in prison, sometimes you can get into debt, if you see what I mean."

"You're in this to pay off debts?" Holloway asked. "How much?"

Jacob smiled coldly. "He doesn't mean the kind of debts you pay with money, do you, Kevin?"

"No, exactly right, Mr Jacob. I don't mean the kind of debts you pay off with money. See, I needed to be looked after in prison a little bit from time to time. I helped people out, people helped me out. See, I'm a big lad but some people take advantage of me when they see I'm not really very good at looking after myself. I look big, I am big, but when push comes to shove, I'm not very good at looking after myself."

"So, somebody gave you protection in prison from some trouble you were in?" Jacob asked.

"That's about the size of it, Mr Jacob. Frankland can be a pretty ugly place from time to time, and I was having a bit of grief from a gang in there, a druggie gang, and then someone looked after me and told me that maybe one day I'll be able to pay him back."

"And this person said the debt would be covered if you got him some coins."

"Well, that's right, see. He told me that I needed to buy some coins and take them out to a forest somewhere. I don't know why – I don't ask questions, especially not with this geezer. But the thing is I didn't really fancy doing the job myself. I kind of lost my nerve as I thought these coins might be leading to some kind of trouble and of course, I was right, wasn't I?"

"So that's when you went to talk to your mate Teddy Curtis in Leyhill?" Holloway asked.

"That's right. That's why I'm here in Cirencester. It took a bit of doing because I had to get the train from Byker to Gloucester and then another one from Gloucester to Kemble. Then I had to get a taxi up here so I had somewhere to sleep for the night. But anyway I got a taxi down to Leyhill and I spoke to Teddy and asked him if he knew anyone local that could do a job."

"This all sounds a bit iffy to me, sir," Holloway said, now going through Kevin's suitcase on top of the unit beside the television set. "Why not just phone Curtis and ask?"

"I wanted to visit another friend of mine down here in Bristol. His name's Marcus Dunn, you can check it out. It's all above board. He runs a taxi company in Fishponds. Dunn's Cars."

"We'll check it out," Jacob said. "Rest assured."

"Still sounds iffy."

Kevin sighed. "What you don't understand is this bloke that asked me to do the favour and get the coins is not someone you say no to. First of all, I owed him and there was no hope of me telling him to do one. Second even if I didn't bloody owe him I'd still do what he asked. He is one of the toughest blokes in Frankland, doing life. He tells me to get those coins sorted so I get the coins sorted. Problem was, I didn't want to get involved but I couldn't tell him, so that's why I went and spoke to my mate. He knows everyone around here that will do a bit of hooky business."

"So, you spoke to Teddy Curtis in Leyhill and promised you'd send his sister the money if he bought the coins from the shop in Marlborough and delivered them to Ravensroost Woods?" Jacob asked.

"Yeah, which I thought was a bit weird really. I'm not from around here, so I've never heard of Ravensroost Woods, but who wants to have coins delivered to a forest? That was the bit that made me realise I had to speak to Teddy and get someone else to do it."

Jacob's cold smile returned. "You know what I'm going to ask you now, don't you, Kevin?"

Kevin nodded glumly. "You want the name of the man who asked me to get the coins, don't you Chief Inspector?"

"Yes."

Kevin began to flap around, visibly becoming more flustered. He heaved his enormous bulk up off the bed which groaned with relief as the big man made his way over to the window beside Jacob. After glancing outside, suddenly interested in the passing clouds, he now fixed his eyes on Jacob.

"You know I can't do that, Chief Inspector. It's just too dangerous."

"Not giving me what I want is even more dangerous. I assure you."

"See, I was the only person he asked. If you come knocking on his door, he's gonna know who led you there."

"It's a murder investigation, Kevin. It doesn't get any more serious than this. You've read the news, you know about the coins and what they were used for. We've already had three people killed and there could be more if we can't catch this man."

"Three people?" Kevin scrunched his face up with confusion. "I thought it was just them two lasses – one in the abbey and the other one in a castle."

"There was another one found this morning, but I can't give any more details about it because it hasn't been made public. That's three people killed by this man."

Kevin seemed to turn white. "Wait – you can't think I'm the one going around doing all these women?"

"I don't think anything, Kevin. I follow the evidence. The evidence is now pointing to the person who wanted these coins delivered to Ravensroost Wood. You claim this is a man inside Frankland Prison, which means he couldn't be our suspect. This makes me look elsewhere."

Jacob stared at Kevin.

"It's wasn't me!"

"If it wasn't you and it wasn't the man in prison, then who was it?"

"I think the bloke in Frankland who told me to get the coins sorted was told to do it by someone else."

Jacob felt a heavy blanket of disappointment and frustration crashing over the top of him. "Your mate in Frankland was being told to do this by someone else?"

Holloway huffed out a sceptical laugh. "Just how many links in this chain *are* there?"

"Not that many," Jacob said, still staring at Kevin. "The person who asked your mate to get hold of these coins is the copycat killer."

Kevin looked around the room sheepishly and nodded his head, his big fat white jowls wobbling. "I think so, Chief Inspector. The bloke in Frankland who told me to get hold of the coins said he was asked to, he said he was a very unsavoury character."

Holloway scoffed. "That's rich coming from a lifer at Frankland."

"I need the name of this person in Frankland," Jacob said. "Or I'll do you for obstruction and with your record you'll be going right back inside again. I'll do everything I can to make sure it's a Category A."

Kevin deflated once again. "It's Gary Wilson."

Jacob didn't have to search his memory for long before an image of Wilson appeared in his mind.

"I recognise that name, sir," Holloway said.

"He murdered two women in Northumbria back in the 1990s," Jacob said. "He's a very nasty piece of work, nothing ritualistic about it. Brutal, savage sexual assault and murder. Very nasty piece of work. I think they were both killed in Newcastle. I can see why you don't want me to get in touch with him, Kevin."

"The thing is, if a man like that looks after you in prison, you don't get no more trouble."

"But everything's got a price, hasn't it, Kevin?" Jacob said. "Do you know who told Wilson to get the coins?"

"I think he'd been having some kind of correspondence with someone," Kevin said. "Also he hinted at there being trouble if I messed things up. I was never a serious criminal, Chief Inspector, you know that! I just drove the gang away from a few jobs, that's all. I've never hurt no one in my life, not ever. Men like Wilson and whoever was corresponding with him though… they are in another league altogether. These are killers, cold-blooded killers."

"I'd worked that out all for myself, thank you."

"Thing is a man like Wilson's got reach, Mr Jacob. If you go speaking to him about the coins he'll know it was me and then I'd have to spend the rest of my life looking over my shoulder."

"That is very much your problem, Kevin."

"Thanks a lot."

"Ever read Faust?" Jacob asked him.

"Eh?"

"Never mind." Jacob turned on his heel and pointed at Holloway. "We're out of here."

CHAPTER 26

Jacob stared out across the beautiful shining sunlit clouds from the window of his EasyJet A320 as it raced north to Newcastle Airport. Holloway was sitting beside him, with his attention firmly focused on an audiobook he was listening to on his iPhone, oblivious to the world thanks to the earbuds firmly inserted in his ears. His tray was down and he was holding a can of Coke in his right hand. Now and again he would stop and laugh at some joke in the book, tipping his head back and really enjoying himself.

There had been some discussion about interviewing Gary Wilson on the phone or Zoom or Skype, but Marcus Kent objected, wisely Jacob thought, on grounds of security and possible hacking. There were very unpleasant details surrounding Gary Wilson's murders that were never released to the public, and Kent was extremely keen not to be the source of the leak of any of this information simply because they wanted to speed things up by a few hours. After this, it was decided to send Jacob and Holloway out to Bristol Airport, which was a short enough drive and then fly the 300 miles north to Newcastle Airport before driving south to HMP Frankland where they could interview Gary Wilson in person. So far so good, Jacob thought, sipping his sparkling water and looking out across the sunny world beyond the window. From up here he could see why the world under the clouds was so cold and overcast, but now his mind felt the same way.

Gary Wilson was a notorious murderer who had never cooperated with the authorities at any point from his arrest through to his trial and imprisonment. He had helped not one iota, even when he was promised a reduction in sentence. Northumbria Constabulary was particularly keen to track down a rumoured third woman he had murdered, but Wilson always denied it and to this day refused to comment on the matter. Jacob held out little hope that Wilson would offer any information helping to connect him to the copycat killer. But he was still obliged, with a duty of responsibility and care to the victims of the killer and their loved ones, to try. Now he sat back in his seat and closed his eyes, trying to concentrate on the sequence of events that he had learned about the case so far.

Two things were going on here. First, someone whom he had initially believed was Alastair Keeley, but now he was certain was a copycat killer, had killed Tansy Babbington, Jennifer Stanley and now Declan Taylor and put coins in their mouths and wrapped all three in shrouds. He had also left raven's feathers in their hands. He was reminded from reading Jess's old Shakespeare books that the raven feather was associated with revenge. He wasn't sure what that could mean if this wasn't Keeley, but he knew that Sophie was safer out of the country in Italy. While the first two murders had been committed on Tuesday, the day before Sophie had flown to Italy, Declan Taylor was murdered this morning and that meant the killer was still in Britain. Or at least he had been as of two or three hours ago. Jacob knew he had to catch this man before he could get to Sophie, especially since the raven feathers were really being left behind as a symbol for revenge. It was Sophie who had put the copycat killer's hero, Keeley the Ferryman, in prison all those years ago.

The second thing that was going on was the kidnap of Anna Mazurek. Anna was a key member of his team, and a detective sergeant with considerable experience and skill. She was kidnapped over thirty-six hours ago and hope was beginning to fade that they would find her alive. Things had been confusing, but Jacob speculated that the copycat had used Declan to kidnap Anna with a view to sowing confusion in the team and reducing their manpower. Jacob had expected to find Anna dead when he had been called in about the third victim this morning, but instead, it had been Declan Taylor. He presumed this meant the killer had grown tired of Taylor who was no longer useful to him and instead had become a liability. That wasn't difficult to imagine. So the copycat killed Declan Taylor and dumped his body in the same way he had done with the two women before, knowing full well he and the rest of the team would think he was Anna. At some point, he had dumped Declan's blue Honda out at Ravensroost and torched it. Morgan and Holloway had attended the scene and predicably found nothing. Mia had attended and also found no traces of anyone except Declan. More dead ends.

Is that what had happened? he asked himself.

The question was, where was Anna now? Had the killer already taken her life and dumped her somewhere to be found over the next day or so? Or was she still being kept alive somewhere by him, for some grisly reason he didn't even want to consider?

Jacob's speculation was brought to an end by the sound of Holloway's braying laughter to his right. Jacob opened his eyes and looked out across the clouds one more time, the aircraft now already nearly halfway into its flight and approaching Liverpool and Manchester. He speculated in less than one hour he would be face to face with Gary Wilson and that would either make or break the case.

*

After a rough landing in high winds and a long and difficult drive in a taxi through a heavily congested Newcastle, Jacob and Holloway found themselves walking up to the main entrance of His Majesty's Prison Frankland, which was situated in Brasside, to the north of Durham. It was colder here than back home in Wiltshire, and much windier. Jacob was glad to get inside even if it meant going through the lengthy and time-consuming process of signing in to the institution. The prison was a very different kettle of fish to HMP Leyhill, currently hosting Teddy Curtis down in Gloucestershire. This was a large, heavily fortified maximum security Category A prison with dozens of cell blocks separated by various quads and green spaces and even some sports facilities. It sprawled everywhere and hosted hundreds of prisoners, many of whom were some of Britain's most serious offenders.

"If you'll follow me please," said one of the prison guards. He led them down a corridor to the right of the reception area until they arrived at a suite of conference rooms. There was a faint scent of cleaning detergent in the air, and a strange sort of silence as the guard showed them into a room and asked them to take a seat at a desk pushed up against the far wall.

"I'll bring him through in a minute. He won't say anything though."

"When the guard left the room, Holloway turned to Jacob.

"I don't think Teddy Curtis would like it in here very much do you, sir?"

Jacob said nothing. He was listening to the sound of footsteps walking up and down outside the conference room, low murmured voices that reminded him vaguely of funerals he had attended over the years. He had never met Gary Wilson before, but he knew all about him, not just because he was a senior police officer but because everybody in the country knew all about him. Some cases were so notorious that the names of the killers lived on forever as a kind of permanent scar on the nation's face. Gary 'the Newcastle Nightmare' Wilson was one of them.

The door opened and the same guard returned, but this time he was accompanied by a second guard and between the two of them they guided Wilson into the room and told him to sit at the table opposite the two detectives. He was older and thinner than the photographs Jacob had seen of him in the press from nearly thirty years ago now. There was a gaunt expression about him, but he was one of those rare men who had retained a full head of hair even well into their fifties. The hair was short and had a tight curl, mostly dark brown but with unmistakable strands of silver appearing in it here and there. He had a square jaw, and a sharp angular nose, and his eyes were wide and bright and piercingly blue. There was a vague athletic look about him that almost unnerved Jacob to see in a man of his age and he met Jacob's eyes fully and without fear or shame.

"I don't get many visitors," Wilson began. "So, I suppose I should thank you for coming really."

He had a soft, rounded Geordie accent, not the full-on heavy brogue utilised by so many TV drama writers, but something that communicated a gentler, wealthier upbringing.

"I'm Detective Chief Inspector Jacob and this is Detective Constable Holloway from Wiltshire CID."

"My, my. You have come a long way. I was told about your visit a little while ago and I have to say I asked myself, why on Earth would southerners from down in Wiltshire be flying up here to talk to me? I never worked in Wiltshire."

Jacob felt his skin prickle with disgust. Everyone in the room knew very well what 'work' Wilson was referring to.

"We're not here to talk to you about any of the offences you committed in the past, Gary."

Wilson's face changed totally in a heartbeat. The smile vanished, replaced with a menacing scowl. The eyes iced over like frozen ponds. "I don't recall inviting you to use my first name."

"Very well, Mr Wilson," Jacob said, working hard to control his temper. "I'm here to ask you about some of your more recent activities."

"You're talking about them coins! Aye, them coins caused a hell of a kerfuffle in the last few days."

Jacob was not sure how to play this but decided to go in front and centre with no subterfuge or tricks. "I expected a man of your intelligence to have already put two and two together."

"Aye, that's right. I can make four. When I was asked if I knew anyone who might be able to do a favour it was easy for me to say yes. How is that fat fucker Phillips? He's the one that sent you up here crying to me, right?"

"Mr Phillips sends you his regards," Jacob said.

"Aye, well you can tell him to fuck right off. I asked Kevin to get hold of them coins for me and the next thing I know they're turning up in the mouths of dead women all over Wiltshire. I've had nothing to do with that, as I think you can tell." As he spoke, Wilson glanced around the conference room and presumably the wider confines of HMP Frankland surrounding it. "I think I've got one hell of an alibi, don't you?"

"No one can disagree with that," Holloway said.

Wilson's eyes swivelled to the younger detective. "Weh hey! The puppet squeaks."

Jacob paused a beat, then said, "You've been in correspondence with lots of people, haven't you, Mr Wilson?"

Wilson looked rattled for the first time and now shrank down in his chair a little before his eyes began crawling over the table dividing the three men. Jacob noticed both guards standing behind Wilson exchange a quick furtive glance.

"Aye, I write to a few people. You'd be amazed at the number of women who have written to me since I've been here. I'm really popular since I done those two women in the city."

Jacob bristled with revulsion. "I heard it was three women."

"Not that again, man."

"Who wrote to you and asked you to get those coins, Mr Wilson?" Jacob asked, finally bringing the hammer down. "I'm sure you realise that whoever it was is the copycat killer murdering these women in Wiltshire. And I'm sure you want to alleviate the torment in your soul you no doubt feel every day after killing yourself."

Jacob had said this to provoke Wilson, but the man's face now scrunched up a little with a kind of inward confusion. He shifted in his chair, and Jacob heard the handcuffs behind his back rattling.

"There's no torment, Mr Policeman. I feel nothing at all."

"Who told you to get the coins?"

Wilson smiled like a demon. "I tell you what Mr Jacob, if you beg me to tell you who's been writing those letters to me, I'll tell you. But you've got a beg."

Jacob felt Holloway's eyes crawling all over him. Jacob almost felt sweat prickling on his brow; it was only the very cool temperature of the conference room that had prevented it from beading on his forehead.

"Very well, Mr Wilson," Jacob said quietly. "I beg you to tell me who's been writing letters to you."

"Did you hear that?" Wilson turned to the two guards standing behind him. "The great Detective Chief Inspector Jacob, the solver of the Witch-Hunt Murders, is begging me for help!"

"Are you going to keep up your part of the deal and tell me who has been asking you to buy these coins?"

"Nah, but that was fun."

Jacob rose from his chair, which he would have liked to kick out of the way but it was bolted to the floor, as was the table. He leaned forward and only just managed to refrain from grabbing a fistful of Wilson's prison uniform and shaking the information he wanted out of him.

"Tell me who wrote the letter asking for the coins."

After a long pause, Wilson's smile returned. "I won't tell you, but I'll give you a little clue, because big, famous detectives like you like clues, don't you?"

Jacob saw the eyes of the two guards narrowing and was concerned that they might terminate the interview. He sat back down in the chair and straightened his tie.

"OK, Mr Wilson. Why don't you give us your little clue? Because you're right you know – detectives do like clues."

"Alright, well here's your clue so listen up. My friend who wrote to me asking about the coins told me that he'd found paradise."

"Paradise?" Jacob asked.

"Aye, that's what he said."

"Where?"

"In your neck of the woods. Wiltshire. And you can't read any of the letters because I destroyed them all."

"What did he mean when he said that?" Holloway asked.

Wilson arrogantly shrugged. "How the fuck should I know, puppet? He told me that he got some money from a bank job one of his mates did, and he had just moved to paradise in Wiltshire."

Jacob rose from the chair and indicated with a quick glance that Holloway should also get to his feet. He looked down at Wilson who was still slouching sloppily in the metal chair on the other side of the desk.

"Thank you. You were very helpful today."

Jacob headed over to the door, which one of the guards opened for him. Holloway stepped out into the corridor and Jacob went to join him, lingered in the doorway and turned to look back to Gary Wilson.

"And don't let all those women writing to you go to your head, *Gary*. They're not in love with you. They're suffering from hybristophilia. It's a paraphilic sexual disorder in which the sufferer is attracted to criminals. Goodbye."

CHAPTER 27

Jacob and Holloway managed to return on the second flight of the day between the two airports and arrived back at Devizes before four o'clock in the afternoon. Gary Wilson's oblique reference to the copycat killer living in paradise had not been cryptic enough to fool Tom Jacob, who had immediately decided that it must be the name of a property the copycat killer had bought, not to live in but to use as a sort of centre of operations while replicating Keeley's grisly murders. He also thought there was a good chance that it would be the location where he committed the murders and then stored the bodies before driving them out and dumping them at Malmesbury and Old Wardour Castle.

Holloway had the idea of requesting the data from the Land Registry, but Jacob knew there was a quicker way. Back in the conference room at Frankland, Wilson had said that the copycat killer had recently moved to paradise, he also said it was in Wiltshire, so it did not take Jacob long to get on a website listing recent house sales and narrow down his search to Wiltshire and the last three years, which he interpreted as 'recent'. It took less than five minutes for him to locate what he was looking for – Paradise Farm. The deal was sealed when he saw its postcode placed it in between Malmesbury and Ravensroost Woods.

"That's gotta be it, hasn't it, sir?"

Jacob thought so but was reluctant to show too much enthusiasm in case they reached another dead end. Instead, he called Morgan and Innes over to his part of the open plan office and they gathered around his desk.

"You got something out of that bastard in Frankland, didn't you?" Morgan said.

"I think I just might have, Bill."

"Come on then, let the cat out of the bag," Morgan asked. "Is it Anna? Is she OK?"

"I hope so, but I can't be sure. All I can say is that I am almost certain this is an address that is connected to the copycat killer. It's an old property called Paradise Farm, with a large pond and some woodland. It was bought just over a year ago. I checked planning applications for the property and found an application was made to build a basement six months ago."

He watched the faces of his team grow bleak.

"A basement?" Innes asked. "I don't like the sound of that."

Holloway fidgeted with his tie. "British houses don't usually have basements, do they, sir?"

"No, they don't usually have basements," Jacob said. "But this wasn't requested as simply a basement, it was proposed to be a wine cellar. He got permission for it."

"I still don't like the sound of it," Innes said.

Morgan cleared his throat. "What was the name of the person who made the planning application?"

"Dennis Perry."

"As in the 'Den' Delia Wagner said she thought Tansy Babbington was seeing?" Innes asked.

"Could be," Jacob said.

The team fell silent. Eventually, Morgan spoke first. "You think that's the name of the copycat killer then?"

Jacob turned off his computer and snatched up his car keys. "I think we need to get over there and have a chat with Mr Perry, sharpish."

*

Jacob led the way north to Paradise Farm, with Innes sitting beside him in the Alvis. Morgan and Holloway were following in the unmarked Audi directly behind. Jacob had not brought the matter to Marcus Kent's attention, preferring to take full responsibility for the arrest himself, knowing only too well about Kent's propensity to slow down arrests with red tape.

The Alvis ripped past Ravensroost Woods where the coins had been left and Morgan had attended the burnt-out car. Then, Jacob turned left onto a narrow track which he drove along for less than five minutes before a crumbling stone farmhouse slowly moved into view. It was partially obscured by a line of very mature poplar trees, which Jacob now pulled to a stop in front of and climbed out of the Alvis. Innes had barely slammed her door when Morgan pulled up beside them in the Audi and cut the engine. A moment later all four of them were standing outside the abandoned Paradise Farm. There was a large pond to its right, and some woodland beyond it.

"It doesn't look much like 'Paradise', does it?" Holloway asked.

Jacob was more concerned with what he might find in the property's wine cellar than whether the place could ever be described as paradise or not.

"Maybe we should have got an armed response unit, sir?" Innes said.

"What is it with you and armed response units?" Jacob said, trying to break the ice with a weak smile. "There's four of us, Innes. I think we can manage to talk to Mr Perry about his potential involvement in these murders without half a dozen men armed with Glocks."

Jacob made to walk to the front door, steeling himself for the wine cellar, when Morgan spoke.

"Do you hear something round the back?"

Jacob cocked his head and listened. He filtered out the sound of the whistling wind and was able to hear occasional thuds and bangs and what he thought he could make out as footsteps smacking on concrete.

"There's no cars around the front," Morgan said. "I reckon Mr Perry is parked up round the back and is loading a car up ready for an early departure."

"Holloway, Innes!" Jacob said. "Both of you into the house. Do a full search, starting with the wine cellar. Morgan and I will go around the back."

"Sir!"

Jacob and Morgan walked around the back of the farmhouse and when they turned the corner they saw a large expanse of old stained concrete forming some kind of loading bay for tractors, and beyond it an enormous rusty barn, with one side open to the elements inside. It was stacked high with bales of hay. Parked up on the other side of the concrete bay by the house, was a Land Rover. Its boot was up and the back was full of boxes and suitcases and other personal effects.

Then with almost surreal calm, a tall slim man with dark brown hair, wearing a black fleece and a pair of old dirty scuffed jeans and black hobnail boots stepped out of the farmhouse kitchen door with a large box of wooden spoons and other kitchen equipment sticking out of the top of it. He stopped and stared at the two detectives, frozen in time and space like the proverbial rabbit in the headlights.

Jacob reached for his ID. "Mr Perry?"

Perry dropped the box he was carrying and took off at lightning speed past the Land Rover, disappearing out of sight around the side of the barn.

"Get after him!" Jacob cried.

Jacob sprinted across the stained concrete, with Bill Morgan, a former royal Marine Commando, easily keeping up with him until they reached the edge of the barn and burst around the corner to see no sign of Perry.

"Where is the bastard?" Jacob said.

Morgan was scanning the fields. "This wouldn't have happened if we'd got an armed response unit."

Jacob gave his old friend a look. "Thanks for that."

Morgan made to run to the far end of the barn but Jacob caught his jacket and told him to stop. Then he listened to the wind. It was drifting over fallow fields behind the farm, bringing the scent of damp earth and manure with it. Jacob cocked his head again and now zoned in intently on something he could hear off behind a hedge to their right. It was the sound of sloshing – a man was walking through water. Then he heard another sound, the sound of scraping and scratching and rustling.

"He's gone over there and got through that hedge," Jacob said. "There must be a stream on the other side of it. I think he's crossed over the stream and he's trying to climb through another hedge. He'll get clear away if we don't get after him!"

Jacob and Morgan now took off down a short lane to the right of the barn and pulled up at the track that ran perpendicular at the end of it, bordered by a six-foot high hedge of hawthorn and elderberry. For a moment, Jacob was unable to see where Perry had broken through it, but then off to the left, he could see the damage he had caused getting through. He followed him through with Morgan a step behind. On the other side of the hedge, he looked down a metre or so to see a stream around two metres wide and on the other side of it another hedge, just as he had imagined. Then he just caught sight of Perry's boot as he pulled it through the second hedge.

"Stay where you are!" Jacob cried out. "This is the police. You're under arrest, Perry!"

Jacob wasn't surprised when Perry ignored him completely, burst through the second hedge and took off into another field.

Jacob and Morgan gave each other a withering glance and then fought their way over the stream, getting their shoes, socks and trousers soaking wet before clambering up the muddy bank on the other side of the stream. Morgan was significantly more adept at work like this, having been a commando many years ago in his youth. Age had taken the same toll on the Welshman as anyone else in this world, but Jacob had noted with Morgan before that the training commandos received never really left them. Now Morgan overtook him as they climbed up the bank, charged through the hedge and was out of sight by the time Jacob stepped into the second field.

Ahead of him, he saw Perry now a third of the way across the fallow field, stumbling and tripping on clods of earth and tangles of couch grass as he fled, desperately trying to right his balance as Morgan bore down on him from behind. Both men were around the same age, but Jacob guessed Perry had never been in the Marines so now he watched as the broad-shouldered Welshman easily caught up with him and rugby-tackled him to the ground, piling his face down into the muddy earth and pulling his hands up behind his back.

Jacob now slowed to a gentlemanly stroll and caught the two men up just in time to watch Morgan pull cuffs out from under his suit jacket and put them around Perry's wrists, now clamped firmly behind his back. Somewhere above their heads, a raven cried out across the field, an irony not lost on Jacob as he looked down at the muddy bleeding face of Dennis Perry.

"Dennis Perry," Jacob said. "I'm Detective Chief Inspector Jacob from Wiltshire CID. I'm arresting you on suspicion of the murder of Tansy Babbington, Jennifer Stanley and Declan Taylor. You do not have to say anything, but it may harm your defence if you do not mention when questioned something which you later rely on in court. Anything you do say may be given in evidence."

Morgan hefted the man to his feet and the three of them stood in the middle of the muddy field as the cold wind whipped at them and the ravens circled high above.

"Where is Sergeant Anna Mazurek?" Morgan asked. "Is she here at this farm?"

"Of course not," Perry said with an arrogant sneer. "Declan Taylor was keeping her out at a cottage somewhere near Malmesbury, but…"

"We already know that, but she's not there!"

"Let me *finish*," Perry said icily. "He was keeping her near Malmesbury, but when I went over there to kill him, he told me he had moved her because he was getting paranoid the police were closing in."

"Moved her where?" Jacob asked.

"To a small cottage in Castle Combe Woods. By the way, did you like the gift I left for you on your doorstep?"

"You put the dead raven there?" Jacob asked.

"A small indulgence, and not one recommended by the Professor. I thought of it all by myself. If you're interested, it's the same bird where the feathers came from."

"Never mind about that!" Morgan yanked him hard to get him to start walking across the muddy field. "We want the full address in Castle Combe, now!"

Perry reeled off the address and both detectives made a note. Then Innes called Jacob.

"Go ahead, Innes."

"Nothing here, sir. We've made a cursory search of the property and there's no sign of DS Mazurek. Not even in the cellar."

"All right. We've got Perry and we're on our way back to the farm now. Stay put."

Jacob hung up. "Still no sign of her."

"That's because I was telling you the truth," Perry said softly. "Naughty detectives need to talk less and listen more."

"Let's get you back to the car and we're going to go down to the station," Morgan said, turning to Jacob. "I'll head over there right away."

"OK, Bill," Jacob said. "Take Holloway. I'll deal with this."

After a long traipse across the field, through the hedge, over the river, through the second hedge and back into the lane heading towards the barn, Perry finally broke his silence.

"I only did the last one," Perry said.

Jacob stared at him. "What did you say?"

"I said, I only did the last one. The man, Taylor."

"Keep moving," Morgan said. "We can discuss this down to the station."

"I think you'd rather hear what I have to say *now*, Chief Inspector," Perry purred.

Jacob heard a note of something indiscernible in the man's voice, something cold and yet smug and laced with a sense of power. "And why do I want to hear what you have to say now?"

"I already told you. I only did the last one."

"If you've got something to say, then just bloody well say it!" Morgan said, pulling the man forward on his elbow as the three walked down the lane towards the barn.

"Then I will bloody well say it," Perry said. "I only killed Declan Taylor because I was being threatened."

"And who was threatening you?" Morgan said.

Jacob already believed he knew the answer. "It's Keeley isn't it?"

The three men came to a stop. A cold wind rushed down the lane, and above the silence was scarred by the mocking croak of a raven circling them high above.

"That's right," Perry said coolly. "I was never the Ferryman, nor a copycat. The real Ferryman killed the first two women and stored their bodies here at the farm. Then after he told me what he wanted me to do, how to make it look like a copycat on purpose, I was to dump the two bodies at a precise time and place. After he told me all of this, he flew away. The last thing I heard from him was when he told me to get rid of Declan Taylor because he was a liability and a material witness to the crimes."

"What do you mean he flew away?" Jacob asked, feeling a shiver of fear working its way up his spine. He already knew the answer to this as well.

"He flew away like a raven, Chief Inspector."

Morgan grabbed Perry's collar and shook him. "What do you mean, Perry?"

"Have you ever been to Rome in November, Chief Inspector?" Perry asked with a sickening smile.

Jacob met Morgan's eyes and saw the same mix of fear and disgust he was feeling reflected on him. The Welshman now shook Perry again. "If you've got something to say then you'd bloody well better say it now!"

Sensing some reluctance on the part of Perry to say anything further, Jacob played a common gambit. "If you help us, we'll help you, Perry. Anything you tell us now that can bring an end to the murder and the killing will work in your favour during your trial. I'll see to it myself."

"I'm being clear enough, Chief Inspector. Professor Alastair Keeley, the Ferryman, is alive and kicking. He was here in England on Tuesday when he killed both those women and stored them here at Paradise Farm. Then he flew to Italy. He said something about ravens and revenge and how he could only lead a peaceful and happy life once he had finished one more job. He was very insistent about the raven's feathers being left on the bodies. He said he would never forget what she did to him."

"My God…" Jacob said. "Sophie! I need to call her, right now!"

CHAPTER 28

Sophie knew she was an uptight person, and the relaxed casual happiness others seemed to find was something she often had to work at quite hard. It turned out that a few days in Rome had been of immeasurable help in this regard, and now on day three of the conference she was strolling through the Italian sunshine on her way out from buying some lunch and a coffee and making her way back to the conference centre when she heard her telephone ring.

She pulled the phone from her bag and saw it was Jacob. "Tom! How is everything? Please tell me you have some good news about Operation Abbey?"

"Sophie, I need you to listen to me very carefully."

Sophie felt her blood turn to ice. She knew Jacob well enough by now to know that something was seriously wrong. He was notorious for his calm and measured response to crises, now she could hear what could only be described as mild concern in his voice.

"What's the matter?"

"Keeley is alive."

Sophie pulled herself to a stop on the pavement and a woman walking behind her now piled into her by accident, reprimanding her in hurried Italian for coming to a stop without warning, then bustled off down the street. For Sophie, the world seemed to stop.

"What are you talking about? You told me that he'd been killed in a crash! You said Marcus Kent had the evidence sent over from Austria! You said you'd seen pictures of him dead."

"I know all of that and I don't know how any of it was done, but he's still alive."

"How do you know?"

"We caught the copycat killer, a loner called Dennis Perry. He came clean and told us that he'd only murdered Declan Taylor, not the two women. He told us Keeley is alive, killed the two women and was pulling his strings all along."

"Declan Taylor is dead?"

Jacob swore quietly, cursing himself for not telling her before. "Yes. I'm sorry, I haven't had a chance to get in touch with you and tell you. He was killed by Perry when he stopped being useful to him and Keeley. As I say, Perry has been working with Keeley."

"And you're sure you can believe what this man is telling you? Who's to say he's not just making it all up to send you running round in circles again, off in the wrong direction?"

Jacob conceded there was a possibility Perry was lying but doubted it. "I think he's telling the truth, Soph. He said Keeley was very clever and deliberately had the bodies made to look like it wasn't his MO but a copycat. The whole thing was done to fool us and misdirect us. Soph, Perry told us Keeley flew away. He's not in England."

Sophie's heart quickened in her chest, and it felt like her world was closing in around her, choking her, stifling her. "What do you mean he's not in England? You can't mean…"

"Perry says that Keeley is in Italy, Sophie. Now listen to me very carefully. He was leaving the raven feathers behind on the bodies for a reason – this is about revenge. I think this is all about you. The whole thing – Tansy Babbington, Jennifer Stanley, Declan Taylor, the shrouds, the coins, the raven feathers, everything – it's all been about you from the start!"

Sophie felt dizzy and stepped over to the side of the pavement to lean up against the wall, bringing her hand up to her head and squeezing her temples, trying to slow her breathing. "This is, this is madness, Tom! We only have Perry's word for it. He's got to be lying. It can't be true! The Ferryman is dead!"

"We can't assume that, Sophie," Jacob said. "It's just too dangerous an assumption to make. I need you to get to the nearest police station and wait there for me. I'm going to talk to Marcus Kent and tell him everything I've learned from Perry. I'm driving straight down to Bristol Airport right now. I can be in Rome in three hours. Tell the Italian police who you are, tell them who I am, and tell them everything!"

Sophie stared up at the street and saw hundreds of pedestrians moving up and down on both pavements, motorbikes, Vespas and cars cruising past, the smell of exhaust fumes heavy in the warm air. Everywhere she looked were coffee shops clothes shops, tobacconists. She needed to think straight, to get her mind in focus. She needed to get her mind organised and focus on finding a police station.

"OK, Tom. I can do that! I'll Google it right now and I'll walk there straight away, but I don't speak Italian."

"Don't worry about that. You can make them understand you. Just get to a station and tell them you need protection. I'll speak to you in three hours."

Sophie heard Jacob hang up and for a moment didn't know what to do. She was standing in the heart of Rome, surrounded by thousands of people with not a care in the world, and now she knew that one of them was Professor Alastair Keeley, the notorious Ferryman serial killer who had almost taken her life all those years ago. Was he watching her now?

She found herself desperately scanning the crowd for any sign of his face, but after a while, everything just became a blur. There was no hope of finding him in this massive, shifting sea of faces all around. It was completely impossible. Pulling herself together, she slowed her breathing once again and as her heartbeat reduced, she found herself navigating on her phone until she found where the nearest police station was – the Rome Police Headquarters on the Via de San Vitale, only a ten-minute walk away from her current position. She thought about calling Kit or Louise, but they were out in a bar enjoying drinks near the Forum. They would take too long to get here. She had to do this alone. Keeping her head down and staying tucked away at the side of the pavement, she made her way towards the police station as quickly as possible, but no matter how far she walked, she couldn't shake off the feeling that the Ferryman was always one step behind her.

*

Jacob cut the call to Sophie and immediately made another call to Marcus Kent at the station. He used Kent's direct number and was relieved when he answered the phone in his usual brusque manner.

"Detective Chief Superintendent Kent. Speak."

"This is Jacob, sir. We've got a situation."

"Alright, Chief Inspector, calm down. Are you driving?"

"Yes, I'm driving down from the farm. Paradise Farm."

"And what the hell is Paradise Farm?"

"We got a lead from Gary Wilson up in Newcastle, sir."

"Why wasn't I told about this?"

"We needed to act quickly! Wilson was playing games with us. Our copycat killer was corresponding with him in prison and Wilson told us he told him to get the coins, then Wilson told Phillips to get them. It worked like a chain. I think it was just to send us all around the country on a wild goose chase, to waste our time. He also told us he knew where the copycat killer was – he gave us a cryptic clue and we worked out he was referring to a farm that the copycat bought. His name is Dennis Perry. Innes and some uniforms are bringing him into custody now!"

"Why the hell was I not told about any of this? This is a disciplinary matter."

"We can argue about that later, sir," Jacob said, overtaking a dawdling delivery van. "The point is, Perry told us he was being used by Alastair Keeley. He was working with the Ferryman all along!"

"Working with the Ferryman?" Kent said.

"That's right. When we arrested him, Perry confessed to killing Declan Taylor but claimed Keeley killed the two women. Now everything makes sense."

"How does everything make sense? The only thing that makes sense to me is this Perry is obviously lying about working with Keeley just to make mischief. Use your head, Jacob!"

"I don't think he's lying, sir. I think he's telling the truth. He told us that Keeley was very particular about how the bodies had to be wrapped in the shroud, what coins were used and that the feather had to be left behind. He also told Perry to murder Declan Taylor. The feathers were about revenge! This whole thing has been about revenge from the very beginning. He wants to kill Sophie and Perry told us he's in Italy!"

"This all sounds like some kind of extraordinary fairytale to me, Chief Inspector. Where are you now?"

"I'm going straight down to Bristol Airport."

"I do hope you're using your hands-free kit, because… hold on, what do you mean you're going straight to Bristol Airport?"

"I'm flying out to Italy immediately, sir. I've already called Sophie and told her to get to the nearest police station. She needs me."

"*We* bloody need you! And you're not going anywhere without my permission. You're a Detective Chief Inspector in the Wiltshire CID, Jacob. You don't just get to go swanning off to Italy whenever you please. You have to conduct your investigation here! Sending an official to another country requires organisation. There's paperwork. It has to be approved!"

"You can't stop me flying out there, sir. If you can organise it on an official basis so when I land I'm able to work in an official capacity with the local authorities, that will be the optimum outcome. But if you don't or can't or won't, I'm going out as my own man. I won't let Keeley get anywhere near Sophie."

"There are rules, Chief Inspector! You might have noticed they stop us from doing the wrong thing."

"Rules stop us doing the wrong thing but they often stop us doing the right thing."

"Very poetic, I'm sure," Kent said. "Did you find Anna Mazurek?"

"No, sir, but Perry told us where Taylor moved her after keeping her at the farmhouse where we found his body. Morgan and Holloway are on their way over to Castle Combe right now."

Jacob heard Marcus Kent deliver one of his famous long sighs. "Very well. I don't suppose there's much I can do to stop you anyway, is there? You have always been a loose cannon on deck, Jacob."

"I have to do this, sir. Even if there's only a small chance of Perry telling the truth and Keeley still being alive, I can't just leave Sophie to defend herself out there. You've seen what he's capable of! Look at how he fooled the Metropolitan Police for years while he was killing those other women. Look at how he somehow managed to infiltrate the Austrian Federal Police computer system to upload completely fake documents about his car accident. Look at how he orchestrated this entire thing from the beginning, deliberately misleading us by having the shroud wrapped differently, and using the wrong coins just so we would believe it was a copycat killer. The whole thing's been about Sophie from the beginning. She's in grave danger."

Kent's tone changed completely. "Well, just take it easy and concentrate on what you're doing. I will telephone Rome and make the necessary arrangements so that you can work there in a semi-official capacity with the authorities. I'll try and get it arranged for you by the time you arrive. I happen to know a very senior police officer in the Roman police force, whom I met at a European police conference many years ago and we keep up social contact.

That might help to smooth things along. After all, it's the squeaky wheel that gets the grease, isn't it?"

"Thank you, sir. This will make things a lot easier if they're expecting me."

"I'll make a call, you get on the plane."

Jacob heard Kent hang up, as usual without a goodbye, and then he ended the call his end before joining the M4 and stamping on the throttle, tearing out into the fast lane and making as much speed as he could on his way down to Bristol.

CHAPTER 29

Morgan and Holloway made the twenty-mile trip from Ravensroost to Castle Combe in less than half an hour thanks to a combination of the Audi's powerful engine and the Welshman's flagrant disregard for speed limits. The flashing blue lights in the Audi's grille and rear window also helped as they cut their way through any congestion they encountered en route.

"Take it easy, sir." Holloway gripped the door handle as Morgan took another bend nearly twice the recommended speed.

"I'll take it easy when Anna is safe and not before!"

Morgan now indicated left to undertake someone in the fast lane before steering back in front of him and pressing hard on the accelerator to take a few valuable seconds off the journey.

"Just make sure you know exactly where we're going!" Morgan said.

Holloway had been fiddling around with his phone from the second they had climbed into the Audi and was pretty certain he knew the exact location that Perry had told them about. There was a reasonable size of woodland to the southeast of Castle Combe, and Holloway was able to use Google Earth to find an aerial view of the area. He was certain he knew exactly where the cottage was located, just on their southeastern boundary.

"When we get into Castle Combe, sir, you need to go almost completely through the village and I'll tell you when we need to turn left."

Morgan nodded in understanding but said nothing. His mind was flooded with images of Anna, dying or even dead wherever that bastard Declan Taylor had left her. He couldn't shake the images from his mind, no matter how disturbing and awful they were. He had grown closer to Anna over the years and had in his more idle moments wondered if the two of them might get together. They were both single and shared similar tastes in music and pastimes, but he never really had the nerve to front up to her. He decided that if she was safe, he would find the courage to ask her out.

It was late afternoon now and getting cold. Morgan was more than a little relieved to see the sign for Castle Combe up ahead. He changed down from top gear into fourth and then into third, the engine growling with the extra torque as they blew past the 30 mph speed sign at 50 mph. Morgan had been to Castle Combe many times before because it was one of the county's most beautiful towns. So 'chocolate box' was the town, the village's bridge and the rows of Cotswold stone houses stretching away up the hill behind it was one of the most common views when you typed in 'chocolate box English village' into Google. Today, the aesthetic delights of this beautiful place did not even touch the surface of Morgan's mind as he concentrated on driving the car as fast as was safe through the little town and looking out the entire time for the left turn Holloway had told him about back up on the road into the town.

"Is this it?" he asked impatiently.

"No, not this one, sir. It's the next one."

Morgan recognised the road – one of the most photographed roads in the whole country – as Water Lane, but they blew past it at high speed. Holloway now told him to slow down because they needed the next left. Morgan stamped on the brake and locked both their seatbelts, bringing the Audi to a juddering squealing stop just yards away from their turn. Holloway gave the older senior detective a reproachful look, but Morgan's mind was entirely elsewhere, slamming the left turn signal on and then stamping on the throttle in second gear to make the corner as fast as possible.

The road rapidly narrowed to an unsealed lane full of potholes, but Morgan paid little regard to them as he ploughed the Audi over them as fast as he could, smashing the suspension up and down before finally, the cottage came into view up on their right. Morgan turned the wheel, swerving the car to the right and pulling its nose up tight almost against the cottage wall. Both men unbuckled their seatbelts, jumped out of the car, and ran to the door. Holloway hammered on the front door while Morgan immediately made a circuit of the property, kicking his way through a side gate and walking around to the back. Having seen no obvious way to gain entry to the house, he came back to the front and asked Holloway if anyone had answered the door.

"No sir. Nothing at all."

Morgan, as the senior detective, would normally have asked Holloway to do the honours, but the former commando was too charged up to observe protocol and searched for a rock. Finding one about twice the size of his hand, he picked it up and put it through the front door window, smashing it to pieces. Then he reached inside and unlocked the door. Both men charged into the hall.

"Anna!" Morgan cried out.

"No response, sir," Holloway said.

Morgan saw fear in the younger man's eyes. "You search downstairs, I'll do upstairs."

Morgan's heart pounded in his chest as he bounded up the stairs, three steps at a time, reaching the top floor of the little cottage in seconds. It took him less than one full minute to search all three of the rooms and see no sign of Anna at all. He then saw a loft hatch. He went back into the nearest bedroom, grabbed a chair and positioned it under the hatch before pushing it up. He saw nothing but darkness above him. There was a telescopic loft ladder above him which he pulled down until its feet were pushing into the landing carpet. He clambered up the ladder and looked into the loft but found nothing again. Frustrated and scared for his old friend and colleague, he now made his way back down the loft ladder and down the stairs to find an anxious-looking Holloway standing in the hall.

"Have you found her?" Morgan asked.

The shake of the head said it all. "I'm sorry, sir… but no. She's not here. I've searched all the rooms. Perry was lying."

Morgan lashed out, punching a door jamb and not for the first time splitting open his knuckles. "Damn that bastard!"

Holloway looked at Morgan's bloody hand with concern. "We'll find her, sir."

"Let's get back. I'll be damned if he doesn't know where she is! I'll get down there and beat it out of him."

*

Professor Keeley's Elo rating at chess was well over 3000. This was the rating that only the very best chess players, such as world champion grand masters, could attain. Keeley considered that he could probably achieve much more, but had simply grown bored of the game by the time he was in his twenties. The reason he was so good at chess was because he was able to think many moves ahead, many more moves than his opponents could think.

In this case, his opponent was Detective Chief Inspector Tom Jacob of Wiltshire CID, and no doubt by now, the local Italian State Police working here in Rome. These were not difficult things to predict. It was a simple calculus and this was the Endgame. Once Jacob's slow, plodding mind had finally worked out that the copycat killings were a deliberate misdirection, and that the Ferryman was alive and well and in Italy, a piece of information he had very carefully given Dennis Perry because he knew it would alert Jacob to his current location, the rest would be easy to predict. Of course, Jacob would speak to his superior officer Detective Chief Superintendent Marcus Kent.

Pawn to e4.

Then, naturally, Kent would contact the Roman police.

Pawn to e5.

The Roman police would then take Sophie to a safe house.

Knight to c3.

Keeley had used various dark web contacts to find the list of Roman police safe houses in the city and he knew the most appropriate one was just to the east of the city up in the hills in a small village called Sacrofano. He was almost completely certain this would be the safe house the Italian police would retreat to with Sophie in their loving embrace.

Knight to f6.

Unfortunately for them and even more unfortunately for Sophie Anderson, the bitch who had worked so hard to imprison him and sentence him to a life of solitary confinement, he would be at the safe house before they were.

Bishop to c4.

He was thinking these beautiful thoughts as he drove east out of Rome into the hills in the car he had just stolen. On the passenger seat beside him was a small cardboard box, sealed up with some fresh duct tape, which was something of supreme importance in his plan to deliver justice to Dr Sophie Anderson. He looked at the box with a gentle smile before returning his attention to the road and cruising to the safe house. It wouldn't be difficult to deal with the police, and it certainly wouldn't be difficult to deal with Tom Jacob but that would depend entirely on when he arrived in Italy.

Knight xe4… the game would play on. Queen to h5. Knight to d6…

Keeley's mind suddenly filled with the beautiful image of slowly choking Sophie Anderson to death. It was a mesmerising thought, thinking of her dying in his arms. She would resemble a pale and faint Renaissance beauty as she fell away down to the river. Another soul saved.

The Queen is trapped.

Of course, he would return to his original and most sacred ritual to dispatch her. She would be drugged so she was still conscious and able to see and hear everything that was going on, and then she would be slowly choked. He would make this last as long as possible, there would be no expediency involved at all. He wanted her to be choked out for as long as possible before finally dying, then she'd be wrapped in a shroud correctly and properly. Then he would insert one of his silver honeybee coins into her mouth before finishing wrapping the shroud. Then a sad farewell as the Ferryman took her across the River Styx.

The Queen dies.

Then Jacob would die.

Checkmate.

CHAPTER 30

Jacob disembarked from the British Airways Airbus A321 Neo and made his way to customs as quickly as he could. He passed through customs with little difficulty and made his way to the arrivals lounge where a tall slim man in his fifties, with dark black hair, slicked back and slightly greying at the temples, walked over to him and extended his hand. He wore a smartly tailored grey suit over a white shirt, no tie.

"You are Detective Chief Inspector Tom Jacob?"

"That's right. I take it my department forwarded my details and ID to you?"

"That is correct," the man said with a nod. "My name is Carlo Rossi," he said, showing Jacob his identification. "I am an Inspector with the Italian State Police. My superiors were contacted by Detective Chief Superintendent Kent in England and they have briefed me accordingly."

"Where is Dr Sophie Anderson?"

"She is safe, Chief Inspector. Please, don't fear for her safety."

Jacob felt annoyed and frustrated by the evasive reply. "I asked where she is, Inspector Rossi."

"Please, call me Carlo. Sophie is safe. She is in police headquarters which is where we are heading right now. There is an unmarked police car outside waiting for us. We can use the lights and sirens to cut through the traffic."

"But she's OK?"

"Si, she is OK. She is sitting with one of our female officers and they are drinking coffee. She is totally safe, inside the police station. There is no way Alistair Keeley can reach her."

Walking fast as they talked, Rossi now led Jacob out through the airport doors into the warm Roman early evening air. It is just this way please if you will, Thomas."

"Everyone calls me Jacob."

"As you wish. Please follow me."

Jacob followed Rossi along the broad walkway outside the airport where they crossed a road lined with taxi cabs and then went over a zebra crossing. After another short walk to the other side of the taxi collection area, they found their way to the short-stay car park.

Rossi directed him over to a black Alpha Romeo Giulia, which he now unlocked with a remote. Moments later they were both sitting inside and Rossi was navigating the car through the airport traffic, heading towards the main road that led east into Rome.

"I must say, Jacob, I could not believe it when my superiors briefed me about what had happened. I'm a homicide detective with many years of experience here in Italy, and I was very well aware of the Ferryman murders in London. I was also aware that Keeley was killed in a fatal car crash in the Austrian Alps. I was more than a little taken back when they told me that he was alive and not only that but here in Rome."

Jacob did not feel much like talking but guessed it would help pass the time quicker. He also did not want to be rude to this man.

"We don't have one hundred per cent proof that Keeley is still alive, Carlo, but I believe he is. Earlier today I arrested a man in connection with what we're calling the 'copycat killings'. These were three murders that were dressed up to look like copycat killings of Keeley when in fact he was the killer all along, at least with the first two victims. I always had my suspicions that Keeley was still alive and the man we arrested confirmed that he was. Not only that, he told us that he was here in Italy. I don't believe that's a coincidence."

"You mean that Keeley just happens to come to Italy in the same week that Sophie Anderson is here at a conference?"

"I mean exactly that," Jacob said, peering at the speedometer. "This whole thing was about Sophie from the very beginning. Keeley's escape from prison all those years ago, faking his death in Austria, setting up these hideous copycat murders in Wiltshire. The whole thing was about Sophie. He thinks ahead you see. His genius is terrifying because he uses it only for evil."

Jacob swore and cursed loudly at his stupidity.

"Jacob?"

"How could I have been such an idiot? Keeley has always been not just one step ahead, but ten steps ahead. Then you've got the conference in Italy! He knew Sophie would attend. Kit Bailey is a keynote speaker and Sophie has been to every single one of those conferences! The whole thing was planned, Carlo. Planned to perfection."

"Please don't worry, Jacob," Rossi said, indicating left and pulling out into the fast lane. The Alfa Romeo's engine roared in response to him stamping on the throttle and Jacob saw the speedometer push up to 80 kilometres per hour. "Don't get too angry. Sophie Anderson is safe in the police station and we are going to move her to a safe house. No one knows where the safe house is and we can move her there just as soon as you are there with her. We are organising a full manhunt for this Ferryman killer, and when we have him in custody he can be sent back to the United Kingdom and jailed for the murders of those two women. Don't worry. You and Sophie will both be safe here in Rome."

*

The sun was setting by the time Morgan and Holloway raced out of Castle Combe and made the journey back to headquarters in Devizes. Perry was still in a holding cell, waiting until the morning when he was due to be transferred to a Category A prison, where he would await his trial. Morgan once again used the flashing blue lights in the Audi's grille to expedite their journey back to interrogate Dennis Perry.

The engine had barely switched off by the time Morgan was jumping out of the car and then the two men sprinted across the car park through to the main headquarters entrance. The Welshman burst through the door and made his way as quickly as possible to the interview rooms where Perry was now waiting in a pair of handcuffs with two police officers, thanks to a call Holloway had made to the station en route.

"How nice to see you again, Inspector," Perry said.

Morgan found it hard to contain his anger. He knew it had already been two days since Anna's kidnapping, and an unknown number of hours since Declan Taylor had moved her to a new location. If she had been tied to something like a chair or a bed, she would have had nothing to eat or drink since being taken there by him. Morgan was dealing with some very dark thoughts about her fate and the sight of Dennis Perry smiling up at him made him want to punch him in the face.

"You told us Declan Taylor took Sergeant Mazurek out to an old cottage in Castle Combe. The problem is she's not there."

Perry shrugged his shoulders. "There's not much I can do about that, is there inspector? I can only tell you what he told me. All of this was orchestrated by the Professor. His work has an artistry to it, he is a classic genius."

"And by 'professor', you mean that piece of crap Keeley?"

"Tut tut, Inspector. That's no way to speak about your superiors. Professor Keeley has a wonderful mind. I've been corresponding with him for many months, so I should know."

"You seem to enjoy talking to depraved serial killers in your spare time, Mr Perry. It's not *much* of a hobby, but I suppose now you've joined their club you've got a little bit more in common with them."

"I only killed Declan Taylor because the Professor told me to. Anyone could see he was a complete moron and a total liability to the entire operation."

"Operation?" Morgan said with disgust. "Is that what you call killing three people just to get revenge on a young psychologist?"

Perry went quiet.

"You'd better start talking because if anything happens to DS Mazurek, I'll do *you* for her death as well, got it?"

"I've already told you that Professor Keeley orchestrated the entire operation. He organised the purchase of the properties that were used throughout, and he told Declan Taylor and me what to do. He must have told Declan Taylor to move your sergeant at the last moment, either that or Declan Taylor took it upon himself to use his tiny mind to make the decision that she had to be moved. All I can tell you is, he told me that he was going to move her to the place out at Castle Combe in the woods. I've told you that. She's not there. That's the end of it."

Morgan brought his fist crashing down on the table, making the two uniform constables start behind Perry.

"It bloody well is *not* the end of it you little shit. At the moment you're the only person I've got in custody who has anything to do with this case, anything at all to do with the disappearance of Sergeant Mazurek and you're going to bloody well keep talking until I know where to find her. So, just wrack that genius brain of yours until you tell us where you think she might be."

A long pause. "There is one possibility."

"Go on."

"But I tell you this under the same condition that Chief Inspector Jacob promised back at the farm. I expect a good word to be put in at my trial. I expect to be given some sort of a reduction in sentence."

"Aiding the police in a murder inquiry could help you in that direction," Morgan said. "But you'll need to tell me first. If it were to lead to the successful rescue of Sergeant Mazurek, then I'm certain the judge would look upon that favourably."

You little bastard, Morgan added in his mind.

Perry sighed, clearly conflicted between serving his master Professor Keeley, and securing a sentence reduction. In the end, his innate human nature won.

"Very well. The Professor talked about making Taylor take DS Mazurek out to another location and doing her there."

"Doing her?" Morgan said. "You mean you all planned to kill Anna Mazurek?

"Of course," Perry said calmly. "It was always the intention to kill everyone who had witnessed anything to do with the operation. The Professor believed kidnapping the sergeant would sow confusion and chaos in the team and reduce manpower at the same time. For him, it was the ultimate chess move, one of the high points of the operation. Unfortunately, he made it clear she would have to die in the same way he had me tie up Declan Taylor."

"You do realise if Keeley was ordering the killing of all the witnesses, you would be the next one that he eliminated from the game?"

"I hardly think so, Inspector. The Professor always told me how proud he was of me, and how I was one of his finest students. He considered me to have a fine mind. I could never beat him at chess though."

"Well, I consider you to be a perfect bastard, but you're still going to tell me where Keeley wanted you to dump Anna after you'd killed her."

"As a matter of fact, he wanted us to kill her there and leave her there."

"Where?"

"The Cathedral."

Morgan was instantly confused. "What do you mean, Salisbury Cathedral?"

"No, I don't think so. He didn't mean Salisbury Cathedral."

Morgan furrowed his brow in confusion. "Cathedral? What cathedral? There's only one cathedral in Wiltshire and that's down in Salisbury. Do you mean an abbey, maybe?" His mind raced with the locations of various local abbeys; Malmesbury, Bradenstoke, Lacock.

"Poor little mind starting to hurt?" Perry smiled again and leaned back in his chair. "Are you familiar with Aristotle's First Assumption?"

Morgan's urge to plant his fist in the centre of Perry's face grew. "No, I'm not familiar with Aristotle's First Bloody Assumption, Mr Perry. Perhaps you'd like to enlighten me."

"It's very simple really," Perry continued. "Aristotle claimed that the most important principle of all was that it was completely impossible for the same thing to both *be* and *not* to be at the same time. Professor Keeley taught me this."

"That's all very wonderful," Morgan said feeling his blood beginning to boil in his veins. "But what the hell has that got to do with cathedrals and DS Mazurek's disappearance?"

Perry relaxed in his chair, his smile fading. "The question you must ask yourself is this, Inspector: what *is* and is *not* a cathedral at the same time?"

CHAPTER 31

The headquarters of the *Polizia di Stato*, the Italian National Police, was based in the heart of ancient Rome, roughly equidistant between the main Termini train station and the Trevi Fountain. The building was a large, five-storey trapezoid, with an internal courtyard given over to parking for senior officers. Its exterior façade blended in perfectly with the Eternal City, with beautiful honey-coloured masonry, but its interior was no different to any other busy, large office building, at least not the section Rossi now took Jacob through.

"These buildings seem to be the same the world over," Jacob said.

"Some parts of this building are more beautiful than others, but this is where they keep me prisoner for most of the year," Rossi said with a casual smile.

They walked along a linoleum-tiled corridor towards a set of double doors. Rossi pushed them open and the two detectives stepped into an enormous open-plan office buzzing with activity. Everywhere he looked, police officers were speaking into phones, working at computer terminals, and scouring CCTV footage, all in search of the Ferryman. Rossi told him to follow him to a door on the far side of the open-plan office, and when they got there Jacob saw a plastic door plaque with the words: Ispettore superiore C. Rossi. *Senior Inspector C. Rossi.*

Rossi swung the door open and Jacob was overwhelmed with relief and joy when he saw Sophie sitting behind Rossi's desk and a uniformed female constable sitting in a chair by the window. It was fully dark now, and the two women had switched on a lamp on the desk, producing a gentle amber glow in the room and giving the place a cosy ambience.

When Sophie saw Jacob she leapt to her feet and the two of them almost collided with each other in the middle of the office. They embraced and kissed deeply, completely oblivious to the Italian police inspector and constable who stared at them at first, but then politely looked away.

"I can't tell you how good it is to see you," Jacob said.

"Same here," Sophie said. "When you telephoned me, I was so terrified I came straight here. I was certain Keeley was following me all the way. Are you sure he's here in Italy?"

Jacob nodded. "I'm completely sure he's in Italy."

"Have they found Anna yet?" she asked.

Jacob shook his head. "I don't think so, at least not since I boarded the aircraft in Bristol. We have Perry in custody and he's confessed to the murder of Declan Taylor but he was very clear that the first two women were both murdered by Keeley. He sees him as some kind of depraved mentor."

"But don't worry," Rossi said, stepping into the conversation. "We are going to transport you both now to a safe house here in Italy while at the same time, as you can see from how busy our office is, we are working already very hard to find this Alistair Keeley. It is not usual for my team to be working so late, but we consider this to be an utmost top priority. It is very difficult however because we don't even know how he entered the country."

"He could be using a false passport," Jacob said. "I was thinking about it on the flight from Britain. He met a lot of people in prison, and I think, Carlo, you will appreciate that prisons can be a kind of university for criminals. I don't put it beyond the realms of possibility that he met someone inside who either was a forger or knew a forger. The alternative is that he somehow boarded a ferry or the Eurostar, dodging passport control and came in that way. We both know there are ways to do that as well."

Rossi nodded. "Yes, this is sadly possible. Right now our search is mainly focusing on the CCTV network here in Rome. We have a full file from both the Metropolitan Police and the Austrian police authorities so we know what face to look for. We are also asking questions about any British man answering his description who has checked into hotels here in the city. We start with a wide net but gradually we make it tighter."

"I just don't understand how he's still alive," Sophie said. "I thought the Austrian authorities were adamant he was dead and even had photographs of his dead body."

"I always had doubts about that story," Jacob said. "I don't need to tell you, Sophie, that Keeley is an extremely high IQ genius. I don't think it's particularly difficult for a man like him to stage photographs of his own death, the trickier part would be getting them onto the police computer system in Austria, but again I'm pretty certain Keeley could find a way around that, too."

"It's time for us to go to the safe house," Rossi said, opening his door and gesturing for them to step back out of the office. "Although it may seem safer here, it is an obvious place to bring you if he knows you are in Rome. And you have to leave at some point, he may be waiting and watching. The sooner we get you out of here the better. We all agree here in the force that Keeley is a lethal danger and that you must be protected from him. We have been permitted to share details of the investigation with you, Jacob, and we would appreciate any help you can give us on the way to arresting this dangerous man."

"Of course," Jacob said. "I'm happy to work alongside you to catch him."

Sophie looked at him, horrified. "Wait, I thought you were coming with me to the safe house?"

"There's no need, Soph," Jacob said. "Nobody knows about the location of the safe house, not even I do yet. You'll be taken there and guarded by armed police and you'll be completely safe. I must work with Inspector Rossi. You've told me so much about Keeley over the years, plus I have experience working on this case."

"No one knows Keeley as well as I do!" Sophie said. "If anyone's going to be helping the Italian police, it should be me."

"That's just crazy, Sophie," Jacob said. "He already nearly killed you once, and this time he's very serious about getting revenge. He's killed two people and had a third killed, and we still haven't found Anna. The whole thing is becoming completely out of control."

Jacob paused a beat, taking her hands in his.

"This is about *revenge*, Sophie. This is about getting you back for what you did when you played such a crucial role in getting him arrested and sent down for life. He'll never forget that. Some never forget, and Keeley is one of them. I am not going to use you to catch him, not your experience and knowledge and I'm certainly not going to use you as bait."

"But…"

"I'm not arguing with you about it. You're going to the safe house. If I need any help with psychological profiling, I can call you."

"Jacob is right," Rossi said. "It is far too dangerous and we will not allow you to be part of the investigation, Dr Anderson. I'm sorry, but it is not Jacob's call anyway, it is mine. You are a civilian and not only that you are a specific intended target of this killer. Jacob is not. Also, Jacob is an official Detective Chief Inspector from the English police. He has been permitted to work with us on this case, but you have not. The Italian authorities are perfectly clear on this and my superior has been unequivocal on the matter. You will go to the safe house and you will be protected by armed guards."

"He's right Sophie, you need to go."

A young police officer ran up to Rossi. They spoke in hurried Italian, and then Rossi turned to Jacob and Sophie.

"We just had a call. A woman was found murdered in her apartment this evening. Strangled. An officer checked the building CCTV and they made a positive ID of Alistair Keeley in the building. It is not far from here, in Prati, just over the river. Just four kilometres north of us."

"Who called it in?" Jacob asked.

"Anonymous."

"That does it," Jacob said. "He's right on top of us and he's already started killing. You need to get out to the safe house, Soph."

Sophie relented. "OK, but I want you to stay in touch frequently."

Three police officers were waiting across the other side of the room. When Rossi called them over, they immediately joined them, saluting Rossi.

Rossi said, "Sophie, this is Sovrintendente Colombo – a sergeant. This is Agente Romano, what you would call a constable..." and now Rossi pointed to the female officer. "And this is Agente Lombardi. They will drive you out to the safe house and keep you under armed guard until we have caught Professor Keeley. Should we fail in our duty to catch him quickly, you can be flown back to the United Kingdom in the next day or two when adequate security arrangements have been made for you there."

Sophie met Jacob's eyes, and he saw a look of fear emanating from them that was impossible for her to hide.

"You'll be fine, Sophie. Just get out to the safe house and sit tight. Inspector Rossi and I will do everything we can to bring Keeley into custody as soon as possible. As he says, if we're unable to catch him, we can both be back on the plane to England in the next day or two.

Jacob and Sophie kissed, and then he watched her reluctantly break away and follow the three armed police officers out of the office.

*

"I'm not in the mood for any of your bloody riddles, Perry!"

Morgan circled the desk like a bird of prey, never once taking his eyes off Perry. The other man stared back at the detective, determined not to break eye contact, but in the end, Morgan won and Perry broke away to stare at the desk.

"It's not really a riddle, Inspector. More a test of intelligence or at the very least, local knowledge."

Morgan wracked his mind. Originally from West Wales, he had lived in Wiltshire for a long time, but he kept himself mostly in the orbit between Swindon where he lived and Devizes where he worked. He had never heard of anywhere called a 'cathedral' unless it was Salisbury Cathedral.

"I don't know about my local knowledge," Morgan said. "But I know about my police knowledge. If you don't stop messing me about with this nonsense you can forget about anyone putting in a good word at your trial. Last chance you nasty little man. What was Keeley talking about when he mentioned this so-called cathedral?"

"The Box Mine," Perry said at last.

"Box Mine?"

"Box, as in the village Box," Perry said. "It's an old mine dating back to the Roman occupation of Britain. They dug there for Bath Stone. There's a particular part of the mine which is 125 feet high. Its nickname is the Cathedral."

"I think I know the place he means, sir," Holloway said. "It's also an old Ministry of Defence site. Top Secret, at the time. Some say it's the British Area 51. Urban explorers go there a lot but the authorities are trying to block up all the entrances because it's in such a state of disrepair."

"You mean that bastard Declan Taylor took Anna Mazurek to a dangerous, abandoned mine?"

"It's the last place I can think of, Inspector," Perry said. "If she's not there, I really cannot be of any further help."

"Get a car, Holloway. And get Innes. If Anna is OK, she'll want Innes."

"Oh, Inspector," Perry said. "If you're interested, Declan Taylor cried when I choked him to death."

"I'm not interested actually," Morgan said, tapping the tape recorder. "But the trial judge will be, you nasty little shit."

Morgan turned to the two police officers. "Take this bastard back to his holding cell. Holloway, you're with me.

We're going to Box to have a look at this mine. And call some paramedics up as well, in case Anna's in need of medical help."

CHAPTER 32

Police officers in Rome are usually armed with handguns, which is not something Jacob saw on a day-to-day basis back in Wiltshire, despite them becoming gradually more common due to the increase in violent and disruptive behaviour in the county. Now, as Jacob and Rossi and two uniformed agents piled out of Rossi's car into the warm Prati night, the uniformed agents both drew their handguns. Jacob followed Rossi into the lobby area of the dead woman's apartment and waited as he rang the bell.

"There is no reply," Rossi said to Jacob. "We will take the elevator."

Rossi operated an old birdcage lift, situated in the heart of the building, and now all four of them stepped inside and rode their way to the fourth floor. When the lift reached its destination and Rossi opened the cage gate, they stepped out into a shabby-looking hallway and were immediately confronted with Apartment 41, the dead woman's apartment. The door was ajar.

Rossi shook his head and reached into his suit jacket, lifting his lapel and pulling an automatic handgun from a shoulder rig. He turned to the two young police constables standing beside them. "Andiamo, e tenete le vostre armi pronte!"

Jacob heard the words but did not know what they meant, but Rossi politely informed him.

"I told them to keep their weapons ready and that we should go forward."

Rossi took the lead, approaching the door stealthily, before nudging it open with the toe of his shoe and peering down inside the corridor. Seeing nothing obviously threatening, he opened the door further and slid inside the hallway, gesturing with a waving motion of his left hand that the rest of the team should follow him inside. Jacob followed Rossi down a white-painted corridor with wooden floorboards and some simple generic paintings on the wall, before reaching the main living area. Sprawled on the sofa was the dead woman. There were no serious head injuries, gashes, stab wounds or gunshot wounds, but Jacob could see the telltale purple shade of bruising marks around her neck and throat as the damage from being strangled slowly showed itself.

Rossi and the police officers checked the rest of the apartment was clear and then the Italian inspector exchanged a few sentences in Italian with the two police constables. Rossi turned to Jacob. "I just ordered an ambulance and a forensic team to get here as soon as possible."

"This is him," Jacob said. "This is the work of the Ferryman."

"We don't know that, Jacob. There is no shroud."

"I know it, I know it in my blood. He's here in Rome and he has strangled this woman but there must be a reason for it. This isn't one of his ritual murders. As you say, she's not wrapped in a shroud…" he walked over to the woman and gently opened her mouth. "And there's no coin."

Rossi shrugged. "Maybe he's decided to change his modus operandi."

Jacob shook his head, staring around the room, scanning for any clue. "Who was this woman?"

"Her name was Francesca Sartori,' Rossi said. "She was a student studying art at a nearby college."

"This just doesn't make any sense," Jacob said. He paced across the woman's apartment and pulled her blinds apart so he could stare down into the dark street. He counted the cars along the road, all parked bumper to bumper, and saw there was one missing.

"What did she do for money?"

"She drove an Uber."

Jacob felt a shock of realisation as the epiphany struck him. Cars. He must have hired Francesca to drive him somewhere and then killed her for her car. "We need to know what car she drove. Keeley is in her car."

A flurry of Italian filled the room for a few moments along with the crackle of radios. Moments later the answer came back in. Rossi stared at Jacob with some hope in his eyes.

"She drove a metallic silver Fiat Bravo. We have the registration number."

"Get looking for it on city CCTV," Jacob said. "Keeley killed this woman for the car and that meant he wanted to drive somewhere without hiring a taxi or a hire car. Are you absolutely certain he doesn't know where the safe house is?"

"It shouldn't be possible, but…"

Jacob now detected a momentary flash of uncertainty in Rossi's eyes. "You can't be certain can you?"

"There is no need to panic. I will speak to the detectives guarding Sophie at the safe house and tell them to look out for the Bravo. I can also get a police helicopter out looking for it too."

"I need to get there as fast as possible," Jacob said. "Will you drive me?"

Rossi holstered his weapon. "Of course."

Rossi ordered the police constables to guard the apartment and wait for the forensic team and ambulance to arrive before stepping briskly out of the apartment and ordering the birdcage lift to their floor. As they waited for the old lift to creak and whine its way up to the top, Jacob gave up and turned to the stairs.

"What are you doing, Chief Inspector?" Rossi asked.

"I'm saving the woman I love!"

*

Sophie was standing in the kitchen of the safe house out in the Lazio countryside with her hands wrapped around a warm cup of milky coffee. Of the three armed police officers who were with her, it was the woman named Lombardi who had made the coffee and the two of them had tried to maintain a conversation despite not knowing each other's languages. Sophie did not feel safe but tried to persuade herself that the Italian authorities knew what they were doing and had moved her to an entirely unknown location. She quietly prayed that Jacob and Rossi had made good headway in the manhunt for Alastair Keeley, but knew she would not be able to relax until he was behind bars and she was with Jacob again.

Sergeant Colombo now stepped into the room also holding a mug of coffee. His English was better than Lombardi's and now he smiled at Sophie as he set his coffee cup down on the table. "Sophie, I've just had a call from Inspector Rossi."

"I heard the telephone. Is everything all right?" she asked nervously.

"I don't want to lie to you, I want to be honest. They think Alistair Keeley has killed again, here in Italy. In Rome."

Sophie felt her heart almost stop beating and had to stop herself from crying out. "In Rome? He's murdered someone else?"

Colombo nodded. "They believe so, but nothing is proven yet. There is a woman who was found murdered in an apartment in Prati. They think he killed her to take a car. He had already hired her to drive him somewhere. She was an art student who drove Uber in her spare time for money. So they think he killed her to take the car. They found her dead in her apartment. She had been strangled."

The words flew at Sophie like a maelstrom. "To take a car? You mean he's on his way here? I thought you said that no one knew where this place was!"

"That is true," Colombo said, keeping his voice calm and reassuring. "No one knows where this place is. It is a very confidential location used as a safe house in the witness protection scheme here in Italy. We have used it many times before and it is very safe. They don't know where Keeley is driving, but the CCTV picked up his car driving out of the city in this direction. It could be a coincidence, but if he is heading here I want to reassure you that we will not let anything happen to you. Inspector Rossi is on his way and he has ordered a helicopter to search for the car Keeley stole. This Ferryman might be clever but he cannot get past three armed police officers. If he comes here he will be arrested. It will be the end of him."

It will be the end of him. Sophie heard Colombo's words going round and round in her mind. She knew he meant well. She knew he was trying to reassure her and calm her down, but at the same time, she knew he was underestimating Keeley. Keeley was far from stupid. He would not put himself at the mercy of armed police officers. If he knew where the safe house was and he was heading up here to get her, he would have a plan. He would already know how to handle the situation. He would have thought ahead. Keeley would have presumed the presence of armed guards in a witness protection safe house and would have planned accordingly.

"Where is Jacob?" Sophie asked. He was the only person she wanted to see right now.

"As I say, he is on his way here now. Inspector Rossi is driving him and they will be here very shortly. I know that it will make you much happier when Chief Inspector Jacob arrives. And that is two more men, which makes a force of five in total against the so-called Ferryman. If he comes here, he stands no chance of gaining anything but his own arrest."

Sophie stared down into her coffee cup and saw her own terrified eyes looking back at her in the reflection. She wanted to believe Colombo more than anything, but her experience with Keeley taught her never to underestimate the Ferryman. If he was coming for her, he would get her.

*

Anna Mazurek bolted awake. She was in darkness, on stony ground and her hands tied behind her back. Everywhere reeked of petrol – no engine oil. She realised it must have been a cloth Dex had stuffed in her mouth to gag her when moving her here, to this new place. But now the cloth had been loosened and was hanging around her neck. Everywhere was damp and cold. How long had she been here? Was she alone? She knew he would be going to prison for what he had done this week. He was a violent and aggressive man who had treated her very badly and yet still there was some small part of her, some tiny slither of her inner maternal nature that just wanted to make everything alright for Declan. But this time he had gone too far. That was the last thing she had said to him.

You have gone too far, Dex!

"Why have you brought me to this place?" she cried out.

Silence.

"Dex? Are you there?" She had called him Dex as a way of endearing her to him. It was something she had picked up on back in the last place he had taken her to, the old abandoned farmhouse, wherever the hell that was.

She licked her lips. They were dry, split, cracked and bleeding. She was so thirsty. She realised she'd had nothing to drink for at least thirty-six hours. She looked up and saw a rock ceiling hundreds of feet above her. She was in some kind of a cave. She licked her dry lips again, her mouth as dry as sand. When she swallowed, it was just blood from her lips; its coppery taste disgusted her. She felt weary and tired and wanted to go to sleep. She knew she had to fight the urge to fall asleep because she wasn't just sleepy, she was dying. She had had nothing to drink for several days and she was dying of thirst. The only time that she'd had water was when Declan had given her a bottle and it had contained salt water. She had drank greedily from it for a few moments before realising what it was and tried to spit it out as it ran all down her top.

"What the hell are you playing at, Dex? This is salt water!" she had said. "Is that what Keeley told you to give me? It could kill someone making them drink salt water!"

"He's gonna kill you anyway. He's gonna kill us all."

"Why don't you just let me go, Declan? If you let me go, I can help you! Don't be an idiot. You can't trust Keeley."

"I think it's gone way beyond that now," Declan had said as he paced up and down the enormous cave, his hands in his pockets, staring down at the floor as he talked. His voice was low and his words fell out like mumbled regrets. "I think he's gonna kill us all. I should never have got involved with him, Ania. Do you think he'll kill me?"

"Not if you let me go!"

He paced faster, his boots crunched on broken fragments of limestone.

"You have to shut up now, Ania! You have to stop talking. He told me you would beg for me to let you go. He told me you would tell me all kinds of lies. He said you would try to put poison in my ears. That's the truth, now isn't it? You're lying to me, pretending you can help me! If I let you go all that will happen is you'll have me arrested and then I'll go to prison."

"That's not true, Declan! Everyone knows Keeley is a complete and utter psychopath. I can help you get through this, but we need to work together. The longer you keep me tied up down here, the more danger you're in of going to prison for a very long time."

"Going to prison for a very long time is better than being hunted by the Ferryman, Ania. Wouldn't you agree?"

The conversation slowly receded from Anna's memory. Declan was gone now and had been for some time, although how many hours she just couldn't tell. She was in here all alone. The cave was almost entirely pitch black, except for the weakest rays of moonlight shining down through some kind of break at the top, lighting the rocky walls stretching up above her head. It smelt musty and damp and cold and she could hear the wind whistling through the cave system behind her. If only she knew where this place was, maybe she would stand a chance of getting out. What was she thinking? Declan had stuck her arms and legs to her body with duct tape and positioned her directly in the middle of this cave. She couldn't see behind her, and when she cried out, her sad, terrified voice was too weak from the terrible thirst and simply echoed away into the darkness, mocking her. She tried to strain against the tape but she was just bound too tightly, like a worm. She tried to call out louder, but nothing more than a humiliating mumble left her lips. Unless Declan Taylor returned here in a hurry, Anna Mazurek was going to die in this place, but she had no faith in that happening. Instead, she closed her eyes and prayed for God to make her end quick.

CHAPTER 33

Rossi's Alfa Romeo growled as they navigated the nighttime streets of Rome. The two detectives were determined to escape the city fast and head out to the safe house in rural Lazio, but despite Rossi using the sirens and blue lights, they had been caught in heavy traffic caused by a road traffic accident on the Ponte Flaminio, a bridge crossing the River Tiber. Now, as Rossi dipped the clutch and changed gear, taking yet another roundabout at high speed, Jacob pulled out his phone and made a call to Sophie.

"Sophie, it's Jacob. I suppose you've already heard from Rossi's men about Keeley?"

"Sergeant Colombo just told me that Keeley killed a woman to steal her car and he's driving out of Rome in this direction. I'm scared Tom. You know how dangerous this man is and we both know that he's coming for me. As you said, this is about revenge."

"Just take it easy, Sophie."

Jacob didn't know where to look. Outside the window of the speeding car, Rome was rapidly disappearing behind them and the rolling hills of rural Lazio were beginning to unfold on either side of the car. The traffic was thinning out and Rossi was going faster than ever before but it wasn't fast enough for Jacob. He found it difficult to find words that were both reassuring and truthful at the same time.

"Nothing's going to happen. You already have three armed policemen up there with you now, and Rossi and I will be with you soon. We'll regroup at the safe house and think things through."

"Does anyone know where Keeley is right now?" she asked frantically.

Jacob heard the terror in her voice. He wanted to be there with her, to hold her, to calm her down, but instead, he was stuck twenty kilometres away. Better than anyone, he was aware of what the Ferryman had subjected her to all those years ago, as she used herself to lure him out. The Metropolitan Police had struggled to track him down after he murdered several women in his notorious ritualistic style, but working with Dr Sophie Anderson, hired because of her experience in the United States in hunting down those with the most depraved criminal minds, they managed to catch him, but only after she had used herself as bait to lure him out.

She had a brilliant mind and had manipulated him. She got close to him, posing as a student and spent many weeks without ever letting on who she was, carefully moulding his mind until he saw her as the perfect victim, the ultimate woman to choke to death and send over the River Styx into the Underworld. Mistakes were made at the end of the operation which resulted in him nearly choking her to death before he was finally arrested and put on trial. He was found guilty and given a life sentence without parole before being moved to Wakefield prison, the notorious Monster Mansion up in Yorkshire where he was to spend the majority of each of his days in solitary confinement for the rest of his life. After his escape, Sophie had been put on high alert but when they heard about his fatal accident in Austria she relaxed for the first time in years. The nightmare was finally over. But now it was back once again and more terrifying and awful than ever before. Jacob struggled to find the words that she needed to hear.

"We're going to be with you in just a few minutes, Sophie. Stay in the house. Stay with the police officers."

"OK. Just get here as fast as you can."

Rossi had been talking on the police two-way radio fitted to his car, now he jabbed a thumb at Jacob to get his attention.

"That was my superior back in Rome. They sanctioned the police helicopter to try and track down the stolen car and stop him from getting anywhere near the safe house. They believe they know which road he's on. It's just taking off now. It will overtake us shortly. Please tell Dr Anderson it is not far away."

"I don't know if you heard any of that, Sophie," Jacob said into the phone. "But Inspector Rossi has just told me that the Italian authorities sanctioned the use of the helicopter he requested. It's taking off from Rome now and it's going to fly above the road they believe Keeley is on, just ahead of us. There's no way he can get to you. I'll be with you in a few minutes. Just sit tight. I love you."

"OK Tom," Sophie said. "I'll wait here for you. I love you, too."

Jacob heard her hang up and then cut the call at his end and slid the phone into his pocket. Searching the sky through the window, he waited anxiously to see the first sign of the police helicopter, knowing there was no way they could get to the house before Keeley.

*

At the same time, nearly 1000 miles northwest of Jacob's frantic pursuit of Keeley in the Lazio countryside, Morgan was racing an unmarked police Audi, with Holloway and Innes at his side, through the Wiltshire countryside. Full dark now, the powerful German car's headlights cut through the pouring rain in two giant arcs, lighting the way through narrow lanes, whose borders were lined with thousand-year-old hedges, tangled with nettles and cow parsley, as he navigated as fast as he could to the small village of Box.

Following the road around a small copse, they eventually reached Box and Holloway navigated Morgan along the High Street. This eventually became the London Road leading to the even smaller hamlet of Box Hill. Morgan strained to see through the rain as it piled down and the windscreen wipers sloshed back and forth. Ahead of him, the headlights still lit the torrential downpour.

"Which way now Holloway?" Morgan asked desperately. "Which way am I going, man? I can't see a bloody thing!"

"We need to turn right here, sir, and then there's a sudden left after that."

Morgan slowed for the village road Holloway had navigated him onto and now Holloway asked him to turn right down Barnett's Hill and then left onto Love Lane before finally turning onto White Ennox Lane.

"It's just up here, sir. I just hope we can get into the place."

"What do you mean?" Morgan asked, rounding on him angrily. "You told me to drive here and I've driven here. We haven't got the time to waste!"

"It's just that several of these entrances have been blocked up by steel and concrete to try and stop urban explorers from getting inside it. The authorities are frightened someone's going to get injured because it's a very extensive cave system down there. It's one of the largest limestone quarries in the region."

"It's also a bat preservation area according to what I've just been reading," Innes said. "Another reason why the government is so keen to keep people out."

"Yeah, well... there's one bastard that wasn't kept out of it, wasn't there?" Morgan asked. "That bastard was called Declan Taylor. Now you're telling me the entrance you've led me to, we might not even be able to use!"

Morgan didn't wait for a response from the younger detective before swerving to the side of the lane and crunching over some cow parsley before pulling over and braking to a stop. "There's a couple of Maglites in the glove box, Holloway. Get me one and one for yourself."

"I've got a pocket torch," Innes said, rummaging around in her bag.

"There's a fresh bottle of water in there too," Morgan said. "Bring it."

Morgan leapt out of the car, slammed the door behind him and sprinted across the lane. He was already climbing over a fence, only dimly aware of Holloway and Innes crossing the lane behind him, in less than a minute.

He vaulted over the fence and crashed down in a small thicket of brambles, cursing as the thorns cut into his shins and calves, and then kicked his way through them until he found himself standing in the middle of a small field surrounded by trees. He stared wildly around trying to see through the torrential rain with only the Maglite for light.

"It's over this way, sir!" Holloway called out.

Morgan now followed Holloway, with Innes at his side, as they traipsed across the field and then broke through a thick hedge into another small piece of woodland. The wind had got up now and the rain was lashing and slapping at their faces as they searched through the woodland floor for the entrance to the mine.

"And for God's sake be careful!" Morgan said. "If there's a bloody mine under here we could go through the ground at any moment."

"Sir," Holloway said.

Morgan frantically searched the woodland for the entrance, praying to God that the authorities hadn't blocked up the one Holloway had found.

"Are you sure we can get into this place?"

"I told you most of the entrances have been welded shut, others have been blocked with stone and concrete but there are other ways in because they might need to be able to access it. One of the most recent grilles to get blocked up was at a place called Brewer's Drift, which the MOD used to ventilate an area of the mine called Tunnel Quarry, also known as Heart Attack Alley. We're quite near there. If I'm right, when we get down there, we should be near a drift that leads to a red blast door highly prized by urban explorers."

"What's a drift then?" Innes asked.

"Any horizontal opening in a mine is called a drift."

"You're a mine of information," Innes said.

Holloway grinned. "I see what you did there."

"Look, you two can get a room after we find Anna, OK?" Morgan said, moving deeper into the woods. He wiped the rain off his face with his hand and swept the torch from side to side, desperately trying to find any sign of the stone entrance to the mine.

As they searched, Holloway continued to read on his rain-splattered phone.

"I think we need to be careful if we get down inside, sir. They say that this particular mine is in an extreme state of decay and there are collapses all over it on the inside on routes heading towards the Cathedral and the Red Door."

"There's no *if* we get down inside it, Holloway," Morgan said. "This is where that bastard Keeley ordered Taylor to bring Anna so they could kill her here. Now we know he was doing it because he was going to order Perry to kill Taylor and he knew that Anna would be left to die slowly of thirst and exposure in an abandoned mine! So there's no *if*. Not on my bloody watch! Now keep looking for this bloody 'drift' or whatever it's called!"

CHAPTER 34

Was Alastair Keeley the Ferryman? Professor Keeley knew better than anyone that he was merely assisting the Ferryman, putting the coins in the women's mouths so the real Ferryman would be paid his fair wage to take them across the River Styx into the Underworld. The Press had called him the Ferryman, an egregious error that only a bunch of Fleet Street simpletons could make, but more lately he had come to see himself in that way. He rather liked it. Perhaps in some warped and depraved way, he really was Charon, the Ferryman. And it was the Ferryman who now pulled the stolen Fiat Bravo off the road and climbed into another car he had stolen hours earlier and left in preparation for this very moment.

One step ahead, some people thought. One step ahead and you'll be alright. Of course, a man with Keeley's chess rating knew that five, six or seven steps ahead or even ten steps ahead was even better than one step ahead. He knew the murder rate in Rome was rare enough for the murdered

Uber woman to be instantly connected to him, and he knew Jacob would immediately deduce he had murdered her for the use of the car. This wasn't Hollywood, where any fool could climb into a car, punch the housing off the steering column and have it running ten seconds later. Besides, Keeley was a man of breeding, a genius, with an intellect second to none. He was not technically minded and would never lower himself. With the Uber woman, whatever the hell her name was, Keeley had enjoyed the opportunity to murder again, but had made a slight misjudgement with the timing so was unable to wrap her up and put a coin in her mouth. Now she would have to merely decay in this world, not having the requisite payment to pay the Ferryman to take her across the river.

Keeley now stepped into the frontloaded black Mercedes, closed the door and savoured the smell of the beautiful leather seats before pushing the ignition button and hearing the wonderful three-litre engine purr like a sleeping tiger. He put on his seat belt, checked his mirrors and gently pulled the car around in a sweeping arc before driving back up to the main road and turning north to the safe house. While he had transferred between the two vehicles, he was certain he had heard the sound of a police helicopter's rotors whomping menacingly somewhere to the south and had deduced in his mind almost one hundred per cent correctly that this must be a police helicopter in search of the Bravo. He doubted they would be able to see where he had parked it in the trees but even if they did, they would have no idea what vehicle he had driven off in.

Twenty moves ahead.

Magnus Carlsen, one of the world's greatest-ever chess grandmasters, often talked about thinking twenty moves ahead when playing chess. The Ferryman now marvelled and admired such a genius. Imagine thinking twenty moves ahead and now imagine how many variables each of those twenty moves produced. He was certain he could beat Magnus Carlsen in a fair fight but doubted the Press would ever allow such a Battle of Champions to go ahead. It didn't stop him from closing his eyes from time to time and imagining delivering the hammer blow, eventually killing the Queen before finally capturing Carlsen's King.

That was what was happening tonight as he opened the Mercedes's engine up and roared along the road to beautiful Sacrofano. He was about to kill the Queen, and then Jacob the King would be forced to surrender. Stripped of dignity and self-respect and saddled with the burden of having let the Ferryman take his beloved after all this time, Jacob would be a broken man. The Ferryman liked to imagine Jacob would retire from the police and live in isolated misery in his horrible little watermill for the rest of his life. Then again perhaps the Ferryman would visit Jacob one night and send him across the river, too? Such wonderful thoughts eased his journey as he surged the Mercedes forward towards its final dreadful destination.

*

"Over here, sir!" Innes cried out. "I think I found it."

Morgan was standing several yards away from Innes as was Holloway. The three of them had spread out to expedite the search for the mine entrance. Now both men swung their torches around, shining them where Innes was standing, bedraggled and soaking wet with her lank-wet hair down over her face, pointing her pocket torch down to the woodland floor a metre in front of her.

Morgan and Holloway padded through the wet undergrowth until they were standing opposite her and shone their torches down to meet hers on the ground at their feet.

"Does this look like what you're talking about, Holloway?" Morgan asked.

"Yes, that's it, sir," Holloway said excitedly. "Look!"

Morgan now looked on Holloway's mobile phone and saw the photograph he had found of one of the last few remaining unblocked entrances to the mine. It was identical to what they were looking at on the ground – a perfect square of concrete with a latticework of iron bars over the top of it, that looked a little like a drain.

"It looks like those bars are set into the concrete!" Morgan said. "Are you sure this isn't one of the drifts they blocked up recently?"

Holloway's response was to drop to his knees and study the grille. As his knees squished down into the wet mud, he leaned forward and heaved at the metal latticework, pulling it away from the entrance.

"It's supposed to look like it's been sealed off, sir! I think it was originally but some urban explorers might have opened it up. You can see where the concrete's been chipped away."

"Thank God for that," Morgan said.

"You think this is the entrance Declan used to bring Anna down here?" Innes asked.

"We don't even know if she is down here yet," Holloway said.

"She'd bloody well better be down here, Holloway, because there's nowhere else we can go and look for her!"

Morgan had barely finished speaking before dropping to the ground and shining his torch down inside the hole. He saw a series of stone steps leading down into total darkness.

"This has got to be it. I'm going in. Holloway, you're with me. Innes, radio the station and tell them that we found the mine entrance, get an ambulance out here right away then join us."

Morgan made his way down the steps carefully, instantly being struck by a horrible musty smell of mouldy concrete and damp earth. The temperature dropped away drastically, and they could soon see their breath pluming in the air in front of them. Shining his torch out along the stairwell, the Welshman soon reached the bottom. A moment later Holloway was beside him.

By the time they reached the bottom, they heard Innes's heels clicking on the concrete steps above them. Before long, all three were making their way along the narrow concrete tunnel. Morgan noticed the ground gradually sloping down and realised they were walking down deeper into the Earth. After several minutes of this, they noticed the concrete had come to an end and they were now standing in the proper mine. The walls were of roughly hewn limestone, and slick with water that had run down off the surface of the land high above.

"This place gives me the creeps, sir," Innes said, shivering and pulling her collar up.

"Me too, but we keep going," Morgan said. "If Anna is down here, then she's down here alone."

They pressed on, but things soon deteriorated until they were forced to clamber over massive refrigerator-sized chunks of stone and crawl through tight spaces barely wider than their bodies.

"I don't like this, sir," Holloway said. "Maybe we should call in potholing experts or something."

"We haven't got time for that Holloway!" Morgan said. "If Declan Taylor brought Anna down here then we can bloody well get down here too."

"But that's just it, sir!" Innes said. "We don't know if he *did* bring her down here. For all we know, Perry is just sending us on another wild goose chase."

Morgan stopped halfway over another boulder and turned to face the two younger detectives. "Listen, I've had many years working as a senior investigating officer in CID, and I'm telling you now that my nose tells me Declan Taylor's been down here."

He turned to face the darkness ahead of them and called out Anna's name. "Anna! It's Bill Morgan!"

Silence was the only response.

"Bastard probably gagged her," Morgan said.

He didn't notice the nervous glance between Holloway and Innes as he now began clambering back over the boulders on his way deeper into the mine. Now and again, he stopped and shone his torch off to his left or right side, sometimes revealing nothing but a stone wall very close to him, other times, the beam disappeared down an enormous tunnel stretching into nothing. There was a lot of graffiti sprayed all over the walls, and if those idiots could get down here and vandalise a place like this and get back up again, then, so could he.

"Damn, these heels!" Innes said.

"Low flat heels are a requirement for a reason," Morgan said. "How high are those heels?"

"Less than an inch, sir but still!"

Morgan pulled up to an area where the tunnel widened slightly into almost a vestibule and saw a rusted metal ladder on the wall to his right disappearing up into a shaft. He ran over and shone his beam up the shaft and watched the beam just stretch up into the darkness. "That shows you how deep we are! I can't even see the top of the ladder."

Behind him, Innes was shining her torch up on the roof of the mine shaft and noticed several deep fissures, with rainwater running down through them. "It looks like this could collapse at any moment!"

"I think we're underneath the MOD facility around now, sir," Holloway said.

"Oh, you mean the British Area 51?" Morgan said, managing to raise a slight smile at the young man's naivety. "Better hope the Men in Black aren't down here, then."

They carried on in the direction they were going and the shaft narrowed again until they heard a loud crashing sound coming from ahead of them. The three spun around to face each other as the noise echoed down the mine shaft and rapidly receded away again.

"What the hell was that?" Innes asked.

"Maybe Keeley's got more serial killer friends down here waiting for us?" Holloway said.

Innes gave him a sideways look. "Oh, my God! I never thought of that."

"It's not that," Morgan said. "I think it's Anna. She heard me call out for her and she somehow made a noise. Looks like she's dead ahead C'mon, hurry up!"

CHAPTER 35

The Ferryman drove the stolen Mercedes through the small Lazio town of Sacrofano, enjoying the beautiful terracotta buildings stacked up on hillsides lined with the olive trees and umbrella pines that made this part of the world so instantly recognisable, and even more desirable. This was a place for Professor Keeley to live, so it was an indescribable tragedy when he realised that Keeley had almost completely gone now and all that remained was the Ferryman. The Ferryman didn't care where he lived, although perhaps Greece might have been more appropriate. All the Ferryman cared about was finding beautiful women and ensuring they got safely across the river to the Underworld. Perhaps the Ferryman would stay in Italy for a while, then maybe he would finally go to Greece.

The River Styx was always in his mind. Its name described both a goddess and a river and meant 'shuddering', a word expressing the fear and loathing of death, but the Ferryman knew that death was nothing to fear. All one had to do was pay a price to get across the river and then one would find oneself in the Underworld. Many believed, and the Ferryman was one of them, that the River Styx, a fictional river supposed to lead into the Greek Underworld, was based on the River Acheron, a river in northwest Greece.

The Ferryman let these thoughts drift from his mind as if he had set them adrift on a small raft, allowing the River Styx itself to float them away from him. Then he took a turn on a southerly road, leaving Sacrofano in a northeasterly direction until he found a small, mostly concealed, entrance up on his left.

The safe house.

It was a house, but it was not safe.

The Ferryman now turned into the driveway, pulling up only a few yards along it into a passing place where he stopped and killed the engine. Then he stepped out into the warm Italian autumn air, noting it was a few degrees cooler than Rome up here in the hills. Dusk had come and gone and now night had fallen over the land, but the air was still warm and sultry, even in November. Another reason to love Italy. He had spent time here this summer, making his preparations, and enjoyed one of Lazio's hottest days on record when the heat had left the ground parched and its clay-bearing soil riven with mud cracks until a wild electrical storm had cleared the air and left an earthy petrichor scent hanging like mist over the potato fields. That storm was now gone, but the thunderclouds in his mind lingered.

He leaned into the car and pulled out his cardboard box, then began to walk down the lane towards the safe house. Before long, he was peering up the lane through a tunnel of umbrella pines and saw a modest villa in the traditional Lazio style, with metal Juliet balconies on the upstairs windows. The crumbling biscuit-coloured plaster that warmed the property's façade in the day was now silver in the moonlight. There was a marked police car parked in front of a garage and lights were on inside the villa, both up and downstairs.

The Ferryman now stepped into the trees on his left and moved closer to the villa until he was within just a few metres of it. He opened his cardboard box and began work. Inside was a beautiful silk scarf, a vial of gamma-hydroxybutyrate and a syringe. There were also some ancient silver Greek coins with honeybees on them, and a shroud wrapped up tight into a bundle. There was also a small plastic box, which contained a 5G signal jammer, specifically covering the frequency range used by 5G networks. The device was sufficiently powered to disrupt 5G signals across the entire property and a substantial radius around it.

He took it from the box and switched it on, then he set it down against the trunk of one of the pines.

Pay the Ferryman, pay Charon. Charon the psychopomp.

The Ferryman picked up his cardboard box, rose to his full height, and moved stealthily to the safe house. There couldn't realistically be more than four police officers in there, because of the size of the police car parked out the front. He knew Dr Sophie Anderson would have been one of the passengers. That left three police officers comfortably or four uncomfortably. The Ferryman knew instinctively there were three who had travelled up here with Anderson, but that Rossi and Jacob would be on the way. There was also a helicopter. Right now that helicopter was flying up and down the road looking for the Fiat Bravo, but it wouldn't be long before they gave up and flew here to the safe house. He had to work fast.

Lurking outside in the shadows, staying out of the moonlight, and peering in through the windows, he made a slow circuit of the property in the dark. Many of the windows had their blinds drawn, but there were several, particularly upstairs, which were unobstructed and he was able to look through them and see inside. Slowly he counted off the police officers, one, two, three. A chunky older man with grey hair in a sergeant's uniform. A young male officer in his twenties, and a young female officer also in her twenties. Then he saw her.

Dr Sophie Anderson.

The bitch was sitting in the kitchen with the female officer, chatting away as if they were old friends. It looked like they were drinking cups of coffee. A man of his extreme genius had been left to rot in a solitary confinement cell for the rest of his life, while this pinhead of a woman was sitting out here in Italy, as free as a raven. At least now she was frightened, he thought with great pleasure. At least now the fucking bitch was running for her life. But not for long. Soon that life would be over, and she would be starting a new life in the Underworld.

The warm breeze blew again. He heard Mozart singing in the air.

Sull'aria

On the air.

The Ferryman continued his circuit of the property, watching as the male police officers moved from room to room until finally settling in the living area on the opposite side of the villa to the kitchen. This was on the east side of the house, made dark by neighbouring pine trees. The Ferryman decided this was where he would begin the ritual.

Che soave Zeffiretto

Questa sera spirerà

That gentle little Zephyr

This evening he will pass away.

With the beautiful libretto of *Le nozze di Figaro* still singing in his ears, he set the cardboard box down on the ground a few metres into the small grove, what the sergeant would call a *boschetto*, then he stepped away, casually snapped off a low hanging branch from one of the trees and scratched the living room window with it. Then he stopped. It was difficult for him to hear inside the house but he just about made out the conversation of the two Italian men. He was fluent in Italian and listened with amusement as they discussed what the noise was. After he had waited for a minute or so he scratched the window again. Their conversation again turned to the noise at the window. The older man, he knew he was older because he had a deeper voice, now said he was going to open the blinds. The Ferryman slid back into the shadows and watched the confused officer open the blind and stare out. He reported nothing but said he was going outside to take a look and that the younger man should stay inside. This was exactly what the Ferryman wanted to hear.

Questa sera spirerà

Sotto i pini del boschetto

This evening he will pass away

Under the pine trees of the grove.

Stepping back into the cover of a tree trunk, the Ferryman selected a heavy rock and watched as the side door opened then the older police sergeant stepped outside with a torch. He switched the torch on and at the same time opened the button on his leather holster on his hip in which he was carrying a gun. He now pulled the firearm from the holster and stepped out onto the gravel parking area at the side of the house, sweeping his torch through in an arc, the beam bouncing off the tree trunks.

"Se c'è qualcuno là fuori, è meglio che esci dove posso vederti con le mani in alto!"

THE FERRYMAN

The Ferryman was out here all right, but he was certainly not going to comply with the sergeant's words and come out with his hands up.

The Ferryman now scraped his foot in the soil, causing the police sergeant to slowly move forward. The Ferryman watched the intensity of the beam grow in strength indicating the proximity of the police sergeant to him. He waited patiently until the beam finally landed on the cardboard box deeper in the grove. He knew what must happen next. He had thought several moves ahead. The sergeant made his way over to the box and after sweeping the torch around the trees one more time and reassuring himself there was no one out here within immediate range, he sat on his haunches and set his gun down on the ground. He raised his torch and shone the beam at the box. Now he brought his other hand up to open the box. The Ferryman knew this was what must happen. Men in the dark did not set down their torches and hold their guns while they opened a box.

This evening he will pass away.

Under the pine trees of the grove.

The Ferryman stepped out from behind the tree and brought the rock crashing down on the sergeant's head with a sickening crack. The man slumped instantly down to the ground, unconscious but not yet dead. The Ferryman now took the rock and hit the police sergeant on the head three more times, killing him. Now he picked up his cardboard box, and the sergeant's gun and walked over to the open side door.

He stepped inside the villa and casually, as if walking back into his own home, he walked into the room in the living area where the young police constable was waiting for his sergeant to return. The young man's face instantly paled, suddenly ashen with terror as he saw the Monster standing in the doorway holding his sergeant's gun. He fumbled to open the holster on his hip, to pull his weapon on him, but the Ferryman opened fire, planting three rounds in his chest and sending him crashing back into a standard lamp and falling in a bloody heap in the corner.

In the kitchen, he heard Sophie Anderson and the female officer explode with cries of fear.

"It's nearly time for your journey across the river, Sophie," he said quietly.

*

Sophie heard the three gunshots and kicked back from her chair at the table so violently that she slopped her coffee all over it. The cup rolled off the table and smashed on the floor and she stared at the female police constable, barely knowing what to do. Lombardi fumbled for her gun, pulling it from her holster and now holding it at the door with shaking hands. After she tried to calm herself by blowing out some short sharp breaths, she now reached for her shoulder-mounted police radio and was astonished when it didn't work. Now she grabbed her phone from her pocket and Sophie saw a look of terror and confusion on her face as she stared at her phone, shaking her head, mumbling in Italian.

"Non funziona! Il mio cellulare non funziona! Non c'è segnale! Non capisco!"

Sophie didn't understand the words she was saying, having almost zero Italian knowledge.

"What are you saying, Maria? I don't understand."

Maria Lombardi now passed her mobile to Sophie with a shaking hand, still covering the open kitchen doorway with her handgun. "Is not working," she said in heavily accented English. "No signal!"

Sophie looked at the phone with horror and now immediately pulled out her own telephone and saw that Lombardi was right – there was no signal to the house at all. She didn't understand because just moments ago she had used her phone to speak to Jacob. She also knew that Sergeant Colombo had been in regular contact with Inspector Rossi. She tried to contain her fear and tell herself that there was some kind of technical glitch, that she knew happened from time to time in isolated regions like this, but in her heart, she knew the true darkness and horror of the situation unfurling around her.

"We have to get out of here!" she said to Lombardi. "We have to get out of here right now. It's the Ferryman… he's killed them both, don't you understand? He's cut the phone signal and he's killed both your colleagues and now he's coming for us."

"No leave," Lombardi said. "No leave without permission. I stay and guard. My orders."

Sophie watched the brave young policewoman as she continued to stand in front of her, shielding her from whoever was about to walk through that open doorway, covering it with her gun. "I shoot him if he comes here."

With Lombardi's words hanging in the air, the lights went out and both women screamed. Then Sophie heard something that made her skin crawl. It was the Ferryman's voice, which she remembered only too well from her last encounter with him. Cool, calm, smooth, cut-glass posh English accent, words sliding from his lips like honey from a warm spoon. He was speaking from the corridor outside the kitchen, the villa in total darkness.

"Dr Anderson, are you there? Are you hiding in your hidey-hole? I can *see* you."

Sophie watched Lombardi step across the kitchen until she was parallel to the door. She heard the Italian policewoman fire her weapon but she must have missed because the Ferryman returned fire and struck Lombardi in the chest. Sophie screamed as the Italian woman slumped down against the kitchen cupboards, gasping in horror. Then she heard his voice again, floating across the darkness.

"I've come to see you, Dr Anderson. The Ferryman is going to send you over the river tonight."

*

Morgan led the small team to the end of the tunnel where they stepped into an enormous cavern of slick grey stone walls, tapering inwards as they stretched up to an aperture over a hundred feet above them. Rain poured in through the opening and tumbled down to a vision that made Morgan feel a blend of rage, disgust and fear.

Anna Mazurek was lying on the floor, her arms and legs covered in so much duct tape she looked like a worm. Rainwater slid over her face, half-covered with wet hair, and her cheeks were stained black with mascara. She looked at him not with wide eyes full of hope, but with half-shut eyes drained of all life. The cold in the cave made his bones ache, so he knew how bad she must feel, down on the ground with no coat.

"Anna!"

As Morgan spoke, he gently held her shoulders and told Innes to pass him the bottle of water he told her to bring. Anna was mumbling incoherently, looking up at him with blinking eyes, trying to focus as he pulled her around into a more comfortable, upright sitting position and now gently raised the bottle to her lips.

"Just take small sips," he said, a thick cloud of breath pluming in front of him like smoke. "You're going to be alright."

As he carefully poured the water on her lips and watched her drinking, he told Holloway to get started trying to unwrap the tape.

"You're going to be alright," he repeated, raising his hand to her head and gently sweeping her hair away from her face. "It's me, Bill Morgan, I'm here with Holloway and Innes. Can you speak?"

She nodded her head. "It was Declan after all." Her voice was dry and hoarse. "Dex brought me here."

"Don't worry about any of that," Morgan said, having made the decision not to tell her about Declan's murder until she was back up on her feet. "All we have to think about is getting you safely out of here."

Morgan looked up at the hole in the mine ceiling over a hundred feet above their heads, the rain still lashing down through it and running onto the four of them. He considered the possibility of a crane or some kind of abseil rope being lowered down and winching her back up. He even considered the possibility of using a helicopter to lower the rope down but the whole thing would just take too long and could be dangerous, especially if the top part of the mine collapsed in the middle of the operation to extract her. He thought about the route they had come and realised nearly all of it was easily navigable apart from the small section where they climbed over the boulders.

"Anna, if we get you back on your feet, will you be able to walk?"

"Yes," she said, her voice now growing in strength. "I'm sure I can walk. I need more water."

Holloway was finished ripping the duct tape from her lower body and began unravelling the tape holding her arms to her sides. While he was doing this, Morgan was still holding the bottle of water to Anna's lips, allowing her to drink. She had now taken nearly a quarter of the small bottle. Morgan could see the hope and life gradually flooding back into her eyes. When Holloway had finished with the tape, he helped Anna up until she was sitting on one of the loose boulders, and handed her the bottle of water so she could give herself a drink.

"As soon as you feel strong enough, we'll get you up on your feet and the three of us will walk you back out of here. It's not such a bad journey and then we'll be back at the car. From there, we'll take you straight to the Great Western Hospital."

"I don't need to go to hospital, Bill. I just need a good night's sleep and then I'll be back on the case."

"That is the most ridiculous thing I've ever heard in my life," Morgan said. "You really can be obstinate at times. You're going to the hospital and that's the end of it. I am your senior officer and you'll do as you're told."

Anna managed to smile as she made her way through the second quarter of the bottle.

"Let's get out of here," she said. "I'm cold and soaking wet."

Morgan was impressed by her strength as she pulled herself up onto her feet and after a moment to regain her balance, she began to walk. Swaying a little, Morgan and Holloway both rushed her, each taking one of her arms around their shoulders.

"This is how we go, all the way out," Morgan said. "There's a small area where you have to climb over some rocks, but we'll manage that when we get to it. Let's get you out of here and into a nice warm hospital bed. As soon as we're on the surface, and back in the car, we'll radio everything in."

As they slowly made their way back through the crumbling, collapsing mine shafts towards the entrance they had used, Morgan felt a surge of warmth and affection for the brave police sergeant with her arm around his shoulder. He decided that when all this was over, he was going to ask her out on a date and that scared him more than the Ferryman.

CHAPTER 36

As Rossi's Alfa Romeo roared up the narrow track leading to the safe house, Jacob felt a wave of nausea when he saw the entire house was in darkness.

"Why are there no lights on?" he asked Rossi.

Rossi stared at the villa as he brought the Alpha's nose around in a gentle curve and parked up in a clearing halfway up the lane. "This is not right. This is not protocol. It is not late enough for them to be in bed and they know about the threat tonight. Something is wrong. I will park here so we are not heard. We will have the element of surprise."

"My phone has no signal," Jacob said.

Rossi checked his. "Nor mine."

"Keeley is here," Jacob said. "He's cut all power and phone signals. We need to hurry."

Both men grabbed torches, climbed out of the Alpha and gently closed the doors. Jacob saw Rossi pull his handgun from the shoulder rig under his jacket and slide a round into the chamber.

"I am the lead officer in this investigation, Chief Inspector. This is my jurisdiction and you will follow my orders. Do we understand each other?"

Jacob raised his hands showing his palms. "I won't tread on your toes, Carlo, but we have to get in there and make sure Sophie's alright."

Rossi was already moving up the lane. When they reached the top, Rossi noticed the side door of the property was wide open. He indicated to Jacob with a hand gesture that they should go around to it and Jacob followed him around the side of the property until they were parallel with the door.

Jacob stared inside the house, now in pitch darkness and was about to suggest both men go in as soon as possible when Rossi nudged him, his finger to his lips to indicate silence. Jacob shone his torch where Rossi pointed and they both saw someone slumped on the ground just inside the tree line of the woods beside the house.

"Come with me!" Rossi whispered.

Jacob followed Rossi into the woods and was horrified to see Sergeant Colombo, the man he had met earlier back in Rome lying dead on the woodland floor, his head stoved in with a bloody rock now left a few inches beside the cooling corpse.

"My God, that bastard!" Rossi spat. "He has killed twice tonight."

Jacob feared the worst. "We have to get inside the villa, Carlo."

"I'm worried about how silent it is in the villa," Rossi said. "If Romano and Lombardi were still alive and on duty it would not be silent and dark like this. We have to presume the worst. Watch out for yourself in there, Jacob. Take Colombo's gun."

Jacob reached down towards the dead man's holster but then stopped. He looked up at Rossi. "It's already missing. Keeley must have the gun."

"My God, this is out of control! Now he is armed. Let's get into the house."

Jacob followed Rossi, who was walking slowly towards the side door with his gun raised into the aim, while Jacob lit the way from beside him with the torch.

Rossi now stepped over the threshold.

"This is it. If the bastard is in here, we will get him tonight."

Jacob prayed that was so.

*

With fear coursing through her veins, Sophie scrambled forward, grabbed Lombardi and pulled her across the kitchen to the far side. She crouched beside her and saw she was bleeding out all over the kitchen floor. She tried to comfort Lombardi as she thought of a way to stem the bleeding, but then she heard the man's voice once again.

"Time to sail across the river, Sophie."

She heard something else now, something tinny and metallic a scraping scratching sound and realised with terror that the Ferryman was rubbing together his coins. Those beautiful ancient Greek silver coins with honeybees on them. They instilled a terrible fear in her because she knew their true meaning, she knew what he intended to do with them tonight. The hideous vision of him killing everyone here tonight, herself and all three police officers and sending all four across the river with coins in their mouths, wrapped in shrouds, made her blood turn to ice in her veins.

Now, as if in some horrific nightmare sequence, she saw the Ferryman's monstrous black silhouette appear in the open doorway. There was a bright moon tonight, and its light streamed in through the Venetian blinds and lit him in silver and black stripes. He was tall and slim and gaunt with a fiendishly evil grin on his face and dead eyes staring down at her as he pointed the gun directly in her face. Its menacing matte black muzzle terrified her.

"Throw the police constable's gun over here, Sophie."

She thought about snatching Lombardi's gun up and firing it, but she had no idea how guns worked. She knew the difference between an automatic and a revolver, and this was an automatic, but was the safety catch on? If it was, how did you take it off? By the time she'd worked it out, the Ferryman would have put a bullet between her eyes. Now pathetically and with an overwhelming sense of failure and humiliation, mingling with the fear and terror she felt, she obeyed meekly and slid Lombardi's handgun across the kitchen floor. The Ferryman picked it up and put it on the sideboard. In his other hand, he was holding a syringe and a silk scarf.

"Come across the river with me, Sophie. It's time to send you over. You nearly went before but you were such a silly woman. But don't worry, we can finish what we started tonight. You'll love it when you're there. You'll love the journey."

Sophie felt Maria Lombardi's body go limp in her hands and realised with disgust and horror the young female police constable had died. Her eyes stared at nothing and her head slumped down onto her shoulder. Sophie laid her gently down on the kitchen floor and recoiled away from the body as the menacing figure of the Ferryman approached her from across the kitchen.

Without warning, the Ferryman surged forward and lunged at her. He was all over her in a second. He was a big, powerful man and she had no chance of fighting him off. Instinctively, she reached out to the kitchen sideboard behind her, trying to grab hold of one of the knives in the wooden knife block, but it was too far away. The Ferryman stuffed the dead policeman's handgun in his waistband to free his other hand. Grabbing her roughly from behind and manoeuvring himself around until he was behind her with his left bicep crushing up against her throat, he forced her against one of the walls. She was unable to fight back as he gently lifted the syringe to the smooth, pale flesh of her neck.

"I'm going to make this last a very long time for you, Sophie," he said. "I'm going to inject you with this ambrosia and you will lose all control. Then I'm going to choke you half to death but bring you back so you can tell me what you see. I want you to tell me if you see Charon. I want you to enjoy it, my love."

Sophie felt the injection prick her neck with a sharp metallic sting and then the pressure as the Ferryman pushed down on the syringe and pumped the sedative deep inside her, she felt instantly when it hit her bloodstream and travelled to her brain and then her entire body went limp. It was only the pressure of the Ferryman's big body pushing her up against the wall that allowed her to remain on her feet. She felt sick, terrified, but strangely relaxed as the sedative worked its magic on her now completely uncontrollable body.

She felt the smooth silk scarf as he wrapped it around her neck.

"I love you, Sophie."

The Ferryman began slowly tightening the ligature. She felt the pressure increasing on her throat. She felt it slowly crush her windpipe. She began to choke to death.

"Are you there yet, Sophie? Can you see the river?"

Slowly, Sophie's world began to shrink. She saw stars and then her vision became tunnelled. The stars increased in number and she began to lose her power of vision. Her world began to grow black, it was the dusk of her life. The sound of the Ferryman's soft, eerily caring voice was quieter in her ears. She knew this meant she was seconds away from death.

*

The first room Jacob and Rossi came to was the living area, just to the right of the corridor leading in from the side door. Both men saw the young police constable Romano on the floor. He had clearly been shot dead. He was lit black and white by the moonlight coming in through the window. Rossi lowered his voice to a whisper.

"Take his gun. You'll need his gun."

Jacob strode across the floor, working hard to remain calm, focused and as professional as he could be under such personal and horrifying circumstances. Luckily this time, Keeley had not taken the gun. Jacob unbuttoned the holster and pulled the weapon out. He recognised the gun from his firearms training. It was a Beretta. He immediately clicked off the safety catch.

"You search it downstairs," Rossi said. "I will go upstairs and search there. You are authorised to use lethal force."

Jacob nodded in response but said nothing. He followed Rossi out of the room, his gun raised into the aim. Both men turned into the corridor and Rossi now moved up the stairs to his right. Jacob was facing a long internal corridor with two doors on either side of him and a door at the far end. He thought he heard voices, perhaps a man whispering, but it could have come from anywhere, so now he made his way along the corridor, carefully turning into each room and ensuring that each one was clear as he made his way to the final door.

When he pushed open the door at the far end of the corridor he was horrified to see the hideously tall and gaunt figure of Alastair Keeley towering over Sophie, who was entirely limp in his grasp, her eyes rolling up into their sockets and her tongue hanging out of her mouth. Keeley was wrapping some sort of shiny silk ligature around her neck and pulling tight on it. Jacob could see Sophie's face was a strange dark grey colour. He knew that her face was purple but made this way by the moonlight.

"Hello Chief Inspector Jacob," Keeley said. "How very good of you to join us."

Now manipulating the ligature so he was holding it with one hand and still forcing Sophie's body up against the wall to keep her on her feet, he pulled the handgun from his waistband and pointed it at her head. "I'll blow her brains out if you don't put that gun down."

"I think we both know that's not going to happen, Keeley," Jacob said. "Take the gun away from her head and set it down on the side and release the ligature now."

"But she's going across the river. I can't stop her now. Tell me, who's cleverer now – you or me?"

"You're cleverer," Jacob said, eyes crawling hopelessly over his dying fiancée's tortured face. "You're a genius."

"You think so?"

"That coin trail you led me on, the wild goose chase… choosing Tansy and Jennifer because they were reclusive loners with no one to miss them, and giving us no leads… it was all pure genius."

"I thought so, a merry dance perfect for a fool like you. The two women I murdered both thought I was Dennis Perry, by the way. In case anything went awry."

Jacob wanted to take a shot but Keeley was just too close to Sophie. Their heads were less than ten inches apart and if Jacob's aim was just a fraction of a degree wrong, he would end up shooting Sophie in the head. He knew it and even worse, Keeley knew it.

"Put the gun down, Jacob. Just as you've been told."

Jacob knew he had to comply. With rage and fear coursing through him like adrenaline, he now set the gun down on the kitchen sideboard and raised his hands in the air to show Keeley he was unarmed. "Just let her go, Keeley. She doesn't want to go across the river."

"Everyone wants to go across the river, Jacob. After I've sent Sophie across, I'm going to send the other police officers here… and eventually you too. Don't worry – you'll be with her in the Underworld before you know it."

Jacob, who was standing in the kitchen doorway with the corridor behind him was now able to hear Rossi's footsteps as he stepped on the stair treads behind him. Keeley was too far away on the other side of the kitchen to hear. He knew that Rossi was now on the ground floor and would see him standing at the door with his hands raised. A man of Rossi's experience would know what this meant. Carlo Rossi was now Jacob and Sophie's last chance. All Jacob had to do was keep Keeley talking and get him to release the ligature. He had to buy Rossi time, but Sophie was almost dead.

"I still can't work out how you got the world to believe you were dead."

"A simple chess move. I dated a senior policewoman from Vienna for a few weeks, then I threatened her family's life unless she uploaded the false report into the Austrian Federal Police's computer system. Then I sent her across the river."

Jacob knew Rossi needed more time, but with each second he gave the Italian, Sophie got closer to death.

"What's it like on the other side of the river, Alistair?"

"I don't know. I have never been there myself."

"Why don't you ask Sophie? She must have been there by now – look at her."

Keeley's face changed from one of almost rational evil control to one of almost childishly bewildered curiosity.

"As a matter of fact, I was going to bring her back and ask her what it's like there."

Keeley now released the ligature and Jacob heard the sickening sound of Sophie trying to draw breath into her lungs. Keeley was still holding the gun to her head as Sophie slowly gasped and clawed her way back to life.

Jacob was now calculating how long it would take Rossi to get around to the kitchen window, where he had a clear shot through the glass at Keeley's head.

"What's it like, Sophie?" Keeley now leaned into Sophie and lowered his voice to an immeasurably creepy whisper. "What's it like on the other side of the river? Have you seen Charon the Ferryman? Will you tell him that I'm the Ferryman now?"

Sophie was still gasping in pathetically short breaths, and Jacob wanted nothing more than to surge across the room and break her away from the arms of this madness, but he knew any attempt to do so would result in Keeley instantly firing a bullet through her head and killing her on the spot. Jacob brought his hands back down to his sides and balled them tightly into fists as he tried to maintain control of himself. One false step and Sophie's death would be on his conscience for life.

"It's beautiful," Sophie said in barely a whisper.

Jacob's heart raced. Even now, half-dead, she was still able to manipulate this deranged bastard.

"What was that you said?" Keeley leaned in even closer to her until he was almost brushing her ear with his lips.

"It's beautiful across the river," she whispered. "I've never seen anything like it."

"Did you see Charon? Did you tell him that I'm the Ferryman now?"

"Yes."

Keeley gasped. "What did he say?"

The gunshot was explosively loud, fired from outside by Inspector Rossi through the kitchen window. The quiet, eerie moonlit scene in the kitchen changed instantly as the kitchen window shattered into a million shards and the bullet punched up through the back of Keeley's skull, killing him where he stood.

Jacob was across the room, pulling Sophie from Keeley's dead arms. The big man crashed down onto the floor beside Maria Lombardi as Jacob held Sophie in his arms, pulling her up and carrying her to the kitchen door which Rossi now kicked open. It smashed back against its hinges, allowing Jacob to walk outside into the moonlight.

Rossi now ran inside the kitchen to confirm Alastair Keeley was dead, and then he appeared in the doorway. "I'm going to find the fuses and turn the lights back on. Then I will call an ambulance."

Jacob carried Sophie in his arms across the drive to a soft sloping grass bank, laid her down on the grass and pulled the ligature away from her throat. She immediately gasped and filled her lungs with air just as the police helicopter arrived over the property, shining its searchlight down on them at the side of the villa. Jacob heard a confusion of sounds as someone barked Italian commands through a loudspeaker from the helicopter. Their hair and clothes were buffeted by the aircraft's powerful rotor wash, and Jacob struggled to sweep Sophie's hair from her eyes. He stared down at her now, feeling a rush of relief and joy as she opened her eyes fully and looked up at him, managing half a smile.

"What took you so long?" she asked, trying to smile.

Jacob was almost too moved by her defiance and bravery to respond, but now brought his face down and kissed her softly on the lips.

"I couldn't get across the river."

EPILOGUE

Nearly twenty-four hours after Morgan, Holloway and Innes had pulled Anna Mazurek out of the abandoned mine at Box, the Welshman was standing awkwardly at a nurse's station in Swindon's Great Western Hospital, holding a bunch of flowers. He had also put on his best suit and tie. Waiting for the nurse to tell him which ward Anna was in, he realised he had not felt fear like this since his tours of Iraq and Afghanistan with the Royal Marine Commandos. His heart was beating unusually fast and his mouth felt dry.

"Are you family?" the nurse asked.

"Work colleague. I'm her senior officer at Wiltshire CID."

"We all heard about what happened," the nurse said. "I read about it online. I think you're all very brave. She's just down there."

Morgan followed the direction of the nurse's pointing finger and thanked her, then he made his way down the antiseptic-smelling corridor, lined on each side with windows letting the grey English November light into the hospital before finally arriving at a ward. It was full of patients, but at the far end, on his left, he saw Anna Mazurek sitting up in bed. She was on a rehydration drip and reading a paperback. Morgan proceeded with caution.

A few metres away from her bed, she noticed him out of the corner of her eye, folded the paperback down on her lap and smiled at him.

"My first visitor."

Morgan rustled up next to her, still feeling very nervous and sat in the chair beside her bed.

"I heard Kent told you about Declan. I don't know whether to say I'm sorry or not." He smiled awkwardly.

"We don't have to worry about Declan anymore."

He nodded. "Right. OK. All good is it?"

She nodded. "I think so, yes. The doctor says it's really just a case of being dehydrated, but says I was lucky. If I'd been in there much longer it could have gone a very different way. Thank you, Bill. I think you saved my life."

"You can thank Holloway and Innes and their little GPS navigation. That's what got us there so fast."

She smiled and now picked her book up, closed it and put it on the side table. She didn't have to do it, but she was deliberately finding something to do. Morgan recognised the symptoms of awkwardness only too well.

"I'm glad you're doing well and everything, Anna."

Anna pointed at the flowers. "Are they for me?"

"No, I'm going to take them around to Holloway later and thank him for being so good on the GPS."

She gave him a look as he set the flowers down on her side table. "Thanks, they're beautiful."

"Anyway," he began. "So, the thing is I'm so glad that you're doing well and everything. Seeing you in the mine the way that you were, got me thinking you see. I'd already been thinking after that bast... sorry, after Declan took you. I started to think about you in a different way."

Anna looked at him now, her usual inscrutable features for once beginning to warm up and he got the sense she was receptive to what he was about to say next.

"What kind of a way?"

He cleared his throat and threw a glance around the ward, genuinely hoping a hole would open up in the floor, or at the very least a fire alarm might sound. "What I was thinking, was maybe you might join me for a drink one night, go on the town and show these youngsters how it's done."

"I think I'd like that, Bill. All I ever seem to do these days is work, so I'd like that very much."

Morgan felt a wave of relief. "It has been a bit crazy of late down at the station."

"I was thinking about taking some leave – some long-term leave, if I can get it out of Kent."

"Oh yes? Want to go somewhere interesting?"

"I was thinking about going back to Poland, where my grandfather was born. I have never even been there, but I think about it all the time. I've seen photographs of the farm where he grew up, and I think it's about time I went back and had a look at it. I can't explain it. It feels like I miss the place even though I've not been there."

Morgan smiled. "There's a word for that in Welsh. It's called *hiraeth*. A longing for something, maybe in your past, maybe not."

"This place definitely wasn't in my past, but I feel like it should have been, so maybe that's what you're describing. Have you got any leave owing to you?"

"As a matter of fact, I have. Like you, I've been working my ars… working myself very hard lately and I've got a lot of leave accrued. Since Leanne walked out on me all those years ago, I never really had any reason to use it. This year is the same. Why?"

"Why don't you come with me, to Poland? We can explore it together."

Morgan felt a surge of joy as he realised the conversation had gone not only as he had wished, but even better. Anna had agreed to go out with him for drinks one evening and now she was asking him to go on a holiday with her back to Poland. He reached forward and gave her hand a gentle squeeze. "I think I'd like that very much, Anna."

"Good, then when I'm up and about we'll look into booking some flights and a hotel."

Morgan met Anna's eyes and the two of them shared a warm smile. He leaned forward and kissed her on the cheek and realised how life could turn just like that, on a silver sixpence.

*

"Apparently," Anna said with a flourish as she gestured at the Colosseum, "the building was finally completed in the year 80 AD, making it 1944 years old, this year. They believe the name Colosseum is derived from a colossal bronze statue that used to stand right here, almost where we are right now, of the Emperor Nero."

"How fascinating," Jacob said catching her up and putting his arm around her shoulder. "But I think I've had enough Roman emperors to last me a lifetime. Shall we go and get some wine and maybe a pizza?"

"I think I did enough of that while I was going out with my conference friends," Sophie said. "Maybe tonight we should just go back to the hotel and order some food up to the room?"

Jacob pulled her to a stop on the pavement and stared into her eyes. The Italian sun was setting now, lighting the Colosseum and Sophie's face a soft amber colour. She was wearing a simple light cloth scarf around her neck to cover the bruising marks made by Keeley the night before. Just thinking about it made Jacob seethe with rage, but then he remembered how lucky he was that she was still alive and that they would be able to spend the rest of their lives together in the knowledge Alastair Keeley was well and truly dead. Thanks to Keeley, Sophie had spent the night and much of the morning in a hospital here in the city, before being discharged with a warning to take things easy. She had not passed into full unconsciousness at any point, and there were no concerns about any negative effects from the asphyxiation Keeley had performed on her the night before. She was going to be just fine. They both were, now that the Ferryman was dead.

"Come on," she said. "Let's get back to the hotel room."

Jacob and Sophie now weaved through the tourists milling around outside the Colosseum in the setting sun and with the warm Roman air softly brushing their faces, they stepped across the road and headed back to their hotel. All seemed to be well at last. Jacob had received a text from Morgan a few hours ago telling him that Anna had agreed to go out with him and they were even thinking about planning a holiday together. He was pleased for both of his friends and hoped they would be able to enjoy what he had found with Sophie.

As the minutes rolled away and the couple walked calmly through the back streets of Rome to their small boutique hotel, Sophie suddenly surprised him with a question he had not expected.

"You think he finally got across the river?"

It was a sentence that would mean nothing to anyone but the two of them.

"I don't care if he got across the river or not," Jacob said. "He was completely insane and he murdered countless people in a deranged fantasy about sending them to the ancient Underworld. The important thing is that he's dead and he'll never hurt anyone again."

"I know, you're right," Sophie said, lifting her chin into the warm breeze.

Jacob pulled her to a stop once again, watching the warm air stirring her hair, trying to ignore what the scarf around her neck was concealing, but seeing nothing but hope and optimism in her bright eyes. They embraced and kissed for a long time, completely oblivious to the crowd of tourists and Romans passing them by on the pavement and then they continued on their way back to the hotel.

"Maybe we should go on holiday like Bill and Anna?" he said.

"I don't think so," she said. "I just want to go back to the Old Watermill and live a quiet life with you and Drifter."

Jacob wanted the same thing. They wandered through the fading daylight until they finally reached the ancient

River Tiber. They pulled up and watched it sparkling in the sunset. He felt Sophie shiver and put his arm around her.

"Don't worry," he said. "We don't have to cross it. Our hotel is on this side of the river."

About the Author

Rob Jones has published over forty books in the genres of action-adventure, action-thriller and crime. Many of his chart-topping titles have enjoyed number one rankings and all of his Joe Hawke, Hunter Files and Jed Mason books have been international bestsellers.

Printed in Dunstable, United Kingdom